David kissed Ac

It was, of course, entirely casual, she told herself, keeping her smile steady as she said, "Thanks for a fabulous dinner, David."

They were in plain sight of neighbors who might be—and probably were—watching them from their front windows.

"Thanks. Maybe I have a new career path as a chef. You know, in case the prosecutor's office decides I'm a liability."

"You could move," she suggested. *Say, to Sacramento to be closer to me.*

"Maybe." His lashes briefly veiled his eyes. "What about you, Acadia? Are you going to be glad to get home?"

"For a minute, all I could think was—"

"That *this* is home."

His hand dropped to his side, where it stayed fisted. His eyes, intense an instant ago, grew opaque and he finally took that step back.

"Good night, David. I'm glad we did this." Acadia closed the door, leaned back against it and touched her cheek with her fingertips. Despite all that was happening around her right now, one thought occupied her.

David Owen kissed me.

Dear Reader,

I'm a small-town girl—can't imagine living in a city. There are pluses and minuses of small-town life, of course. Writing this book, I found myself thinking about a small town in California where I lived from the age of nine until high school graduation. El Granada has undoubtedly grown hugely, since it's right on the ocean and is—if they ever built that new highway—an easy commute to San Francisco. In those days, though, a narrow, winding, perilous highway that clung to the cliff high above the ocean kept El Granada and its small sister towns—Half Moon Bay, Moss Beach and Montara—isolated. Devil's Slide, as the road was known, had a distressing tendency to slide away in winter, isolating us further and aggravating my father, who had to commute daily into San Francisco. I suspect to this day that some of my fear of heights I can blame on our frequent trips over Devil's Slide.

But I digress. El Granada was mostly residential then— schools were in Montara and Half Moon Bay. About all we had in El Granada was a grocery store and a post office. There was no mail delivery in town then, so everyone had to pick up their mail, which made the post office gossip central. I can still picture sitting in the car, drumming my heels and probably whining as I waited while my mother caught up on the news. Everyone, of course, knew everyone else and all their business. Even the kids heard every unsavory tidbit.

Horrific events have long aftershocks wherever they happen, but the effect can be more devastating yet in a small town with a tight web of relationships and a long history of petty resentments and deep loyalty alike. Grow up in a small town and it's bred into you. Memories, good and bad, so easily sweep you back to your hometown....

Hope you enjoy *A Hometown Boy*. Please contact me c/o Harlequin Books, 225 Duncan Mill Road, Don Mills, ON M3B 3K9, Canada.

Janice Kay Johnson

A Hometown Boy

JANICE KAY JOHNSON

HARLEQUIN®

entertain, enrich, inspire™

Recycling programs
for this product may
not exist in your area.

ISBN-13: 978-0-373-71825-2

A HOMETOWN BOY

Copyright © 2013 by Janice Kay Johnson

www.Harlequin.com

Printed in U.S.A.

ABOUT THE AUTHOR

The author of more than sixty books for children and adults, Janice Kay Johnson writes Harlequin Superromance novels about love and family—about the way generations connect and the power our earliest experiences have on us through-out life. Her 2007 novel *Snowbound* won a RITA® Award from Romance Writers of America for Best Contemporary Series Romance. A former librarian, Janice raised two daughters in a small rural town north of Seattle, Washington. She loves to read and is an active volunteer and board member for Purrfect Pals, a no-kill cat shelter.

Books by Janice Kay Johnson

HARLEQUIN SUPERROMANCE

SIGNATURE SELECT SAGA

*The Russell Twins
**A Brother's Word

Other titles by this author available in ebook format.

Wanda, this book especially would never have been written if not for your enthusiasm and faith in me. I feel so lucky.

This one is definitely for you.

CHAPTER ONE

How COULD SHE still love someone who was the source of most of her misery and grief? Someone who had ruined her life?

Joyce Owen sat behind closed drapes in her living room, the TV flickering but unwatched although *Days of Our Lives* was on. She had scarcely left the house in two weeks, had become so accustomed to keeping the blinds closed she never noticed anymore how dim the room was. Her world had narrowed gradually as she cut off contact with that hateful Marvella Hatcher first, then the Daleys, Kirk and Marie Merfeld, Alice Simmons, once her dearest friend, the Jurgens…until no one was left. Once she'd enjoyed gardening and talking over the fence with the neighbors to each side, grocery shopping here in town, going to the library, catching up on gossip. It had been years since she'd stepped foot in the Food Emporium here in Tucannon; she drove all the way to Walla Walla now to buy her necessities, just so she didn't have to pretend not to hear the whispers when townsfolk set eyes on her.

All because of Robbie, who couldn't help himself—oh, she knew he couldn't—but he had made her life hard. There was no denying that.

Two weeks ago, she'd had to tell him this was no longer his home, not if he wouldn't take his medicine. He was her oldest, thirty-four years old and no more capable of taking care of himself than a five-year-old. But she had finally become so frightened of him she couldn't live with it anymore.

Since he'd stormed out, she had understood that this wasn't any better. Joyce felt as if a tornado was approaching. The sky was sickly yellow, the stillness absolute, and by the prickling of her skin she knew, *knew,* that something terrible was coming. She was just waiting to find out what that something terrible was. She slept only in uneasy bursts, every creak of the old house jerking her to wakefulness. Come morning, she did her housekeeping chores out of long habit, hurrying when she had to step outside to water her poor pitiful roses in the backyard or haul the garbage can out to the curb. Then she sat, pretending to watch TV. And all she could think about was what he was doing right now. What he was thinking. How scared he was.

She knew Robbie hadn't left town, the way she'd half hoped he would. She didn't answer the phone, but she did listen to messages. Several neighbors had called to complain that they'd caught him sleeping in their garage or under their lilac bushes beneath the front windows. Sounding mad as hell, Wayne Tindall said, "I looked at him down the barrels of my shotgun and told him if he steps foot on my property again I'd let him have it."

Of course, Wayne hadn't liked the boys even when they were just normal high-spirited kids. He'd called the police when David hit a baseball through his plate-glass window. As if he hadn't known perfectly well that Pete and Joyce would pay for the replacement and then make David work it off in chores. Joyce just plain didn't like Wayne Tindall. She tried to feel sorry for his wife, Betty, living with a man who lacked even a grain of compassion.

Crack. The crack of a gunshot came from so close her entire body spasmed. Joyce dropped to the floor with her heart racing. *Oh, God, oh, God,* she thought. It had come. Whatever the terrible thing was.

Somebody was screaming, a keen of terror. *Crack.* The second shot, cutting that scream off, was just as loud, just as near, rattling the window glass. It sounded as if it had been fired right outside her living room.

Or next door, she realized with a shudder. At the Tindalls'.

But she'd heard shotguns fired before, and they didn't sound like this, clean and sharp.

Panic squeezed her chest. Whimpering, she crawled a few feet and then lurched to her feet and ran toward the back of the house. She hardly ever went into Pete's den, only to vacuum and dust every week or so. She hadn't emptied out any of his things since he dropped dead of a heart attack near two years ago. She just…closed the door. She had too much grief already on her mind.

Now she flung the door open and stared in horror at his gun safe, standing open and empty. The key. Robbie had found the key. Pete's hunting rifles were missing, both of them, and Joyce knew without looking that the handgun he kept in the drawer at the bottom of the safe would be gone, too. Lord have mercy on them all.

What had Robbie done?

Right that moment, she didn't even care that he might be coming for her. No, she hoped he would. This was all her fault. Her legs sagged, and she sank down onto the floor right there, in the doorway where she couldn't look away from the awful sight of those missing guns. Tears streaming down her face, she waited for him.

REEVE HADFIELD LAY on his back on his wooden creeper under the car, Kanye West's "Heard 'em Say" blasting through his earbuds. He wiped sweat from his forehead, not caring that he'd probably smeared grease on his face, then adjusted his light and started to lift the wrench. A glimpse of his watch surprised him. Crap! Walt said he'd probably stop by before one, and it was after that now. He'd have seen that Reeve was under the car, wouldn't he?

Walt Stenten owned the Shell station out by the highway. Reeve had pumped gas through high school and after he graduated had gone to work for him full-time. It wasn't like they were friends, exactly; Walt was probably Reeve's parents' age, maybe forty-five or fifty or something like that. He was this short guy built like a box, who kept his hair in a buzz cut and had crinkles beside his eyes from squinting. They hardly talked at all, and when they did it was mostly stuff like, "Start with the oil change, then let's take a look at the brakes on the Hargers' Voyager."

Reeve had been working on his own car, a '55 Chevy Bel Air. Not a convertible; that would have been even cooler. This was a sedan, but it was in awesome shape considering. Getting parts was the hard thing. Walt had been helping him with that.

Reeve reached down to his waist and turned off his iPod, so he'd hear when Walt did come. The garage door stood open to give him better light to work by, so Reeve knew he wouldn't go to the front door or anything.

Talk about timing: he heard footsteps coming up the driveway. Grinning, Reeve laid down the light and his wrench, then gave a push with his heels to send the creeper shooting out from under the side of the Bel Air. He spun on the wheels and, still on his back, zipped out to the front of the garage, the bumper rearing above him.

Since his eyes had adjusted to the dim light under the car, the brilliant sunlight blinded him for a moment. All he could see was a dark silhouette against the white-hot background.

"Walt?" he said, hearing his own uncertainty. He blinked

a couple of times, thinking it was weird that Walt hadn't said anything or moved.

One more blink, and he could see again. Only…it wasn't Walt standing there. It was that freak Rob Owen. And— shit!—he had a rifle slung over his back, a pistol jammed in his waistband, and he was holding another rifle loose in his arms.

His hair was matted and dirty. Was that *blood* spattering his face and the front of his T-shirt? He stared at Reeve, his face expressionless except for his dark eyes, which burned. He was crazy, everyone knew that. But this…this was horror-movie crazy.

Reeve heard himself start to say, "What the…?" when the barrel of that rifle lifted and took aim at his head or maybe his chest. Owen sighted down it, and, as if time had slowed down, Reeve actually saw a finger tightening on the trigger.

I'm dead, he thought incredulously.

And then, God, a body flew out of nowhere just as the first deafening boom sounded. Slam! Somebody came down on top of him, pushing the creeper backward.

Boom! Another shot.

It was deadweight on him. Completely panicked, Reeve shoved the body off him and propelled himself under the car with a scramble of heels and hands.

Walt. God, that was Walt, he realized in horror. Walt, with blood spilling from his mouth, and his eyes…

Reeve came out the back of the Bel Air and leaped off the creeper, crouching behind the bulk of the car, straining for any sound at all.

Nothing. Damn it. Nothing.

He measured with his eyes the distance to the door going into the house, and knew he had to try for it. His heart was trying to slam its way out of his chest, and he wasn't sure he *could* hear over the thunder in his ears.

Now!

Still crouching, he threw himself forward, up the two steps, turned the knob, yanked the door open and all but fell through, into the kitchen. He didn't hear a gunshot, didn't see anything. Hand shaking, he pushed the stupid-ass little button lock that wouldn't keep out anyone, then ran for the phone. It took him three tries to dial 911.

The operator had already answered, her voice faraway and tinny, when Reeve heard another gunshot. Not right out in front; maybe a couple of houses away.

"Somebody's shot," he babbled. "God! I think he's dead. My address…"

"I have your address, sir. Do you see the gunman?"

"No!" he screamed. "I don't know where he went! Just… hurry. Tell them to hurry."

Then he dropped the phone and ran for the bathroom. He'd pissed his pants. He couldn't let anyone see. No one.

Somehow he got himself cleaned up, grabbed jeans from his bedroom and raced for the door to the garage again, still hopping to get the jeans on and buttoned.

Somewhere, sirens had started. Not one, but several.

God. He wanted to go out and see if Walt was alive, but he was too freaking scared to do it. Walt might be bleeding to death, after sacrificing himself to save Reeve, and he didn't have the guts to go back out into the garage.

He'd never learned first aid anyway.

Oh, sure. Good excuse.

The sirens screamed right outside. Doors were slamming, feet pounding up the driveway.

Reeve wiped tears from his cheeks and stood up. He had to go out there. He had to explain.

I'm *the one Rob Owen hated. It was supposed to be* me *lying there bleeding my life away. Not Walt.*

Me.

THE WHOLE DAMN town was a crime scene.

David Owen had just pulled off the highway and crossed the bridge into Tucannon. Incredulous, he braked to a stop in the middle of the road, not even looking to see if there was another car behind him.

Not only a crime scene, he saw, a thriller-movie crime scene, bigger than life. And this wasn't any town, it was his hometown.

Dear God. He'd known, in one way, since his mother's phone call nearly five hours ago telling him Robbie had taken Dad's guns and killed some people, then himself.

"I saw his body," she'd said, her voice shaky. "He's dead. Robbie's dead."

"Is that all you can think about?" he had asked sharply. "How many is 'some' people? Who else died?"

She either didn't know or couldn't say. David had a number now; before he'd reached the summit at Snoqualmie, an hour out of Seattle, the massacre in the tiny Eastern Washington town of Tucannon was all newscasters could talk about. Five people were dead, plus the gunman, and two more clung to life at St. Mary Medical Center in Walla Walla. More were wounded. Victims had yet to be identified.

This had been coming for years, in David's opinion. His parents hadn't listened to reason, his mother even less so than his father. All they could see was that Rob was sick. They ridiculed any suggestion that he could be a danger to anyone.

David had turned the radio on compulsively every half hour during the drive across the bleak, empty center of the

state and again as he passed Walla Walla and the basalt out-
crops gave way to rolling hills covered with vineyards or
wheat. As he sat there now, staring in shock at the police
cars with flashing lights blockading side streets, the TV
news vans clogging Main, the clusters of people hugging
each other out on the sidewalks, the commercial jingle on
the radio ended and a newscaster declared gravely, "Today,
tragic news from Whitman County, Washington. Townsfolk
in little Tucannon were gunned down by a man known to
all, raised by his parents…"

In a violent gesture he rarely allowed himself, David hit
the button to turn off the radio.

A man known to all. Robbie, the big brother he'd adored
and shadowed when they were children.

He made a guttural sound. No, that Robbie had been
gone for a long time, drowned out by the voices he heard
in his head.

Tucannon should have been sleepy at seven-thirty in
the evening, with August heat lingering and the sun still a
couple of hours from setting. Kids out on bikes, neighbors
on porches, most of the businesses closed. But it looked
as if nobody had gone home today. People congregated
outside the storefronts along Main, as if they'd been there
ever since they rushed out to hear what others knew, then
clung together in shock. Maybe they weren't being allowed
to go home.

Traffic crept the half a dozen blocks past police cars,
lights rotating, that blockaded Maple, Sycamore and Elm.
Inching forward, David looked with disbelief at faces wet
with tears. Faces of people he knew.

As a King County deputy prosecuting attorney, he had
seen plenty of crime scenes and always succeeded in main-
taining the necessary dispassion. What horror or revulsion
he felt stayed hidden well enough that he'd acquired a rep-

utation. "He's a calculating son of a bitch," he'd overheard another assistant prosecutor say, and David had taken it as a compliment. On the job he never betrayed emotion unless it served a purpose.

But this… Shock washed over him in icy waves and he turned off the air conditioner. Until now, nothing he'd heard had seemed real. Knowing intellectually and seeing his hometown transformed by horror were two different things.

Robbie did this.

Robbie is dead.

Had Robbie looked around in the end, seen what he'd done and remembered that those people lying lifeless at his feet were friends and neighbors? Or had he still been enmeshed in madness and thought death was his only escape from Satan's creatures—who would not stay silent however he pleaded?

As cold as if the damn air-conditioning were still on, David thought, *It doesn't matter.* They would never know whether Robbie had been obeying his voices or trying to silence them. What he'd done was so terrible nobody would care.

Except Mom, who would be bereft without the son who had been at the center of her life.

David was able to turn onto Poplar, but Third, Fourth and Fifth were all blocked. Finally, at Sixth, he pulled up to the sawhorses and rolled down his window.

God, he wanted to wake up and discover he'd been having a nightmare.

The state patrolman manning this barricade came around to the driver's side of David's Lexus. "Sir, I can't allow anyone to pass…." He took in David's face and stopped. "Are you the brother?"

There had been a time David had been glad he looked

like his brother. But from the time he'd turned thirteen and Robbie fifteen, he'd cursed the resemblance.

Now he nodded curtly. "I'm David Owen. My mother needs me."

"Yes, sir. If you'll wait for a minute, sir."

The patrolman returned to his own vehicle and consulted someone on the radio. Through the open window, David could just hear the crackle of incomprehensible voices.

Then the officer came back, bent down to look David in the eye and said, "You may proceed directly to your house. Please don't turn into the driveway. Park at the curb."

Jaw muscles knotted, David dipped his head. When the state patrolman pulled back one of the sawhorses, he edged carefully through.

The first couple of blocks were deserted. The sun reflected off seemingly empty windows. He felt as if he were driving through a ghost town, and his skin prickled. Had the police gone door to door and asked everyone to leave? Was that why they stood downtown? Or were people watching his car pass from behind cracks in the blinds and asking themselves why he'd never done anything, being a prosecutor and all.

Out of habit, he used his turn signal before going left on Maple. Even he knew the blinking light, the click, click, click of the signal, was absurd. *If a tree falls in a forest, and nobody is there to see...*

A block ahead, he saw police cars and crime-scene crews.

How far from home had Robbie gone on his killing spree? Or was it only the nearest neighbors he'd shot? David dreaded learning who the victims were.

It seemed everyone paused and turned to watch his car glide to the curb in front of his house. His mother's house, he corrected himself harshly; it had been a long time since he'd considered it home. He and she hardly knew how to carry on a conversation anymore, and he hadn't been able to talk to Robbie in a long time.

But his mother had to be shattered. She had no one else to help her bury Robbie and decide what she was going to do next. After that, he had absolutely no idea whether it was possible to mend their relationship. And yet he felt an obligation to try.

A law-enforcement officer walked over the minute David got out of his car. County, not city; Tucannon boasted a five-man police department that handled traffic control, drunks and minor theft. Anything bigger happened and they called in the county.

"David Owen."

"I'm Lieutenant Sykes." The guy looked like an aging football player: thick neck, shaved head, not especially smart except for the eyes. He had a cop's eyes. Shrewd, curious, compassionate.

David hated meeting those eyes but did it anyway. "Is my mother in the house?"

"Yes, sir. She's pretty shocky. I had an EMT check her out, but she's refused to leave. She told us she'd called you."

"All right if I go in?"

"We'll ask you to stay out of the den and the basement."

The basement, where his parents had created an apartment for Rob that allowed him some illusion of independence.

David nodded and started up the walk, ignoring the stares and the concentration of crime-scene personnel at the Tindalls' and Charlie Henderson's beyond.

While feeling sick to realize who some of the victims were, he wasn't surprised that Wayne Tindall had been one of them. Rob had hated Wayne. But Betty…*God.* Betty was a nice lady. And Henderson was always decent to the Owen boys. David hoped like hell his brother hadn't killed Charlie Henderson, or Betty Tindall, either.

Sweat trickled down his back as he mounted the front porch steps and opened the door. Inside was complete silence. The drapes were all drawn, and it was so murky he stopped in dismay. Was she sitting here in darkness?

"Mom?"

A woman police officer appeared from the kitchen. Young and Hispanic, she didn't hide her reaction to his face as well as Sykes had. An expression between fear and distaste flickered in her eyes before she conquered it. "I'm Officer Martinez. I persuaded your mother to lie down. She's in her bedroom." She hesitated. "I've been checking on her every few minutes. I hoped she'd fall asleep."

David nodded. "I'll go up."

The fifth stair creaked under his tread, as it had ever since he'd been a boy. He and Robbie had learned to skip it when they were sneaking out.

The upstairs hall was dim, too, the doors closed to the single bathroom on this floor, his bedroom and the room that had been Robbie's and later converted to a combo guest room and sewing room for his mother. Only the door to his mother's bedroom stood open.

"Mom?" he said quietly.

The bedside lamp was on, the pool of light welcome since the blinds were closed up here, too. She lay on the bed with her back to him, but at the sound of his voice she rolled over. "Davey?"

He hated being called that, but in the midst of his shock at the sight of her, graying and painfully thin, old before her time, he only said, "I'm here, Mom," and went to the bed where she struggled to sit up.

"Thank you for coming." For a moment she sounded

formal, as if he were an attorney she'd called for advice. But then her face crumpled. "Oh, Davey!"

The mattress gave as he sat down and wrapped his arms around his mother. She burrowed her face against his chest as if it was the first refuge she'd found and began to cry, huge coughing sobs that alarmed him. She felt so frail, nothing like the steady, competent woman his earliest memories conjured, or even the mother who had gone to bat against the world on her oldest son's behalf. It was as if she'd aged ten years in the past two, since Dad died.

Or maybe she'd aged all of those years today, since she found out what Robbie had done.

David knew better than to tell her it would be all right, because it wasn't and wouldn't be. He just laid his cheek against the top of her head, his own face wet, and rocked her as she wept.

"ACADIA? Honey, have you seen the news?" her mom asked.

Stepping out of the hospital, Acadia Henderson immediately wondered why she'd thought it was a good idea during her too-brief break to return her mother's call.

Uh-huh, sure, the middle of the day in a busy hospital E.R. and she was watching TV. Snatches of news did often find their way to emergency-room staff, of course, usually the scores of big games. But today had been chaos. It seemed as if every crazy in Sacramento was trying to kill himself or someone else today.

"The moon's full," someone had said wisely early on. Acadia didn't even know if it really was, but the explanation was as good as any other.

"No." She groaned and settled herself on the curb at the ambulance entrance. It was blisteringly hot out here, but she tipped her head back and let the sun bake her. For just a second, eyes closed, she could imagine herself lying on a beach somewhere sunny. Maui, or maybe the deck of a cruise ship off the shores of Belize or Honduras. She could just reach out her hand for that mai tai....

She tuned in to her mother's voice in time to hear, "This man shot up the whole town. They don't know how many people are dead. I tried to call your dad but I didn't get any answer."

Jolted, she opened her eyes. "What?"

"Aren't you listening?" Mom sounded the next thing to hysterical. "Somebody's gone crazy and killed a bunch of people in Tucannon." She made a sound. "Somebody. Right. You know it had to be that Rob Owen boy. Except he's not a boy anymore. But you remember how *strange* he was."

Acadia did remember. She'd had a major crush on the strange Rob Owen's younger brother, David, so she'd paid lots of attention to the Owen boys' comings and goings. Funny how well she could still remember his face…

Alarmed now, she shook her head to dislodge the idiotic memory of a sixteen-year-old who, in reality, was probably skinny and the furthest thing from sexy. "Oh, God. What do you mean, Dad isn't answering?"

"I mean, I've called half a dozen times and left two messages! Oh, why is he so stubborn? If he just had a cell phone…"

Suddenly Acadia couldn't bear the heat for another second. She was having trouble breathing. Pushing herself to her feet, she said, "Isn't he still teaching a couple of classes at the community college? He's probably at the college. Or just out doing errands."

"Didn't you tell me he didn't have classes on Tuesdays or Thursdays anymore? And, Acadia, he's only two doors down from the Owens."

Acadia paused just inside the automatic glass doors,

chilled instead of grateful for the air-conditioning. "You *know* it was Rob Owen?"

"They haven't said yet, but it has to be, doesn't it?"

"Oh, God," she said again. "I'll call, Mom. I'll go watch the news. Let me know if you hear anything."

She went straight for the lounge, where half a dozen nurses and doctors had congregated during a lull they all knew wouldn't last long. The TV was on, the volume low and nobody watching. Acadia stood right in front of it.

"We're told the death toll in Tucannon, Washington, stands at seven now," the pretty blonde newscaster said. "Marsha? Can you tell us more?"

The camera panned Main Street in the small, hilly town Acadia remembered so well and hadn't seen in… three years? Four? But now, in a scene of universal tragedy, lights flashed atop police cars and groups of people cried and held each other on the sidewalk in front of the hardware store. Then it focused on a woman with a microphone, yet another attractive blonde, who shook her head gravely. "Word has just come that one of the victims rushed by helicopter to the hospital in Walla Walla has been declared dead. The police have not yet released names, saying they want to speak to family members first. There are rumors—you can see how frightened townspeople are—" Once again the camera moved over the faces of grieving residents before returning to her. "But no one knows anything for sure, as residents who live in the six-block radius where the shooter chose and murdered his victims are not being allowed to return home."

Acadia made a sound, just a small one, but Keith Gresch, an E.R. resident, asked, "Are you all right?"

At almost the same moment, the phone she hadn't turned off vibrated in her hand. She looked down at it, and her heart constricted. The exchange was 509 for Eastern Washington, but the number wasn't her father's.

"Excuse me," she said, and hurried out. The phone had quit ringing before she got outside, but she immediately hit Send. It rang only once before a man said, "Lieutenant Sykes."

She turned to face the stucco wall of the hospital and leaned her forehead against it, glad of the rough texture. "I… You just called me. My name is Acadia Henderson."

"Are you Charles Henderson's daughter?"

Are. Not *were. Please let him mean it,* she prayed.

"Yes," she whispered.

"Are you aware of events in Tucannon today, Ms. Henderson?" His voice was kind, sad. She'd heard police officers and doctors both speak to distraught family members like that, right here in the emergency room. A few times, she'd had to tell them herself that their beloved son or mother or baby hadn't made it.

"Yes," she said again, pushing her forehead harder against the wall, until it hurt.

"I'm sorry to have to inform you that your father was one of the victims. He was killed outright."

"Are you sure?" She sounded and felt like a frightened little girl who didn't want to understand. "How can you be sure it's him?"

"A neighbor identified him, Ms. Henderson. Your father was shot right on his front porch. We don't know if he was an intended victim, or whether he came out to investigate when he heard gunshots next door."

Something made her ask, "Was it Rob Owen?"

His tone sharpened. "We haven't made the knowledge public yet, but…yes, it was. You knew him?"

She started to nod, then realized he wouldn't see it. "I

moved away when I was thirteen. I saw him a few times when I was visiting my dad. Everyone knew he was crazy."

"So I'm being told." He paused. "Had your father complained about any confrontations with him?"

"No." Grief was thickening her throat, making it hard to say anything else. "No, my father wasn't the confrontational kind."

Not even with her mother. Not even when her mother took his little girl and left him. He hadn't known *how* to rage or cry or laugh exultantly.

Acadia had nonetheless loved him, and had never forgiven him for taking their departure so well.

Now…now she would never be able to tell him that she knew every marital failure was two-sided, or that she had kept loving him even when she was angry.

How many times, in her job, had she seen people bitterly regret what they hadn't said? How could a woman who saw as much death and tragedy as she did have made the same mistake?

"I'll get a flight," she said numbly. "I won't be able to get there until tomorrow."

Lieutenant Sykes started talking about when they could release the body. Acadia didn't want to know.

"I have to go," she told him, and hit End. Then she dropped the phone in her pocket, flattened her hands against the rough wall and cried.

CHAPTER TWO

STANDING OUTSIDE HIS mother's bedroom, David felt about the night ahead the way defendants probably did their stint in the witness box. A grieving parent, an empty house with too many ghosts, his constant prickling awareness of what was happening right next door, images of the brother he'd loved despite everything… It was pretty safe to say he wouldn't be sleeping like a baby tonight.

Once his mother had cried herself out, she hadn't wanted to talk. She'd curled away from him on the bed and he had spread an afghan over her. She'd never napped in her life, but he hoped she would make an exception. Or better yet, fall asleep and not awake up until tomorrow morning.

He shook himself and headed downstairs, startled to see the woman officer waiting for him at the bottom. He'd forgotten he and his mother weren't alone in the house.

"Unless you need me, I'll be going now," she said with that same freezing civility.

"No. Thanks."

She opened the front door and stepped out on the porch. "Investigators will need to speak to your mother."

He knew all too well what was coming in the days ahead, every exhausting, wrenching moment. The cops weren't trying to be cruel. It was their job to understand what had happened. Still, he felt a flash of anger on his mother's behalf.

"Surely they can wait until tomorrow."

"I doubt they'll be ready tonight anyway."

Involuntarily, both of them turned their heads toward the cluster of law-enforcement personnel working the scene next door. A camera flashed, and he felt it like a blow. The bodies were probably gone, but he pictured blood staining the front porch where his mother used to go and sit with Betty sometimes on hot nights, their voices soft murmurs in the dark.

No, crime-scene personnel and investigators were busy right now determining the sequence of action. Who had Rob shot first? Second? Third? God. Fourth, fifth and sixth? David scrubbed a hand over his face. There were more than that. A few that had been treated here in town, at least one other critically injured victim who'd been transported to Walla Walla. He didn't know how many victims there were altogether.

He imagined this as a traffic investigation, the kind that happened after a pileup on the freeway with fatalities. The freeway would stay closed for hours while skid marks were measured, speeds estimated, centrifugal force calculated by obscure formulas. That's all they were doing here: getting the sequence of events straight, the hows and whys for reports. They knew who the shooter was, and he'd made sure there would be no trial. But the chart still had to be drawn, the dots connected.

David went back inside and closed the front door, shutting out all sound. Dusk had barely begun deepening the blue of the sky, but in here it was dark already. He wanted to open blinds but didn't like the idea of anyone looking in.

He made a sound in his throat. Anyone? Just wait until the police barricades came down and the vultures clustered outside! He'd have to talk to his mother about writing a statement. But the fourth estate wouldn't be satisfied with that. They'd wait for either of them to step outside. Their belief the public had a right to know would extend to displaying his mother's ravaged face on the six-o'clock news. Or his. God. He could hear it now. *King County Deputy Prosecuting Attorney David Owen refused to comment on his brother's rampage....*

Would he even have a job waiting when he got home?

He'd have to call tomorrow. Most of his current cases would need to be reassigned. David could already foresee being here for at least a month. He couldn't imagine his mother wanting to stay in this house. But since she'd lived here all of her adult life, leaving wouldn't be easy, either. Packing meant sifting through the past, discarding, keeping. Hurting with every decision. And where would she go? She complained about the noise and rush when she visited him in Seattle. He couldn't imagine her wanting to live with him. The Oregon Coast to be near her sister, Jackie? But she didn't like the damp climate.

Too soon to think about it.

God. Aunt Jackie. Would Mom have called her? Somehow he doubted it. He took out his cell phone, thought, *Lucky me,* and dialed.

She answered after the first ring. "David? Oh, thank heavens! It's so late I didn't want to call if Joyce was asleep, but I've been pacing the floor!"

"You heard, then?" He leaned one hip against a kitchen counter.

"Not until I turned on the ten-o'clock news. I've been busy all day and hadn't even gone online." Unlike his mother, Aunt Jackie had taken to computers like a duck to water. He and she had stayed closer than they might have otherwise because they emailed regularly. She forwarded him Maxine cartoons that were pretty funny.

"Then you know the story," he said. "I haven't heard the names of victims yet, except it's pretty clear Rob killed

Wayne and Betty Tindall next door." She visited often
enough to know the near neighbors. "And Charlie Henderson, too, I'm afraid."

"Oh, no!" She was silent for a long moment, but he could
hear her breathing. "I thought Joyce was exaggerating,"
she said finally.

"Exaggerating?"

"When she'd gotten so afraid of him."

He straightened. "She didn't tell me she was."

"No. She wouldn't. She thought you resented him, you
know."

He closed his eyes and pinched the bridge of his nose
where it burned. "I probably did, back when I was a kid."
Right. Sure. I'm so mature I outgrew that resentment.
"Mostly," he lied, "I thought he needed more help than
they could get him. When he was in one of his rages…"

"You were afraid he might hurt them. Your mom and
dad."

He had to swallow hard before he could say, "Yeah. Mom
wouldn't hear it. After a while…"

"She quit telling you anything," his aunt said gently. "I
know. I argued with her, because I knew you wanted to
help and with a law degree and your connections you might
have been able to pull something off."

"Instead, I alienated Mom so she didn't feel she could
come to me at all. I know damn well I bear a share of responsibility for what happened here today."

"What are you talking about?" She sounded mad. "It's
not your fault, and not your mother's—although I know
perfectly well she's telling herself it is. She did everything
she could. They wouldn't let her commit him…"

"What?"

She was quiet for a moment. "You didn't know?"

"That she tried? No." He felt sick, understanding at last how completely his mother had shut him out.

"Twice. She and Pete did their best, oh, maybe five years ago."

Not only his mother, then; his father, too.

"Then last year again," his aunt continued, "Joyce had an attorney over in Walla Walla have a go, but she couldn't prove to the board's satisfaction that Rob was violent enough to be a danger to anyone. Apparently, committing an adult against his will isn't easy."

"No," David said again. "But I would have thought Rob would meet the criteria." Shit, anyone should have been able to see how angry Rob was, how out of touch with reality. The voices in his head were more real to him than his parents' voices. Had anyone with authority *talked* to him?

"They wanted to know if he'd killed neighbors' cats or dogs. But you know how much he loved animals. He'd never do anything like that."

No, he hadn't killed anyone's pet. Just people.

David had to draw a shuddering breath, the grief swelling so there wasn't much room for air. "Yeah. I know."

"He'd shoved Pete or Joyce a few times, and put his fist through the wall, but that wasn't bad enough."

"He had to kill someone first."

"I guess so."

This time, they both fell silent. What else was there to say?

Aunt Jackie offered to come if Mom needed her. He felt a cowardly burst of hope that she would just take over, absolving him of responsibility so that he could go back to his life.

"If I come tomorrow," she said finally, "I'll have to leave Sunday. Or I can wait until Tuesday to drive up."

He could tell she was hesitating rather than being done with what she had to say. He waited.

"There's something I haven't told you."

The *something,* it developed, was that she had colon cancer. Her doctor was confident she'd win the battle, but she was having regular chemotherapy treatments.

"I can't miss one, of course."

"Is it making you sick?"

"Not yet. Monday will only be my third. I'm feeling a little tired, and I have already bought a wig for when my hair falls out."

"God, Aunt Jackie. You should have told me."

"I'm…having a little trouble saying even to myself, 'You have cancer.' Joyce is about the only other person I have told. Except Warren, of course."

The timing sucked royally, too, but he didn't have to say that. When shit happened, it happened.

"You stay home for now," he said. "I'm here for as long as Mom needs me. If you're up to it, I'm thinking she might want to come visit you for a while. Patting your back while you puke would give her something to do."

She gave a choked laugh and said, "Boy, that sounds fun. You know how to raise an old gal's spirits."

"I'll have Mom call tomorrow," David promised, and they left it at that.

After checking on his mother, who hadn't moved since he left her, he opened the door to his bedroom, where he still slept on his rare visits home. It looked exactly as it had when he left for college. Wanting a clean slate, he hadn't taken much with him. The result was that when he'd closed the door behind him that day, he'd encapsulated himself at eighteen. He hadn't spent enough time here after that to bother changing anything.

His teenage self hadn't hung sports posters. Not him.

He'd gone for travel posters. The Spanish Steps in Rome. A lone boatman poling through reeds along the Nile, pyramids a distant mirage in the background. He'd been confident that he was more sophisticated than his peers, more curious, more *worldly*. He'd probably just seemed like an ass to them.

The bookcases were stuffed. He'd read widely. The honors-level English teacher popularly known as Baron von Trapp—Mr. Baron—had encouraged David to try great American and British writers. He'd already been interested in law and the shelves held some case law and biographies of famous judges and attorneys.

His rueful gaze went to the twin bed, wearing a twenty-year-old corded brown spread. At home, he had a king-size bed. He was six feet three inches. His feet hung over on this one. They had when he was eighteen, too, but then he hadn't minded as much.

He left the door open when he went downstairs. Why shut it? There were too many closed doors in this house.

The kitchen drew him into it, if only because the light was still on. This time he noticed that the wallpaper was new, ivy on a white background instead of the floral pattern he remembered. Mom had probably had to do it to cover the holes Rob had punched in the wall, if Aunt Jackie was right.

His stomach rumbled, reminding him that he'd skipped lunch and now dinner. An exploration of the cupboards didn't excite him, but he put on water to boil for boxed macaroni and cheese, his boyhood staple. There had to be a dozen boxes in the cupboard.

It had been Rob's favorite back then, too. God, his mother probably stocked it for Rob.

He shoved the memory out of his mind. *Don't think about him. Not now. Not yet.*

He kept opening cupboards, investigating. If he were

going to drink coffee, he wasn't surprised to find it would have to be instant Folgers. He'd have to do something about that if he was going to be here more than a week.

His hands knew where to find everything, from a pan lid to the jar of coffee. Part of him was the adult looking on, noticing that the linoleum was aging and the freezer needed to be defrosted—did anyone defrost anymore? But inside him was the kid who was home again, who nudged a drawer shut with his hip exactly as he'd done a thousand times, who knew the milk would be on the door in the fridge and the margarine on the middle shelf. The familiarity was disconcerting because it wasn't only physical—knowing how to curl his hand around the knob without even glancing, that one step took him from sink to refrigerator, that recycling was on the right under the sink, trash the left. It was more complicated than that. He felt more as if he'd just discovered his adult self was a layer of pancake makeup hiding the boy he'd been, cockiness and insecurities unchanged.

How easy it was to step back into his role. The Good Son. The one who was never any trouble, who by his achievements balanced the troublemaking son and let his parents feel relief and pride. Who was there when they needed him.

On those occasions when they noticed they had another son.

With an almost savage motion, he dumped the macaroni in the boiling water.

He went upstairs again. His mother still lay with her back to the door. He could tell from her rigidity and the shallowness of her breathing that she wasn't asleep. But when he said softly, "Mom? Are you hungry?" and she didn't answer, he didn't push it. In fact, he was relieved. If they sat at the table together, they'd feel they had to talk, and that wasn't going to be easy for either of them.

He ate at the kitchen table, then drifted around the house,

so achingly familiar. He'd swear even the knickknacks in the living room were unchanged. The kitchen wallpaper was the only change he saw anywhere.

The yellow crime-scene tape that sealed his dad's den jarred him enough that he didn't go down the hall toward the laundry room or the stairs that led to the basement. There would be yellow tape sealing that door, too.

He waited until the activity outside seemed to have ended for the night before he went out to his car and got his overnight bag from the trunk. He hurried, feeling the need to be invisible.

The single change of clothes he'd brought wouldn't hold him, he reflected. He'd either need to make a quick trip back to Seattle, or get a friend to pack a suitcase and send it to him.

At ten o'clock, he turned on the TV for the news. The police hadn't yet released names. The only victims so far identified were the two who had been transported to St. Mary in Walla Walla. Walt Stenten who owned the Shell station here in town had died in the hospital. It was Wendi Rowe, a pharmacy assistant, who still clung to life.

Stunned, his chest aching, David pictured them: taciturn Walt, a short, square, red-faced man with grease embedded in the cracks of his skin on his hands; and Miss Rowe, who must be in her fifties, with a tight blond perm and a Tootsie Roll for every kid who came into the pharmacy. Why them?

More residents wept on camera. The difference between this and coverage of other tragedies he'd seen on the news was that he knew these people, too. With a sense of shock, he saw his sixth-grade teacher, Mrs. Skott, wiping away tears and saying she didn't know if she'd ever feel safe again. Marge from the Bluebird Café declared venomously that everyone had known it would come to this, with a paranoid schizophrenic allowed to roam the town and terrorize people, and the police chief never willing to do anything about it.

With a soft groan, David closed his eyes and hung his head. Could he have made a difference if he hadn't absented himself, his pride and his feelings stung by his parents' refusal to listen to his suggestions?

Too late to wonder.

He made himself go upstairs and step into his mother's bedroom. "Mom, kitchen's closing. Last call if you want something to eat."

Without rolling over, she shook her head.

"Then why don't you get ready for bed for real? It's ten-thirty."

"What difference does it make if I'm on top of the covers or under them?" she asked dully.

"If there's one thing that keeps people going at a time like this, it's routine." Countless victims had told him that they wouldn't have gotten out of bed at all, except for the morning routine that was so ingrained. They always put on slippers and went out for the newspaper, had two poached eggs on a slice of whole-wheat toast, brushed teeth starting with the right upper molars, shaved just before getting in the shower, and so on, and out of habit they kept doing it. He'd noticed before that people whose lives were more chaotic handled extreme stress and tragedy less well. Structure meant everything.

He thought for a minute that Mom was going to ignore him, but at last she sighed. "You're right," she said, then rolled over and put her feet to the floor. "Did you find something for dinner?"

"Yeah."

He hesitated, watching as she went to her dresser and got a nightgown, then walked toward him like an automaton, her face utterly blank. He wasn't sure she wouldn't have walked right into him if he hadn't stepped aside. A moment later, the bathroom door closed.

Still he hesitated. Did he hang around to tuck her in? Or give her the credit of assuming she was an adult and could make her own way back to bed?

The grunt he gave might have been a laugh under other circumstances. Role reversal never came comfortably to anyone. Parenting your own kids seemed to come naturally to most people. Parenting your parents didn't. He didn't even know if she needed more than a listening ear and an occasional reminder.

Tomorrow would tell, he thought, heading downstairs to turn off the lights.

Back in his bedroom, he called, "Good night" when he heard his mother come out of the bathroom. She said the same. Empty words. Neither of them would have a good night, in any sense of the word.

MARGE PERKINS SET her alarm to get her up an extra fifteen minutes early. All those reporters would be coming into the café for breakfast this morning, and in case they wanted to interview her again today, she should look her best.

Not that it had mattered yesterday; why, everyone had been distraught! But today...well, her dignity demanded that she pull herself together and represent Tucannon well. And who would be spending more time with all those cameramen and reporters than her? There were only two places to eat out in town, and the Bluebird Café had the best food.

Last night Marge had been interviewed by newscasters from two different channels. One was that good-looking John Nolan whose grin when he did his lighter pieces on KOMO had always given her a little shiver. To think she'd not only seen him in real life, right there outside the café, but he had actually wanted to talk to her! He'd held out the microphone and listened to her with deep concern in his brown eyes. What's more, of all the interviews KOMO ran, the longest was hers!

Marge knew why that was. She'd said what everyone else was thinking. That Rob Owen should have been in an institution from the time he was fifteen or sixteen years old. Townsfolk were scared of him even then, but would Pete or Joyce listen? No. He was their son, and they had been determined to pretend nothing was wrong.

Marge thought there was a good chance John Nolan or that other reporter—Brenda Matthews from KING 5— would want to talk to her again today. The Owens had always had their advocates in town, like that Alice Simmons, who Marge herself had heard not two months back telling anyone who would listen that Joyce was doing everything she could, and nobody should cast stones unless they'd been in her shoes. Well, Alice hadn't been on TV last night defending the Owens. Two months ago, this tragedy could still have been averted if only people had spoken out.

She certainly wasn't in the Owens' camp, and it was important for people to hear the truth: a mentally ill man had been allowed to run wild because townsfolk didn't want to hurt Joyce Owen. Joyce, who had never had to work to support herself the way Marge had, and who was practically a stranger here in Tucannon. She didn't even do her shopping here!

Marge wouldn't have told another soul, but it had been exciting to see herself on TV. She'd taped the news on one station while she watched the other. Now she wished there'd been some way to tape both news programs, but at least she had John Nolan interviewing her so she could watch it whenever she wanted.

After using her curling iron and even a touch of makeup

this morning, she studied herself carefully in the mirror before finally nodding. If she did say so, she looked her best. Tucannon would have no reason to be embarrassed by her.

Just in case those cameras did turn her way again today.

JOYCE SAT UPRIGHT in a chair, her only concession to daylight. She had never been one to lie in bed all day. Earlier, David had brought her breakfast, which she'd picked at. Otherwise, all she seemed able to do was wallow in regrets. They spun in her head as if she was a hamster on a wheel going nowhere, yet driven by some primitive instinct to keep trying.

But now David was standing in the bedroom doorway telling her the investigators were here and hoping to talk to her. "I already told them what I know," he said.

A terrible rage swept over her and she flared, "You don't know anything! Why pretend you do? Of course I'll come down!"

His face went utterly expressionless, in that way of his. She'd hurt his feelings, she supposed. But David hadn't known Robbie in years, not really. Joyce didn't even like to think what he'd told those investigators. Of course he'd been trying to help, maybe save her from answering some questions, but he shouldn't have tried to speak for her.

"You might want to brush your hair," he said.

She flicked a fiercely angry gaze at him but stomped into the bathroom and closed the door.

For all of Robbie's illness, she'd understood him. At least he'd talked to her! But not David. He hadn't since he was a little boy. Back then, he'd been serious. And so smart! But not cold, like he was now. Cold and...impenetrable. She could never tell what he really felt. He was more a stranger to her than Jason, the clerk at the Albertson's in

Walla Walla who often rang up her purchases and told her what he'd done on his days off or about a movie he'd seen.

Her hair needed more than brushing, but she did the best she could and came out to find him waiting.

Several uniformed men were in her dining room. They all rose when she appeared, then sat back down when she pulled out her chair and sank into it.

Chief Bolton she knew, of course. He wouldn't meet her eyes. And Lieutenant Sykes was the one who'd walked her to the ambulance and opened the body bag to show her Robbie's face. The others introduced themselves; she didn't even try to take in their names. She didn't care who they were.

"Dr. Cole has already spoken to us about Robert," one of those nameless investigators said.

She stiffened in outrage. "Patient records are confidential."

"He felt he no longer had anyone to protect."

Still angry, Joyce said nothing.

"He indicated that you had expressed increasing concern about Robert's capability for violence."

Joyce pressed her lips together.

David had continued to stand. Now he touched her shoulder. "Talk to them, Mom." He sounded weary and yet detached. "The doctor was right. Rob doesn't need you to protect him anymore."

Abruptly she bowed her head, grief backing up in her throat like bile. "I made him leave. This was my fault."

Lieutenant Sykes leaned forward. "You asked him to leave the house? Is that what you mean?"

She was shocked to realize tears were running down her cheeks again. All she could manage was a nod.

"Why?"

She wasn't sure she could speak. David pressed a tissue

in her hand. He was always such a good boy, she thought drearily, even when she didn't deserve him.

"He wouldn't take his medicine. We've gone through this before…" The truth was, more often than not Robbie had resisted being medicated. He hated the way those drugs made him feel. As if all the colors had been dulled, the sounds muffled, he had told her. And he forgot so quickly the hell he would descend into once the colors became vivid again.

Staring defiantly at them, Joyce said, "He quit showering. When I brought him food, he threw it at me. He liked to sneak up on me. Sometimes, when I thought I was alone, I'd turn and bump right into him. I couldn't tell if he thought it was funny that I was afraid, or…" She pressed her lips together.

"Do you know anything about the injury on his hand?" the lieutenant asked.

"I turned the stove on to start it heating and was filling the pan with water. When I looked back, he had pressed his hand to the burner." The memory was horrible beyond words, like a glimpse into the mouth of hell. The smell of burning flesh… "He had this expression on his face of…" Exultation. But she simply could not say it, only shuddered.

"What did you do?"

"I dropped the pan and grabbed his arm. He fought me. And then…and then…"

David squeezed her shoulder. The contact, so small, gave her the courage to finish. "He took my hand and started to force it down to the burner. I…somehow I wrenched away and fell. That was when I told him. I could not bear to have him in the house if he wouldn't take his medicine."

He had stared at her with dead eyes, turned and walked out the back door.

Behind her, David said nothing. She knew that, whatever

his shock, his face wouldn't reveal a thing. He had learned long before he left for college to hide his emotions.

Joyce made herself finish. "I knew he was still around. People told me. I caught…glimpses."

Chief Bolton stirred. "As I said, Joyce called me to let me know. We stepped up patrols in the neighborhood. The only complainant was Wayne Tindall. And, well, he called so often to complain about everyone and everything, we didn't do much but say, 'Uh-huh, yes, sir, I'll make a note of that.'" The red of shame stained his face, but he finished anyway. "I told him once that I didn't know how to separate the wheat from the chaff with his grumbles, that he needed to think through what was important before he picked up the phone and called us."

The boy who cried wolf. They were all thinking it. Joyce didn't remember whether, in the fable, the boy had in the end triumphed or been eaten. But Wayne's fate they all knew.

"What was his last complaint?" a balding man asked.

"He caught Robbie pissing on his rosebushes."

Joyce cringed. They all stole looks at her before their gazes slid away.

They asked more questions. So many questions, she felt empty when they were done, an overused well gone dry.

Lieutenant Sykes was the last to go. "We appreciate your cooperation, Mrs. Owen. We'll undoubtedly have more to ask you, but we got a good start today." He nodded and left, David behind him.

She heard the murmur of voices, then the front door opening and closing a last time.

A good start? They would be back? In that moment, she wished as she'd never wished for anything that Robbie had come for her. That he had killed her instead of poor Betty or Charlie Henderson. She had borne responsibility! She had!

And she no longer knew if she could stand the weight of it.

CHAPTER THREE

EXACTLY HALFWAY across the bridge, Acadia let her bike clatter to the sidewalk and swung herself up onto the broad stone half wall that separated pedestrians from the drop into Tucannon Creek.

"Ouch!" she mumbled. The stones were baked hot from the August sun and she wore shorts. Which meant she couldn't let her legs dangle the way she wanted to. Instead, she had to sit on her butt and draw her knees up, wrapping her arms around them.

The bridge had been built during the Depression by the Works Progress Administration; there was a bronze plaque at one end that said so. Tucannon High School also boasted a wall mural painted by WPA artists. Acadia got that the government had put people to work building stuff like bridges and public buildings, but art? She was pretty sure her neighbor Mr. Tindall would say that was a waste of taxpayer dollars.

Right now, she didn't want to think about her dad. Or about the high school she'd never attend.

She stared down at the creek, running so low in late summer that most of the rocks were dry. Clear, shimmering ribbons of water slipped between, deepening just downstream into a pool that was year-round and where all the boys fished.

She suddenly wished she'd gone farther across the bridge. Maybe practically to the other side, instead of stop-

*ping exactly where she was supposed to stop. It was one of
her father's dumb rules. Tucannon was safe, but the highway on the other side of the river represented the big, scary
outside world from which she had to be protected.*

*Tears spurted in her eyes, making her mad. Acadia Hen-
derson did not cry!*

"Hey," a voice said behind her. "I heard."

Her heart took a sickening leap. It was him!

*Frantically she swiped away the evidence that she did,
in fact, cry, and swiveled on her butt. There he was, David
Owen, the absolute most gorgeous guy in the world, standing not two feet away. He was fifteen, two years older than
her, and already at least six feet tall. His dark, wavy hair
was shaggy and damp with sweat. His mom would probably cut it before school started, but she liked it this way.
He had a basketball tucked beneath his arm, which probably meant he'd been down at the high school shooting bas-
kets. He had been a starter this year, even as a freshman,
and everyone said he'd lead Tucannon High School to a
state championship before he graduated. Acadia had been
praying for eighth grade to come and go, like instantly, so
she could go to the high school, too.*

*Even though she'd known him her whole life, she'd got-
ten totally tongue-tied around him these past couple of
years. She blushed every time he even looked her way. "You
mean, that my parents are splitting up?" she said bitterly.*

*"Yeah." He leaned against the stone wall, his clear gray
eyes darker than usual as he studied her. "Mom told me."*

*Her vision got watery again and she looked away. "Mom
and I are moving. She's packing right now."*

"Were they fighting or something?"

*Acadia shook her head. "Mom gets mad sometimes, but
Dad..." Her throat closed up.*

"Dad?"

*Her shoulders jerked. "He just sort of closes up and ig-
nores her. I've never heard him yell."*

*"Do you know where you're going?" he asked after a
minute.*

*She couldn't figure out why he cared. Why he'd stopped
to talk to her at all. When they were little kids, they'd played
cops and robbers and tag and dumb stuff like that in the
street with all the other kids on their block. But she hadn't
exchanged ten words with him in the past three years. His
voice was soft, though, and kind, as if he felt sorry for her.*

*"California. I guess San Francisco. Mom's always
hated it here." She mimicked her mother. "She wants to
go to plays and concerts and talk to people who care about
what's happening in the world." Acadia bowed her head
and squeezed her legs. "She grew up down there. When
she was in college, she went to Vietnam War protests and
she says she's stifled in this little backwater town."*

*He was silent for a moment. She stole a look at him, to
see that his brows had knit. Quietly, as if he wasn't even
talking to her anymore, he said, "I can hardly wait to get
out of here, too." He brooded for a moment, but then the
dark, unhappy expression left his face and he met her eyes.
"I want to do all those things she says. And see the world."
Face clearing, he grinned at her. "So maybe it won't be so
bad. Except for you missing your dad."*

And you. Especially you.

*"I hate him," she said flatly. "I don't think he even cares
that we're going. When Mom tries to talk to him, he just
turns on the TV."*

"So you don't want to stay here with him?"

*She shook her head, even though that was a lie. She
wanted to stay in Tucannon so desperately her chest ached
with the longing. Especially now that David Owen had
smiled at her.*

"But you'll be coming for visits, right?"

"I guess," she said despondently.

"I bet you will. Maybe even come home every summer."

Would she? At the thought, she could almost breathe again. Next summer, she'd be fourteen and maybe not so skinny. She would seem sophisticated and sexy and a little mysterious. David said himself that he was bored with Tucannon. Wouldn't he be more interested in a girl who was from California and who could talk about this concert she'd been to in Golden Gate Park or something her gay neighbor had said or the protest in Berkeley? She didn't actually know if they'd have gay neighbors, or if there were still protests in Berkeley like the ones her mom liked to talk about. But something would be happening that was different from here, where nothing ever changed.

Pain stabbed her. One thing had changed: Deborah and Charles Henderson were getting a divorce. Acadia Henderson would not be entering eighth grade in Tucannon, Washington, this fall. Her group of three best friends would become only two.

"Yeah. Maybe," she mumbled.

David straightened away from the wall. "Uh, I've got to get going. I'll see you around before you leave, right?"

Afraid he'd see the misery in her eyes and guess that she was in love with him, Acadia nodded without looking up. She swallowed the tears. "See ya."

He didn't move for a minute. She thought he was standing there watching her, and she tried to muster the courage to look up to find out what he was thinking. But then he walked away and she lost her chance.

Only...he had talked to her. And she bet he was right. She didn't know that many kids whose parents were divorced, but in the books she read the dad always had visi-

tation rights. So she probably would be back next summer.
Maybe even for Christmas.

So there was hope, wasn't there? Even a few months from
now, she would have changed. She could dream, couldn't
she, that David would be intrigued by her. Maybe he'd
start writing her, or even calling. And there were really
good colleges in San Francisco, weren't there? What if he
chose one of them?

She wondered why he was so unhappy in Tucannon,
when she loved it so much. Was it his brother, who'd gotten
really weird? Or was it because he was too smart, too ambi-
tious, for such a small town? Well, the why probably didn't
matter. She'd been dreading the day he left for college.

Only now, she was the one leaving Tucannon instead.
Forehead pressed to her knees, she let the tears fall.

ACADIA FLEW INTO Seattle and then Walla Walla, renting a
car there for the forty-five-minute drive to her hometown.

She hadn't cried since breaking down in tears at the hospital. Instead, she felt numb. Part of her didn't believe that
her father was dead. Most of all, she didn't believe that Robbie Owen had killed him. If she closed her eyes, she saw the
Robbie of her childhood, with a wide, devilish smile and
the ability to coerce all the kids on the street to play whatever game he had in mind. Sometimes the usual stuff: tag,
cops and robbers, street soccer. But when Robbie was into
soldiers, that's what they'd played. Oh, and dinosaurs. That
was the worst. The older kids had been raptors or T. Rex,
while the little kids had mostly been compelled to take the
role of the plant-eating dinosaurs nervously munching on
grass and waiting for the attack.

She shivered, remembering how she and Shelly Knight
and the Strauss twins and… She couldn't remember who
else had been there. A bunch of them. But clear as day

she could hear the roar, and how she and the others had screamed. Instead of huddling together they had fled shrieking in every direction.

Was that what it had been like when Robbie started shooting? Had people run to hide?

Her father had died on the porch. Had he been outside watering or getting the newspaper, and had run for the house? Or when he heard shots, did he step outside to find out what was happening? Dumb as that sounded, and for a really smart man who'd taught college-level history, it was so like him. Anything out of the ordinary would have provoked only tepid curiosity. Even dying, he'd probably been no more than bemused. She couldn't imagine him terrified, or enraged. Charlie Henderson was a mild man who had died in a way he didn't deserve.

And that made *her* angry. When, that is, any real emotion penetrated the mist that seemed to be muffling her emotions.

She'd visited often enough over the years to know every curve of the narrow, two-lane highway. Rising out of Walla Walla, the hills were planted in wheat and grapes, the one golden and interrupted only by huge sprinkler systems, the grapevines tied in rows that followed the contours of the land. Closer to Tucannon, the dips and rises became sharper, as if they had been formed more recently, the rough edges not yet smoothed.

And then her hometown lay before her, and something like agony clutched at her chest. In her memories, Tucannon was idyllic, lit by the golden light of summer as if Thomas Kinkade had painted it just for her. She saw it through a child's eyes, and it had been a perfect place to grow up.

Built in a V-shaped canyon between hills rising steeply to each side, Tucannon was a pretty town. In spring the creek, really a river, rushed beneath the town's two bridges;

now, in late summer, it trickled, small shimmers of water slipping between rocks. Not much had changed here in eighty years or more; city hall, the police station and the library were housed in a Carnegie-era granite building updated only with a wheelchair ramp. Kindergarten through middle school were all in one building, the most modern in town, built in 1973. The high school was housed in the original granite block schoolhouse, barely updated from the thirties. An old-fashioned department store had survived here, offering boxer shorts, Carhartt work clothes, toasters and office supplies. A gas station and garage, one bank, two cafés, an equal number of taverns, the grocery store that was a new addition to town in the 1960s, the hardware store owned by the Owens' next-door neighbors the Tindalls, a beauty parlor and a barber. At last count the population of Tucannon stood at 1,573 people who could get cuts stitched up at the small clinic in town but had to go to Walla Walla three-quarters of an hour away for tests or hospitalization.

Acadia had ridden her bike everywhere with a freedom most kids didn't have anymore. People didn't worry about their children; this was the kind of town where everyone watched out for each other and felt free to reprimand any eight-year-old who stepped out of line. Benevolent storekeepers gave out suckers to kids. In summer they'd splashed in the creek or run through sprinklers, played street games in the soft light of evening, when parents sat out on front porches to catch the cooler air dusk brought. Doors were never locked and all but the youngest children were latchkey, free to entertain themselves.

She knew better now, of course. No place was that perfect. Beneath the surface, there had undoubtedly been drunkenness and domestic abuse and maybe even, somewhere, a child sexually abused. The gossip wouldn't have been nearly as benign as she remembered. People got fired from jobs, stole from their neighbors and committed suicide, even in Tucannon.

But all her adult knowledge couldn't cushion her from the sight of her town overrun by police cars and news vans. Acadia's numbness gave way to dread as she turned over the old bridge and saw immediately that many of the businesses on Main Street had Closed signs hung in their windows. Only the cafés seemed to be open; well, they'd almost have to be, to take care of all the outsiders here in town. And their profits would be unprecedented. But the hardware store was shuttered, and even the tavern on the corner was dark. The taverns *never* closed. More shocking yet, the gas station was closed.

Not many people were out, and she didn't recognize those faces. She saw a male newscaster talking into a microphone and being filmed from an angle that would show the closed department store behind him.

She took the last familiar turns, leaving downtown behind her, until she came to a police blockade only two blocks from home. The officer manning it came to her car, and she rolled down the window.

"I... My father was killed. Charles Henderson. A Lieutenant Sykes called me yesterday."

After going away to consult someone, he let her through, restoring the barricade behind her.

The dread swelled in her as she drove the last blocks. Oh, God, it was real. She gripped the steering wheel so hard her knuckles hurt.

Daddy, Daddy, Daddy. I'm sorry I didn't come for Christmas. So sorry I never got over being mad at you. Please let them be wrong, let them have discovered you were at the college and someone else was shot on your front porch, maybe the mailman or a utility meter reader or someone, I don't care who even though that makes me an awful person. Please please please be all right, let me say I'm sorry and hug you and cry with you about what's happened to Tucannon.

Eyes dry but burning, she pulled to a stop at the curb in front of her father's house. Yellow police tape circled the front porch, hanging limply from the bushes with no breeze to stir it. She could feel from here how empty the house was, as if it had been deserted for a long time.

Acadia knew, without speaking to anyone, that no mistake had been made. Since she was too much of a realist to have really believed the police officer who called her was wrong, she ignored the twist of anguish and opened her car door.

It was hot out here, even worse than it had been at home in Sacramento. The mercury had to be pushing a hundred degrees, and the air was so still it felt heavy.

She'd just slammed her car door and reached the sidewalk when she heard voices. Men were coming out of the Owens' house, a whole cluster of them. All uniformed, she saw. Most of them glanced her way but went to their cars and got in. Only one paused, then started down the sidewalk toward her.

Acadia didn't really see him, though. She couldn't tear her eyes from the tall, dark-haired man who stood on his mother's porch. He was the only casually dressed one, wearing jeans and a gray T-shirt. He watched the cops leave, then began tracking the one who was walking toward her. She knew the moment he spotted her. His eyes narrowed and he and Acadia stared at each other for a long, tense moment. At last he dipped his head before abruptly turning and going back into the house. The screen door banged.

"You know each other?"

She drew in a ragged breath and finally looked at the law-enforcement officer in a tan uniform. Crew-cut hair, thick neck, brown eyes that were reading how shaken she was.

"I… Yes. I did grow up here, you know."

"Right. Of course you did." He held out a hand. "I'm Lieutenant Sykes. We spoke on the phone."

She let his meaty hand engulf hers, then said, "It's occurred to me belatedly that there wasn't any reason for me to come rushing to Tucannon, was there?" She had followed blind instinct without thinking it through at all.

"No, but sometimes you have to see with your own eyes."

She bit her lip and shook her head. "I kept thinking…" She offered him a wavering smile. "I'm a trauma nurse. I seem to be going through all the same stages I see in patients' families. I feel…predictable."

"Because there's a reason for those stages."

"Probably," she conceded with a sigh. "Um…the whole block looks deserted."

"We asked people within a six-block radius if they could find another place to stay last night, with friends or family. We're letting them all come home today."

She found herself staring at the small frame house that sat on the corner just beyond the Owens'. The one house in the row of four that didn't have that ominous yellow wrapping of crime-scene tape. "Mr. and Mrs. Sonnenberg? Are they all right?"

His gaze followed hers. "They went to the Tri-Cities shopping yesterday morning. I understand they're staying for now with a daughter in Richland."

The Sonnenbergs had to be in their seventies. They had grandkids close to Acadia's age. Still, she remembered their daughter, Margaret, who had visited her parents often.

"I'm glad," she said simply. "They're really nice people."

"So was your father, from all reports."

"Yes." *Oh, Lord*—suddenly she was close to cracking. Her voice did. "He was."

So damn nice, he couldn't stand up for himself or anyone else. Of all the people in the world, he seemed the unlikeliest to end up being gunned down.

The lieutenant gripped her elbow. "Why don't we go inside out of the sun, Ms. Henderson?"

She nodded docilely, and let him lead her around through the side yard to the back stoop.

"We had to go in the house," he said, sounding apologetic. "I left this door unlocked."

She didn't care. The only possessions her father had valued were his books, and no thief would be interested in them. Breathing carefully in through her nose, out through her mouth, she led the way up the two wooden steps and into the kitchen.

"Let's see if there's anything cold in here to drink," the policeman said. "You look like you need it."

He settled her at the kitchen table and opened the refrigerator. He produced a Pepsi—no surprise, her father had been addicted—and opened it for her, then asked if she'd mind if he had one, too.

It had to be pretense, but he sat and talked to her as if he had no place at all he had to be. He seemed to genuinely want to know about her job and her life after she left Tucannon, none of which had anything to do with yesterday's tragedy.

She was the one to bring them back to the here and now by asking how Joyce Owen was.

The lieutenant shook his head. "About what you'd expect. I don't know if it's quite hit her yet."

"You mean the fact that her son has become a monster in the eyes of the world?"

"And that she's lost him," he said, gazing into his Pepsi can as if searching for answers, then taking a long, last swallow and setting the can down. He made standing-up motions, his sharp gaze on her. "Will you be all right now?"

"I suppose." She found a twisted smile for him. "Are you sure you don't need me to identify my father?"

Lieutenant Sykes shook his head. "If you feel the need to see him…"

"I don't know. Maybe. Let me think about it."

"You have my number. Call, and I'll send an officer to get you."

She nodded and saw him out the back door, having promised not to use the front door or go out onto the porch until the police were sure they were done. Then she was left by herself in a silence so complete she knew at last that her father really was gone.

Her knees gave way and dumped her back in the chair at the kitchen table. What was she doing here? Eventually—yes, she'd have to clean out her dad's house, put it on the market. But that could have waited until the loss was less…raw.

And yet, she couldn't have done anything but come when she did. Even if Daddy would never know that, this time, she hadn't hesitated.

HE SHOULD HAVE known that she'd be arriving, but she'd taken him by surprise anyway. Glancing down the street and seeing her had stunned David for reasons he didn't even try to identify.

Acadia Henderson.

Inside the house, he locked the front door, then leaned back against it. Would she be asking questions right now of Lieutenant Sykes, wanting to know where her father

had fallen, or whether he'd died instantly or had lived long
enough to suffer?

His jaw muscles spasmed.

Memories rushed back of the little girl who had been
part of his growing-up years as much as the creek and the
baseball field and Laverne Whaley of Laverne's Café, who
made the best pancakes in the world. Someone he had once
taken for granted, until her parents' divorce created a rift
in the fabric of his hometown.

He could still see the terrible unhappiness on her face
that day he'd heard about the Hendersons' trouble. That
was his mother's word: *trouble.* Perhaps she had thought it
would be temporary, but that's not how it turned out. Acadia
had come to her dad's for visits after that, but David hadn't
seen her, except for the one summer. That first summer he
had worked at the vineyard near Walla Walla and come
home every night sunburned and exhausted. Somehow he
and Acadia had ended up sitting out on one or the other's
porch most evenings, but the year after that he volunteered
building houses in Nicaragua. He remembered telling himself he'd see Acadia other vacations, other summers, except then he left for college and came home only for brief
visits, and he let her drift from his mind.

And yet, she'd been a vivid personality from the time
she was a little girl: fiery and stubborn, never a pushover
even for Rob. At thirteen, she hadn't been mature enough
to interest David; he'd had a thing for Kristy Nordahl, who
had developed early and possessed a centerfold figure by
the time they were freshmen. Too bad that Kristy bored
him cross-eyed when he wasn't making out with her. Not
really thinking it through, he had kept an eye on Acadia,
still skinny and with no more figure than a board right before she moved away. The next summer, when they'd gotten to be such good friends, she was starting to develop,

but *starting* was the operative word. All along, though, he'd guessed she would end up beautiful once the gawkiness passed and those skinny, bony legs became just slender instead. She had an unforgettable face, dominated by huge, chocolate-brown eyes and a fierce, pointy chin. That last year or two, she'd taken to blushing every time she saw him, color that was unbecoming given her skin tone and carrot-red hair. Despite himself, he smiled, remembering her mother's efforts to tame those curls. The worst was the year Acadia's mother had had her hair cut really short. Acadia had been furious, storming to anyone who would listen, "Little Orphan Annie. That's what *everyone* says. What did Mom *think* I'd look like?"

It was still untamed, he thought, picturing her as she stood there on the sidewalk staring at him, curls long since escaped from whatever was holding the whole mass into a bundle on the back of her head. And she had ended up as beautiful as he had imagined.

More beautiful.

If her mother hadn't snatched her away, David suspected she was the girl he would have taken to senior prom. Which would make things even worse now. He should be relieved that the two of them didn't have that kind of history.

Because it was a pretty fair bet that Acadia Henderson now hated with a passion anyone with the last name of Owen.

Nor would she be alone. Once the police barricades came down and neighbors returned to their homes, what would happen? Cold stares? Deliberately turned backs? Eggs flung against the side of the house? A rock through the Owens' front window? Or worse?

Feeling sick, he knew he had to take his mother away from Tucannon. She would be nothing but a reminder of past horror to the children and friends and neighbors of

Rob's victims. Maybe, instead of packing up the contents of the house themselves, they should hire movers to come in. His mother could go through things and make decisions later.

The trouble was, he had no idea whether she had yet given a thought to the future. She was still in shock. Whether she felt guilt, he didn't know. But she'd given her life over to taking care of Robbie, and the grief at her failure probably hadn't yet hit her.

He wondered if people in town knew she'd tried to commit Robbie. She'd had friends when he was growing up. Would they support her now, or turn away in horror at what her son had done?

Would it even occur to his mother that some people in town, like Marge, who'd been interviewed on last night's KOMO news, would be desperate to find a scapegoat, somebody still living who could be punished?

David rubbed a hand hard over his face. Damn it, it was too soon to try to talk to her.

They needed groceries. That was something practical he could do.

Start by finding out whether Mom wants anything at the store. Try to make her think about eating more than a bite or two. Little steps.

He'd drive to Walla Walla rather than try to shop here, where he'd be recognized immediately and find himself having to declare "no comment" over and over as he pushed his cart down the aisle. This was a good time to make a getaway, before the news vans descended on their neighborhood.

He wondered what Acadia would say, when those vans parked up and down Maple Street and she couldn't step out of her house without being pushed to make a statement.

CHAPTER FOUR

"UH…YOU'RE asking *me* to open the gas station?" Reeve's heart had begun to hammer the minute he heard Mrs. Stenten's voice on the phone. What she'd said had blown him away.

"Yes. Walt trusted you, Reeve. Who else can I ask?"

Anyone. Anyone at all.

"He wouldn't have died if it weren't for me." The words came out choked, but he had to say them. *It's my fault he's dead.* She knew that, right? Oh, damn. What if no one had told her?

"No." The stiff way she'd been talking cracked. "Walt cared about you. He was…he was a marine, you know. You've seen his tattoo."

Yeah, Reeve had, but he'd never thought much about it. He closed his eyes and caught a flash: that body flying through the air, jerking as it took a bullet. Maybe this wasn't the first time Walt Stenten had done something heroic. It had never occurred to him to imagine his boss as someone who'd maybe fought in a war. Shot people, or gotten wounded, or carried a bleeding friend to safety. He was just…Walt.

"You don't blame me?" Reeve sounded like a little boy, begging for a kind word, and he hated it.

"No," she said wearily. "Reeve, will you do it? I've been getting calls. People need gas. And…and I don't know how I'm going to keep the station open or whether I should sell it, but I can't afford not to have it open right now. Especially…"

She didn't finish, but he knew what she was going to say. Especially not right now, when so many visitors were in town. When they could be selling two or three times as much gasoline as usual.

"Okay," he said. "Is it okay if I call the other guys who pumped gas and give them shifts, too?"

"Yes. Consider yourself the manager for now, until I figure out what to do."

"Okay," he said again. "I'll do that, Mrs. Stenten." He almost thanked her, but he didn't know what he'd be thanking her for. Trusting him? Not blaming him?

But it is my fault. It is.

Rob Owen came after him, Reeve, because he'd been such a butt that one day. If he'd been even half decent to Rob, Walt wouldn't be dead.

If only he and Rob hadn't gotten into it last week.

Reeve had come out of the garage at the gas station and found Rob sitting on his Kawasaki. It wasn't a Harley, but it had some power and Reeve had worked for years to be able to buy it. He'd told him to get off, that it was his. All Rob did was sit there looking at him with that creepy stare, and Reeve had gotten mad and shoved him.

Why wasn't I nicer?

Now Reeve kept seeing Walt, sitting behind the scarred desk inside the gas station, keeping an eye on the boys pumping gas or doing oil changes. He always had grease under his fingernails, and there was usually a streak on his face. His stumpy hands were quick and in a weird way graceful when they were inside a car engine, but his fingers always looked thick and awkward when he gripped a pen.

Today, if he weren't one of the victims, he wouldn't be

talking much about what happened. If anything, he'd have gone quieter still.

Reeve wished desperately that he didn't have to wonder if he wasn't partly to blame for Rob flipping out and killing a bunch of people. Not only Walt, but the others, too.

He'd give anything for a do-over. Because then he wouldn't know that he was a gutless wonder who pissed his pants and hid while a good man bled to death in his place.

Reeve wished like he hadn't wished for anything in his life that he'd never discovered that about himself.

ACADIA SAW DAVID leave in the black Lexus parked at the curb, and then return several hours later. He had to make three trips to carry in everything stowed in his trunk. She was ashamed of herself because she'd been listening for the sound of his car and had hurried to the front window the minute she heard it. She stood to one side peeking out, like some nosy old woman, only inside she felt more like her thirteen-year-old self, hungry for every glimpse of him.

She was pathetic.

He'd probably turned into a jerk. That's what happened to most guys who were too good-looking, too smart, too successful. He wasn't the boy she'd loved so helplessly any more than she was the skinny girl who grieved leaving behind the boy who barely even noticed her existence more than she did leaving behind her own father.

She shivered despite the sweltering midday heat, glad that from where she stood she couldn't see the bloodstains on the front porch. Acadia couldn't yet make herself believe that dark, rusty splotch was Daddy's lifeblood. Every time her mind tiptoed that direction, she yanked it back. Yet another reason to be ashamed of herself. She was a trauma nurse. Hadn't she seen everything? She'd laughed over gruesome scenes with dark humor like everyone else who worked the E.R., and now she was as squeamish and heartbroken as someone who couldn't look straight at a few beads of crimson on a cut finger.

She stayed absolutely still, wanting to believe she was invisible as David bent once more over the trunk of his car. This time he lifted out a box. It looked as if it held a coffee-maker of some kind. Weirdly, she felt a smile curving her mouth. His mom probably still drank instant like Acadia's father had. That morning, she'd pondered whether it would be worth buying a coffeemaker or espresso machine for the short weeks she might be here to pack up Dad's stuff. She'd decided not, but David had obviously felt differently. She was a little bit jealous, watching him hoist the box, slam the trunk lid and start toward his house.

He paused, though, on the sidewalk, and even though she was absolutely positive she hadn't moved, his gaze seemed to lock right on her. She stared, stricken. After a moment, he dipped his head like he had earlier, then kept going as if he'd dismissed her.

Falling back from the window, Acadia felt raw. As if every nerve ending in her body was exposed.

She'd had the TV on all morning, which was probably a mistake, but she'd found she needed to know who else had died. Acadia had watched with sick fascination as the story was replayed endlessly, new facts knit into it. One by one, victims were being identified. The Tindalls, Walt Stenten, Earl Kennedy. Wendi Rowe was clinging to life in the hospital. Earl's was the only name Acadia didn't know. She couldn't understand how Rob could have shot Miss Rowe, who had had a smile for everyone.

Or Daddy, who would never have been anything but gentle and patient with the crazy Owen boy. She kept telling herself it might have been an accident, a shot that went wild. Would Rob really have looked right at her father and fired the round that hit him square in the chest?

At least one victim hadn't been identified as yet. Police were refusing to give names until families were notified, which she respected.

She'd been horrified to see David's face staring at her from the television, only to realize right away that it was Rob and not David at all. The brothers had always looked alike, although it hadn't been hard telling them apart, not back then when Rob was two years older, bulkier although not taller. He'd had a heavier beard than David, too, and incongruously a voice that never deepened as much as his brother's. David must be cursing that resemblance now. Maybe he had even before she moved away, it occurred to her. Rob was already starting to be strange by then, although no one had yet used the word *schizophrenia*. His eyes—brown, she remembered, not gray like David's—had looked weird, and he'd taken to talking to himself.

But still, it was brave of David to appear in public right now. He must have gone to Walla Walla to shop, but even there people would have seen the resemblance and stared.

Why was she thinking about him and not her father?

Because I'm not ready.

She hadn't done a single useful thing all day. A part of her didn't believe any of this was real, that her father was truly dead. She might have to ask to view his body to convince herself. The bloodstain on the front porch apparently hadn't been enough. When she wasn't staring at the flickering images on the truly ancient console television in the living room, she was drifting around the house consumed by memories.

Or had she been trying to raise her father from the dead? Maybe deep down she *did* believe he was gone, but also that if she willed him to appear here where he belonged, it would happen. She'd hear his voice from the kitchen, or his footstep upstairs. Maybe walk into his den and find him in the easy chair where he'd always retreated to read. When she was little, she would contentedly settle down at his feet and play or turn the pages of books and pretend she was reading, too. The times he'd read to her were the best. Later, she'd become infected with her mother's impatience. When he looked up from his book, she wanted him to *see* her, but instead he would blink myopically and she had to suspect that, when interrupted, it took him a good minute to remember who she was.

She wanted to remember the father she loved, and instead she kept feeling well-worn resentment and hurt. She had to get past it.

How?

Start by doing something practical. Grocery shop, maybe. But there wasn't any great urgency, because the refrigerator and cupboards were reasonably well stocked. Plus, she wasn't very hungry. She'd had trouble choking down a slice of toast for breakfast. Lunch hadn't interested her.

Picking up boxes at the grocery store would be a good start. She could begin to pack then. The books alone would take her forever. She'd have to decide what she wanted to keep and then what to do with the rest of them. The idea of unloading them on a thrift store, though, made her sick. Her father had loved his books so much.

The knock on the back door was surprisingly welcome. Neighbors had been returning to their homes this morning. They would have noticed the strange car out front and maybe guessed she was here. So far, the police must have kept the news vans from entering this part of town, but she knew they would be soon. More warily, it occurred to her that an enterprising reporter might have slipped past the barricades on foot.

Acadia reached the kitchen and saw her caller through the glass pane in the back door. Her heart did another lurch. David. It was David standing there, waiting for her, his expression tight and closed.

She rushed forward and opened the door. "David."

His mouth crooked slightly into a half smile. "Acadia."

She stood back. "Come in. Please."

He hesitated, then nodded and stepped into the kitchen. He scanned it and shook his head. "It hasn't changed."

"No." She crossed her arms in a gesture even she knew was protective. "Last time I stopped by to say hi to your mom and dad, it didn't look like anything over there had changed, either. None of our parents were big on the concept of remodeling."

His eyes sharpened on her face. "Mom didn't mention you."

"It's been years." *Because I was determined to hurt my father's feelings.*

"You haven't been seeing your dad?"

Her eyes wanted to fill with tears, but she denied them. "Yes, but he'd fly down to Sacramento or we'd meet up somewhere. Seattle. The Oregon Coast." That vacation was nice. They hadn't talked much—she wished now they had—but they'd walked miles on the beach, and the silence had felt like those long-ago times when he'd sat in his chair reading, her entertaining herself at his feet. Peaceful.

David nodded. He stood there looking at her, his eyes inscrutable. He wore jeans, as he had when she saw him yesterday, with a navy blue T-shirt today. Denim and tee both clung to long, lean muscles. The ones in his forearms flexed when he shoved his hands in his pockets.

"I thought one of us should say I'm sorry," he said

abruptly. "Mom's not up to it yet. It doesn't make up for a damn thing, but I'd give anything to go back and change what happened."

"It wasn't your fault."

A muscle ticked on his jaw. "I'm not so sure about that."

Acadia frowned. "What do you mean?"

He gave his head a hard shake. "It doesn't matter. Might-have-dones don't mean crap after something like this. Rob did what he did. Those of us he left have to live with it."

She had never heard a voice so expressionless and yet stretched so tight. He did blame himself. She couldn't imagine why and found she needed to know.

"Would you like something to drink?"

Surprise flickered in his eyes. "I expected you to tell me to go to hell."

"I'm an E.R. nurse, David. I've seen more than my share of mental illness. Rob was a classic schizophrenic, wasn't he? I was remembering on the flight up here. It hit him in adolescence. We thought he was talking to himself, but he wasn't. He thought somebody—or something—was talking to him. He was answering."

"Yeah." David swore. He bent his head and pinched the bridge of his nose. "Yeah," he said hoarsely. "Mostly he was begging them to go away."

"Them."

"He had a whole crowd of invisible…God, I was going to say 'friends,' but I don't think even he saw them that way. They taunted him, they tempted him, they tormented him. That's not what friends do."

"No." Instinct had her reaching out and gripping his arm. Briefly, a squeeze only, but she felt those muscles go rock hard under her fingers. "Poor Rob."

He gave a ragged laugh. "I can't believe you can say that."

"You thought I'd be angry," Acadia realized. And she was, but not the way he'd been thinking.

"Hell, yes!" He stared at her with incredulity. "How can you not be? You loved your father. He was a good guy. If Rob was going to go berserk, why would he kill your dad of all people?"

"Or Wendi Rowe," Acadia said softly. "Or even Betty. Wayne, well, I sort of get…" Shame had her stumbling to a halt.

This laugh was a sharp crack. "I thought the same thing. I get why he'd go for Wayne, too."

They exchanged a look of rueful understanding. Then he said, "Yeah, I wouldn't mind something to drink." This smile was the most natural yet. "Say, a Pepsi."

Acadia chuckled and opened the refrigerator. "That was option number one. Dad apparently made a trip to Costco in the recent past. I found half a dozen thirty-six packs of Pepsi in the basement. But I've mixed up some lemon-ade, too."

"Pepsi is fine. I didn't sleep well last night. I could use the caffeine."

She nodded and took one for herself, too. "Ice?"

He shook his head.

"When I was watching you out the window, I was fixated on that coffeemaker. Dad believed coffee came powdered in industrial-size jars. I swear, this morning's tasted stale."

Somehow he was smiling again. "At least Mom doesn't buy her instant in warehouse-size jars. But yeah, I confess, I couldn't stand the idea of drinking her coffee for however long this takes."

They sat at the small kitchen table and looked at each other.

"How is your mom?" Acadia asked finally.

"Not good. She's mostly lying on her bed pretending

she's asleep. I made her get up and have some breakfast, but she refused lunch."

"I can't imagine what she feels."

His gray eyes were cloudy, maybe not seeing her at all. "I got pissed at her when she called to tell me what happened because all she could talk about was Rob. 'He's dead,' she kept saying. 'What about the people he shot?' I asked her. I think still it's unreal to her. She'd made her life all about Rob. It's still all about him. She got angry when one of the cops said that Rob's doctor had talked about him. 'What about confidentiality?' It's as if he isn't gone. She still has to protect him. I don't know what's going to happen when she's really hit with the reality that she can't do anything more for him."

It wasn't the undertone of anger that shocked Acadia so much as her ability to hear it threading the uninflected words. Did *he* realize how angry he was?

"The unreality I understand," she said after a minute. "This morning I was thinking that I can't make myself believe Dad is gone. That the blood on the porch is his. Maybe even that it *is* blood. You know? And for your mother, it has to be way worse."

"She feels guilty." He frowned, as if surprised that he'd said as much. But he kept going. "It's the flip side of having dedicated her life to Rob. If she was responsible for him, his wrongdoings had to be her fault."

"I can understand that."

He was turning the Pepsi can around and around and around on the table without seeming to notice what he was doing. "I'd like to pack her up and get her out of here before the police turn the jackals loose." His eyes met hers. "And what about the townspeople? I expected you to hate her guts, and mine, too. Have you been watching the news? There are plenty of people who do blame Mom and Dad."

"Won't she go?"

He grunted. "She moves like she's eighty years old. She's as frail as if she were, too. Do you know I could never get her and Dad even to visit me in Seattle? I doubt she's been farther than Walla Walla in fifteen years or more. She only drove that far because she refused to shop here in town anymore. She couldn't look her neighbors in the eye." Now his voice was harsh, the anger less muted. "That house is her entire world. I don't think she's ready for me to throw her in the passenger seat of my car and drive her away from everything she knows."

"However hellish that's become," Acadia murmured.

"Yeah." His fingers flexed and there was a popping sound as the aluminum sides of the can dented. He lifted it and guzzled, his throat moving like a man downing three shots of raw whiskey.

An awful thought struck her. "Will she want to bury Rob here?"

David looked appalled. "Oh, damn. I hadn't thought of that." He closed his eyes and groaned. "Of course she will. Dad's here."

The cemetery on the outskirts of Tucannon dated back to the 1860s, when the first white settlers built here on the river. The trees were as old as the early graves they shaded. Dad would want to be buried there, too, Acadia realized. Of course he would. He might even own a plot. One of the many things she hadn't yet made herself do was go through his desk. She'd gotten far enough to find a copy of his will naming her as sole beneficiary and couldn't make herself look further.

"They'll all be buried there," she said, and David grimaced.

"All Rob's victims. Just think what the families of those

victims would say about having him laid to rest in the same ground as the people he murdered."

"Maybe...maybe you could talk her into having him cremated. She could take the ashes with her."

"And guard them for the rest of her life," he said harshly. "Yeah, she might go for that." He pushed back from the table and stood. "I'd better check on her. Acadia...I wish I'd seen you again under other circumstances."

She tried to smile but felt it tremble. "Me, too."

"If, uh, you need any help..."

"You've got enough to deal with, David."

"Yeah." He retreated toward the door, but stopped with his hand on the knob. "You remember that summer you came to stay with your dad? How we'd sit out in the dark and talk?"

"I remember," she whispered. She'd clung to the memories of that magical summer for years. David Owen had overshadowed every other boy and then man she'd ever tried to have a relationship with.

I am pathetic, she thought, for the second time today.

"I said things to you I don't think I've ever said to anyone else."

The pain in her chest grew more acute. "Are you asking me not to repeat anything you said today?"

He smiled. "No, Acadia. I know you won't. I was remembering, that's all."

And then he left, and she stayed where she was for the longest time, not knowing what to think or feel.

BY MIDAFTERNOON, the news vans had begun to prowl the streets. Watching through the window, David bitterly likened them to packs of wolves. Yellow crime-scene tape was a wounded animal to them. He could almost hear the howls.

It wasn't long before the doorbell rang. Fortunately, he'd

been watching and knew an old friend of Mom's hadn't come calling. Did she *have* any friends anymore?

"Who's that?" his mother called down the stairs, sounding alarmed.

He took the stairs two at a time and went to her bedroom, where she sat on the side of the bed. She was shaking.

"There are three news trucks outside," he said. "I've unplugged the phone."

"What if the police need to reach us?"

"They have my cell phone."

Her skin tone was as gray as her hair. "Can they see inside?"

"I've pulled all the blinds."

They sat in silence for a moment.

"When will they go away?"

"Not for days," he told her with regret. Or weeks, but he didn't say that. "We'll need to give them a statement. That will help."

"A statement?" She stared at him in shock. "You mean... me?"

"I can do it for you. On the job, I speak to the press often. But I'll need you to help me draft what we want to say."

"I don't see why we should say anything. What we feel is nobody's business but ours."

"You don't think we ought to say we're sorry? That we hurt for the families of Rob's victims?" He saw on her face that the acerbity he'd let creep into his voice had hurt her, but he wasn't going to apologize. He also didn't let himself say, *Or don't you hurt for anybody but yourself?* Though he had begun to wonder.

She flushed. The color looked more like anger than shame, which had him tightening his jaw. This wasn't the mother he remembered. She'd been burned in a crucible and come out unrecognizable. Was that inevitable?

The doorbell rang again, three insistent peals.

"You're not going to answer the door?" his mother asked.

"No. They're going to pretty well trap us in the house, though, at least until we issue that statement."

"I hardly ever leave the house anyway," she said with sudden indifference, and groped for the afghan she'd spread over herself all day despite what had to be 110-degree heat up here, on the second story.

"I'll put dinner on soon," David said.

"I'm not hungry." She lay back down.

"You need to come down and eat." He made sure she heard the steel. "You refused lunch. You're alive, Mom. Act like it."

He walked out, not knowing if he was being cruel to be kind, or only cruel. Downstairs again, he cracked the blinds. Four news vans now, plus a couple of cars at the curb. Damn it, he thought suddenly: *Acadia.* But he couldn't see her porch from here, with the Tindall house in between. Presumably the yellow tape wrapping her porch would keep the press off it, but that wouldn't prevent them from going around to her back door, which had that glass pane with no curtain. He imagined noses pressed to that glass, Acadia afraid to go in the kitchen and make dinner.

Seeing her today was all that kept him from feeling like a wild animal, penned and frantic.

She doesn't blame me. She doesn't even blame Mom. The relief had all but staggered him.

As a kid, she'd been emotional, living up to the red hair, but this afternoon he'd been reminded that she was Charlie Henderson's daughter. Instead of fierce anger, she'd greeted him with common sense, her father's gentleness and understanding, and the knowledge of a medical professional. She had even given him the gift of a few moments of humor. He wished he could slip back over to her place now. He didn't like to think of her alone in her dad's house, trying to believe in a death evidenced only by a bloodstain and her father's face appearing with monotonous regularity on the newscasts.

He should have gotten her phone number. Chances were she wasn't answering her father's landline, either. It occurred to him that Lieutenant Sykes might have it, but what excuse could he give for wanting it? And what would he say if he did call?

He sighed and paced restlessly through a downstairs made even more cramped by that damn yellow tape barring him from his father's den and the basement. He hoped the police would come back soon and let loose those parts of the house. Mom might not be ready to start packing yet, but surely she'd agree they had to clean out Rob's stuff.

God, he hoped she'd agree.

Eventually he started dinner, a stir-fry he had to make in a frying pan on the stove, having forgotten when he bought the ingredients that his mother might not have a wok. He'd made biscuits, too, and bought a cake. He needed to get some calories in his mother. He'd bought some of those protein drinks, too, thinking that if nothing else he'd insist she drink one or two of those every day.

To his surprise she came down when he called her. She picked at her meal but did eat, although she jolted every time the doorbell rang, which it seemed to do at about five-minute intervals. The fact that the phone was dead and had no voice mail must be driving the TV newspeople crazy.

Mom looked startled when he set a piece of cake in front of her and said, "Oh, I don't usually have desserts," but ate it with more enthusiasm. He ignored the way she stared at her empty plate then, as though ashamed of having enjoyed anything.

She didn't like it when he insisted they figure out what

to say to the press tomorrow. He had to drag a few sentiments out of her, told her what he was thinking of adding and deleted a few remarks that clearly offended her. But when she balked at telling the world she and Dad had tried to get Rob involuntarily committed, David said, "That's the most important thing we can say. I didn't know you'd done that, so I suspect the neighbors and your friends here in town didn't, either."

She set her jaw and her lips thinned as she stared at him.

"I guess that means you didn't tell anyone," he said resignedly. "Mom, they need to know you did everything you could. Even more important is saying, 'This didn't need to happen.' Rob should have been in an institution. Why was the process made impossible, when he'd clearly become a danger to you and himself at the very least? What happened here can be a catalyst to change in the system, if you're willing to speak out."

She heard that. He couldn't tell if she liked it or not, but finally she nodded.

"Say whatever you want," she said distantly, stood up and left the room. He heard her footsteps on the stairs and the sound of the bathroom door, followed a few minutes later by her bedroom door.

David ground his teeth. He looked down at his own piece of cake, only half eaten, and finally stood to scrape it in the garbage. He wished there was somebody else he could call to take his place. Almost anyone would probably be more palatable to his mother. But there wasn't another soul, not with Aunt Jackie sidelined with cancer.

God. Cancer. What if Mom had to deal with losing her sister, too?

No. Not happening. Aunt Jackie said her prognosis was good. The timing sucked, that was all.

Clean the kitchen, he told himself. Write the damn statement. Turn on the ten-o'clock news to see if the name of the last victim had been released yet.

He started with the kitchen. Ended with the news.

Still no name. "Police have not yet been able to notify family," the anchorwoman said with a practiced look of great sadness.

Dark settled late in the Northwest at this time of year, but it had finally come. He had closed his laptop some time ago, and sat now in the living room, a book open on his lap although he was rereading one paragraph over and over again. He wasn't tired enough for bed yet. He'd have liked to go online, but couldn't find an unprotected wireless to hitch onto. Hell, maybe dial-up was the best available in remote Tucannon. Mom and Dad didn't even own a computer, of course. Being cut off from the internet made him feel even more isolated, trapped.

Maybe Acadia was still awake. He could walk over unseen in the dark. Knock only if she had lights on.

No, that was stupid. She'd been civil. More accepting with him than anyone with the last name of Owen deserved. That didn't mean they were allies, far less friends.

Glass exploded behind him. David threw himself down as something crashed to the floor.

CHAPTER FIVE

JOYCE STARED AT the terrible sight of a rock sitting in the middle of the living room floor. It had scarred the hardwood where it hit. Shards and crumbles of broken glass glittered where they'd fallen. The blinds were bent in the middle, where the rock had torn through.

David looked up from a crumpled piece of paper he held in his hand. The lack of expression on his face seemed to her almost as dreadful as the fact that someone had thrown a rock through her front window.

"I've already called 911," he said. "Not that it will do any good."

"You're bleeding."

He frowned. "Bleeding?"

"Your face."

He reached up and found the trickle of blood on his cheek. He pulled out a tiny, knifelike shard of glass, barely wincing.

"The rock could have hit you," she said dumbly.

"By the time it made it through the glass and blinds, it had lost some force," he said, as if that made it all right. He frowned at the sound of a siren. "You'd better put a robe and slippers on before they get here, Mom." He came to her side. "I don't see any glass here, but step carefully."

By the time she made it downstairs again, voices were coming from the living room. One of the officers on the city police force had responded. She saw at a glance that he would be useless. He was absurdly young, for one thing; Joyce wondered if he even shaved. He looked like a child compared to her David, who dominated any room by sheer size alone, given that he was well over six feet tall and broad shouldered. This was a funny time for her to be jarred by the realization that her son was not only a man, but an intimidating one. With his hair ruffled, his jaw shadowed with a day's growth of beard and blood smeared across his cheek, he was unmistakably tough and even dangerous. Yet his voice was, as always, courteous and devoid of any obvious emotion.

So much to regret, she thought, and stiffened when the young officer turned to face her. He was nowhere as successful as Davey was at hiding what he thought. He despised her; it was in his eyes.

Joyce lifted her chin and stared back at him. "Did you even try to find who threw that rock through our window?"

"I took a look around, ma'am, but I didn't see anyone out and about."

And if he had, she diagnosed, he would have offered a thumbs-up and a ride home.

Who would have done this? she asked herself. Or maybe she should ask herself whether there was anyone in town who *wasn't* a possible perpetrator. She hadn't watched the television at all, but the voices coming from it had drifted upstairs. She recognized some of them. The vitriol Marge Perkins vented made Joyce sick. She hardly knew the woman, even as small as Tucannon was. She and Pete hadn't eaten out often, and Marge didn't have children. Their paths hadn't crossed much. But Marge hated her, and she wasn't alone.

Maybe if I hadn't isolated myself... But how could she have done anything else? Even her friends were afraid of Rob, and for good reason. She ached inside, thinking of

Pete. It was all endurable as long as he had been alive, as long as she wasn't alone. But by the time she buried him, she didn't have anyone else at all. And yes, that was her fault. Not all of it, but some. If she could have brought herself to ask for help from Davey, he'd have given it. He was here now, wasn't he? Motivated by duty and not love, but here.

"We'll discuss this with Lieutenant Sykes tomorrow," David said now, his eyes narrowing slightly. He didn't like this officer any better than Joyce did. "I'll wait to give the note to him. He's in a better position to check it for fingerprints."

Face reddening, the other man glared. "I'm the responding officer. There's no reason I shouldn't take it."

"I'll give it to Lieutenant Sykes," David said again, and there was no give in his voice at all. No give in that steady gaze, either.

The idiot kept arguing, and David kept saying no. Finally he said, "I need to help my mother to bed. You're welcome to join the lieutenant and me tomorrow."

Joyce realized she actually did know this police officer. She should have recognized him immediately. He was the Degamos' nasty little boy, who'd grown up into a nastier man.

"Do I know him?" David asked, once he shut the door behind Officer Degamo.

"He's quite a lot younger than you, but you might remember him." She frowned. "I believe Acadia might have babysat him a few times."

He looked startled. "Good God. She'd barely started babysitting. Wait. Not…what was his name? Josh Degamo? The crybaby?"

"Josh," she said, almost pleased. "I couldn't remember

his first name. Didn't he introduce himself when he arrived?"

"Yeah, but it didn't sink in. Huh. Well, he isn't fat anymore."

"No, now he's self-important and small-minded."

Her Davey actually laughed. "That about sums him up." He shook his head. "Josh Degamo. Man. I remember Acadia whining about him and saying the buck an hour, or whatever his parents paid, wasn't enough."

Joyce sniffed. "His father is equally self-important and small-minded."

Why, she wondered, hadn't Rob shot somebody like Miles Degamo instead of Charlie Henderson? Miles had been vocal about why Rob, who he described as a vicious wild animal, shouldn't be allowed to run wild within the city limits. Rob must have heard him sounding off at some time or other.

Of course, it was dreadful for her to think anything of the kind. What Rob had done was unspeakable. Nobody *deserved* to be gunned down in cold blood. Still, she wished she understood why he'd chosen the victims he had. Or had he chosen at all? His voices, increasingly strident and chaotic, might have told him where to go and what to do. Did anything about his recent behavior make real sense?

Davey walked her upstairs and all but tucked her into bed, making her feel cherished until she saw his face, as remote as ever. She'd imagined any softening she thought she saw earlier.

Pausing in the doorway, he said, "I'd better go clean up some. I think I'll tape cardboard to the window from the inside until we can get it replaced."

She nodded although he wouldn't see her, understanding what he wasn't saying. If he were to go outside tomorrow in daylight and stand on a ladder nailing plywood over the broken window, he'd be engulfed by reporters. He had become a shut-in, just like she was.

Joyce lay in the dark after he was gone and knew she ought to start thinking about the future, even if only one day ahead. But she couldn't seem to make herself care what tomorrow would bring. She would gladly have traded her life for Betty Tindall's or Charlie Henderson's or the quiet gas station owner's, Walt Stenten, who had given jobs to so many local teenagers over the years. In another lifetime, Joyce would have called Anne Stenten to express her sorrow, but Anne wouldn't want to hear from her of all people. Closing her eyes, Joyce thought about Charlie's little redheaded girl, Acadia. She must know by now about her father.

As she pictured that girl, freckled and fey, watching Davey with such hopeless yearning, Joyce would have given anything to be able to lose herself in the oblivion of sleep.

ACADIA SLEPT EVEN more restlessly after having heard the siren and seen the flashing lights that stopped in front of the Owens' house. She'd hovered at the window, craning her neck, afraid an ambulance would follow the police car. What if Mrs. Owen had had a heart attack or stroke? It wouldn't be much of a surprise, with the pressure she was under. Would David remember she was a nurse and think to call her?

But no ambulance arrived, and after a few minutes the flashing lights were turned off and the police car drove away, leaving Acadia with no idea what had happened to bring it. She thought wistfully of the long-ago days when she was one of the neighborhood children who would have gathered to stare and whisper. Now, she'd have given a lot to be able to see David's house from her father's. The fact that she couldn't made her feel even more alone. The Tindalls' next door was empty but for ghosts, and Acadia didn't know the people who'd bought the place on the other side of her father's. Across the street…well, as far as she knew the Strausses still lived there, and old Mrs. Winningham next to them, and the Gibbons on the corner. Remembering so much felt peculiar, when she'd moved away so long ago.

Come morning she felt none of her usual energy. It was all she could do to shuffle downstairs, hurriedly pour herself a bowl of cereal before some enterprising reporter could appear and retreat to the dining room to eat breakfast. When the doorbell rang, she started. By the time she crept into the living room, it had rung three more times and someone had knocked thunderously. She heard voices on the front porch. She separated blinds only enough to see half a dozen people out there—and catch the glint of sunlight off a camera lens. Acadia let the blinds close and stood there thinking. Was it her imagination, or was the yellow tape gone?

Oh, God—were those hateful people standing *right on top of her father's blood?*

This, after the newswoman and cameraman who had circled her house and knocked on the back door yesterday. She'd marched over, opened it and snapped, "No comment. And I will call the police to arrest you for trespassing if I see you set one foot onto my property again." She still couldn't believe they could be so insensitive.

Suddenly enraged, she flew to the front door and flung it open, not even thinking about what she was wearing or the fact that she hadn't yet brushed her hair.

They were all a blur, she was so mad.

"You will get off my property and not come back," she said with all the force she could muster. "You're not welcome, and I'll call 911 if I see one of you so much as stumble onto my lawn." Then she slammed the door, panting as she leaned back against it.

Please, God, don't let me appear on the evening news.

She was bound to have been flushed with anger, and red wasn't the best color with her hair and freckles. She was still shaking with outrage that they could be so lacking in respect. Why she was surprised, Acadia didn't know. News cameras appeared in the E.R. often enough. The viewing public had an insatiable appetite for tragedy, apparently.

But this tragedy was *hers,* and that made it different.

She closed her eyes. The interest in her had to be nothing compared to what the Owens must be going through. Probably, in his job, David was used to dealing with the press. He'd know how to protect his mother. But this tragedy was theirs, too, which made it as different for him as it was for her.

She wondered if he'd come back. Perhaps she should sneak over there to tell Joyce the same thing she'd told David: that she didn't blame her. Who could ever have imagined that Robbie would do something like this? Surely not even his parents. Or, perhaps, *especially* not his parents.

Not half an hour later, she peeked cautiously into the kitchen when she heard a rap on the back door. It was Lieutenant Sykes's face she saw, and she let him in.

He smiled. "You surviving the onslaught?" His smile died. "Are you all right, Ms. Henderson?"

"I've been better." She was embarrassed to be caught still in the boxer shorts and sacky T-shirt she'd slept in, her hair tangled around her face where it had escaped the braid. The same way, heaven help her, any TV cameras would have filmed her. "Will they go away soon?"

"A few more days, I'd guess," he said. "David Owen plans to give them a statement this afternoon. That might help." He hesitated. "Have you looked out front?"

"This morning? Well, I opened the door to yell at the reporters." She frowned. "And I did look out last night. Do you know what happened at the Owens'?"

He told her that somebody had thrown a rock through the front window with a message wrapped around it, held in place by a rubber band.

Acadia braced herself. "What did it say?"

He studied her, and she thought he was evaluating where she stood on the "hate the Owens" front. His mouth tightened momentarily. "'Burn in hell, Joyce.'"

"How could they?" she said with quiet fury. Then her eyes widened. "What is it that's out front?"

He sighed. "Flowers. Tributes to your father."

"Oh, my Lord," she whispered.

"They're heaped on the Tindalls' lawn, too."

She knew it happened, but…in Tucannon? For her father? "Who is bringing them?" she asked, feeling shaken.

He shook his head. "Neighbors, I suppose. But not just them. There's a steady stream of traffic into town. I've seen cars going from one crime scene to the next, someone hopping out at each to leave flowers, notes, balloons." He shrugged. "Something like this happens, people want to express their sympathy. There's a bigger pile out front of your house than the Tindalls' next door. Your father was a professor, wasn't he? He touched a lot of lives."

A sob caught in her throat. She didn't know if she was more aghast at the idea of strangers leaving flowers in her father's memory, or people who'd known and loved him. People who might have known him better than she, his own daughter, did.

She couldn't even go out there and study them closely, see what people had written about Dad, not without appearing on television for sure. Imagining the shouted questions, the microphones thrust toward her, she shuddered.

"What time is David holding this press conference?"

"Three o'clock," the lieutenant said.

"You removed the crime-scene tape from the front porch."

"Yes, first thing this morning. You can clean up anytime you want." He looked discomforted. "Maybe you should call someone to do it for you."

Acadia shook her head. There wasn't much she could do for her father, but scrubbing his blood out of the porch boards was one. "I'll manage."

He rose heavily, as if he was weary. "I'll let you get on with whatever you were, er…" Those steady brown eyes scanned her skimpy, slobby getup a little uneasily.

"I wasn't doing a single useful thing," she admitted. "Before I can start packing, I need to get boxes, but that would mean going out."

"And braving the hordes." He nodded. "I can get some delivered for you."

"Really?"

He smiled. "That's the least I can do."

She was choked up after he left. His offer was surely above and beyond. He had to be overwhelmed by a crime of this magnitude. Murder was surely rare in any form in the barren stretches of a relatively underpopulated county. The only good-size towns, like Walla Walla, would have their own police forces to handle the full range of crimes, unlike Tucannon's. That Lieutenant Sykes had taken the time to be kind, too, was amazing.

In case someone else did come calling—someone she'd want to open the door to—Acadia went upstairs, showered and got dressed.

She'd start by sorting Dad's clothes, she decided. Weirdly, that felt less…personal than handling his books. Dad never had cared what he wore, and she wasn't that familiar with his current wardrobe. She could just make piles until the boxes arrived. No, it occurred to her, there'd surely be a box of plastic garbage bags somewhere.

She found some in the basement, and looked around in dismay, realizing how much was stored down here. Might there even be things of Mom's and hers, too? She snatched the box of big, black bags and hurried upstairs.

He'd been a tidy man, and she wasn't surprised to find his closet half-empty. It was as if he hadn't slid open the right-hand door in years. Not even his shoes spilled over onto that side. Dear God, it had probably been that way since Mom packed her clothes and vacated her part of the closet all those years ago. Wonderful thought.

She'd have to call her mother again tonight. The conversation they'd had after Acadia arrived had been brief. Mom had left a message since then, but Acadia hadn't felt like talking. And she still didn't.

She worked steadily, but far more slowly than she'd expected. *Oh, no,* she would think, *I do remember this sweater,* and five minutes later she'd still be sitting on the edge of his bed hugging the darned thing with tears running down her cheeks.

Even laundered, the clothes smelled like her father. He must still have been using the same soap he had when she was a little girl. And he'd smoked a pipe all these years. Mom had made him go outside, but Acadia had noticed yesterday that the sharp scent of tobacco permeated his den. Once alone in the house, he'd allowed himself the luxury of smoking there in his favorite chair. Laundry soap apparently couldn't altogether wipe out the scent of pipe tobacco.

Most of his clothes were well-worn. The nicer slacks and shirts—probably what he wore to lecture in his classroom at the college—she folded neatly to give to a thrift store. Ties, ditto—although to her eyes they looked old-fashioned.

Boxer shorts and white undershirts, she dumped into a bag to throw away. Socks, too. Many of his comfortable, at-home clothes weren't suitable for a thrift store, either. Knees bagged, there were sweat stains beneath the arms, unrepaired snags, unraveling hems.

Clutching a pair of pants that he must, judging from the grass stains, have worn to mow the lawn, Acadia found herself both smiling and tearful again. Daddy had been meticulous about the lawn. Mom thought he should mow in the evening, when it was cool, but no—he'd eat a leisurely breakfast on Saturday mornings, linger over his coffee and finally head outside about the time the day's heat was rising. Acadia hadn't realized then why it made her mother so impatient. Now she realized it had to do with their clashing natures. Dad was a creature of habit, slow and methodical. He must have driven Mom crazy, with her impulsive, mercurial personality.

It wasn't only Tucannon Mom had been fleeing, Acadia thought bleakly. It was Daddy, too. Back then, she'd believed her father had refused to move elsewhere for her mother's sake, but now she wondered if he'd ever been given that option.

Looking around his room, already losing the stamp of his personality, she tried to imagine him in San Francisco, and couldn't. He belonged here, in a way her mother never did.

"Oh, Daddy," she whispered, and—blast it!—began to cry again. She swiped at the tears, dropped those grass-stained pants in the garbage bag and raced to the bathroom across the hall to wash her face. She'd cried more today than she had in the past ten years. She prayed that cleaning out the rest of the house wouldn't be as bad.

Without even realizing she'd been doing it, Acadia had been keeping an eye on the time. At exactly 2:45 p.m., she acknowledged what had been only a half-formed idea until then.

She would go to the Owens' and stand beside David when he issued his statement. If he wanted her. But he'd be dumb not to, she told herself; her presence would be a statement of its own. And from her point of view, she could answer some questions and get it over with. Maybe then the reporters would go away.

She'd have to hurry if she was going to make herself presentable in time.

DAVID HEARD A knock on the back door five minutes before the hour. His mother had refused even to come downstairs for the press conference, much less make an appearance. He hadn't let her see his impatience or frustration. Exposing her frailty and obvious grief would have helped her cause, but she professed not to care what anyone else thought.

And maybe, he thought in exasperation, she didn't. He bet she'd have done what she had to if Rob was alive to need her to speak out, but without her sole motivation for living, she might have nothing left inside.

When he opened the back door, he was stunned to find Acadia standing there. She wore khakis and some kind of filmy short-sleeved shirt open over a camisole. Her glorious hair was neatly French-braided.

She was thinner than she should be—God, she looked as if she'd dropped five pounds in the past two days. There were deep purple bruises beneath chocolate-brown eyes. That pointy chin was held high and defiant as she waited with what he realized belatedly was wariness.

Taking in her puffy eyelids, he said, "You've been crying."

She pressed her lips together and lifted one shoulder in

a half shrug. He felt like an idiot. *Gee, now why would she have been crying?*

"Come in," he said. "Uh, this might not be the best time. In—" he glanced at his watch "—exactly two minutes I'm giving a statement Mom and I prepared to whomever is gathered out front."

Acadia slipped past him into the hall. Her gaze touched on the damn yellow tape still barring the basement door and the door to his father's den, then glanced away. "I know," she said. "Lieutenant Sykes told me. That's why I'm here."

It took him a slow-witted second to understand why she looked nervous. "You're planning to join me?" he said incredulously.

"If, um, you think it's a good idea."

He stood there speechless, his throat working. Rob had gunned her father down in cold blood, and she still intended to step out there at David's side and stare down those TV cameras and all those avid reporters. She was proposing to stand up *with* him.

Nothing in his life had ever moved him like she just had.

He finally got his voice back. More or less. "You know what townspeople are saying." It came out hoarse.

She nodded. "Some of them. But not all. I saw Alice Simmons insisting your mom and dad had done everything they could. The trouble is, defenders aren't news the way the hostile people are." Her eyes were shy now, reminding him of her younger self. "I thought I might be news because my father was one of the victims. And, well, this will give me a controlled venue for making my own statement."

He should ask her what she was going to say in case it would undercut him, but he couldn't insult her that way. David was shocked to realize he trusted her, a woman he hadn't seen in sixteen years.

"Thank you," he said simply. He led the way through the house to the front door and looked at her. "Ready?"

Her smile was only a little shaky. "Or not."

He had to wipe the grin off his face before he opened the door.

IT WENT ASTOUNDINGLY well, entirely thanks to Acadia's astonishing presence at his side.

He hadn't stepped outside before the shouted questions began, but when she followed him, silence fell momentarily. He saw a few gaping mouths—people who knew who she was. The others were obviously trying to figure out who she could be. He had no doubt they'd researched him thoroughly enough to know he wasn't married, so this wasn't the dutiful little wife.

There must have been twenty-five people crowded onto the small front lawn facing the porch. Microphones bristled in front. He was as conscious of the huge eyes of cameras, television and otherwise. David walked to the top of the steps, where he raised one hand.

"I have a short statement to read," he said. "First, let me introduce Acadia Henderson, whose father, Charles Henderson, was one of my brother's victims."

Standing right beside him, she nodded. More like a regal dip of the head, he thought, amused despite the situation. Feisty Acadia had grown into a woman who knew how to stand up for herself.

His voice carried well, so he didn't step any closer to the microphones. He was a strong speaker who could and often did rivet a jury. He let real emotion come through as he told these strangers—and, through them, everyone else following this story—how shocked he and his mother were. He talked about his brother, intelligent, athletic, well liked until schizophrenia manifested itself when Robbie was in his teens. He told them about the struggle to keep Rob on his meds, and his parents' desperate attempts to get their son committed when his behavior became increasingly erratic and even frightening.

"They failed," he said finally, looking from face to face, camera to camera. "He hadn't killed anybody yet. He hadn't hurt anybody yet. My parents couldn't get any help. Nonetheless, my mother blames herself. She is prostrate with grief over the loss of her friends and neighbors at Rob's hands. She grieves for her own son, too, who—despite everything—she loved. I ask that you give us the space to begin to heal." He let a small silence fall, then said, "Ms. Henderson has something to say as well. Then we'll take a few questions."

She drew a deep breath. "I'm not an eloquent speaker. I can only tell you what I feel. My father was a kind, gentle man. He didn't deserve to die by violence. He was never anything but nice to Robbie Owen. He felt so sorry for him, and for Pete and Joyce Owen, who had to cope with a son who would forever be a worry to them. What I know is that my dad would ask me to tell you that Joyce isn't to blame for what Robbie did. David isn't to blame. Nobody is. Not even Robbie, who was tormented for most of his life by voices. He tried so desperately to shut them out, but he couldn't. Robbie was nice to me when I was growing up, as nice as a good-looking, smart guy who is four years older ever is to a scrawny neighborhood girl who trailed after him and his brother like a hopeful puppy."

There was a ripple of laughter.

"Rob had begun to change before I moved away from Tucannon when I was thirteen, but my father continued to tell me about his troubles. When Dad talked about him, it was with compassion. Wherever my father is now, that's still what he feels. He might even…" Her voice hitched for the first time. She looked down, swallowed, then raised that determined chin again. "Dad might have been waiting for Rob, to take him in his arms and say, 'You'll be at peace now, son.'" There were tears on her cheeks. "I pray that Robbie has found peace. And I know my father has."

She turned her back on them long enough to swipe at her cheeks. David discovered that he needed to do the same. When they faced the reporters again, he put his hand on her back.

"How well do the two of you know each other?" someone called.

Acadia laughed. "Until I arrived in town two days ago, I hadn't seen David Owen in sixteen years."

"Were you friends?"

He smiled at her. "We grew up playing together, along with a bunch of other kids on our street. But I became a teenager when she was still a kid. If she hadn't moved, we might have become closer friends later, once she was in high school, too. As it is…" He shrugged. "It didn't happen."

He wasn't going to tell them about the next summer, when she was fourteen and he was sixteen. Those nights they'd sat out on one or the other of their porches, enjoying the night and talking—those nights were their business alone.

There were other questions. They wanted to know about his parents' attempts to get Robbie committed and why they'd been thwarted. He was glad to talk about that, about why doctors and officialdom should listen when parents say, "My son is a danger." They wanted details on the days leading up to the shooting. They wanted to know why Rob had shot the people he had, to which David could say only, "We'll never know. There were a couple of victims he'd clashed with." He shook his head. "No, I won't tell you who.

There were also victims, like Charlie Henderson, who'd never been anything but nice to Rob. I believe there was neither rhyme nor reason to why he shot who he did. I believe he was expressing pain and rage and may even have been blind to the faces of his victims. But I don't know."

There was incredulity that Acadia could be so generous as to forgive Joyce and David, to which she fired back, "There is nothing to forgive. A mentally ill man killed my father. His family had protected him, and other people from him, for all these years. The fact that, in the end, they couldn't keep protecting everyone was not their fault."

At one point David swept the crowd with his gaze and spotted Lieutenant Sykes at the back, standing on the sidewalk listening. He inclined his head and David nodded back.

Finally David said, "That's all. I ask again, please respect our privacy. Mine, my mother's, Ms. Henderson's and the families of the other victims. None of us can begin the rest of our lives when we feel as if we can't even walk out to the street to get our mail or newspapers."

If there was any shame, he didn't see it. As he ushered Acadia inside, questions were still being shouted after them. He shut the door, locked it and leaned back against it, wondering if she'd be offended if he wrapped his arms around her and held on for a long, long time.

No, I don't dare, he knew. Sixteen years was a long time. He might tell himself he knew Acadia Henderson, but he didn't really.

CHAPTER SIX

"WELL, that was fun," Acadia said after a minute.

He'd had his head tilted back, leaning against the door, but now he straightened and looked at her. His eyes were almost black in this light, gloomy with the blinds all drawn against the sunlight.

"Thank you," he said, voice low and gravelly. "What you said was...amazing."

"I didn't say anything that wasn't true." What she would have given sixteen years ago to see that expression on his face. "If you mean the bit about Dad...I meant all of it. But especially the bit about Dad."

David made a strange, huffing sound that was almost a laugh. "Do you know I've barely cried yet? Until I just did, out there?"

"You knew Dad." Acadia tried to smile and couldn't. "He *would* have asked me to say exactly that. And...if it was possible for him to meet Robbie in the hereafter, I'm betting Dad did."

"Yeah." His throat worked. "I hope he did. I hope he could. I hope my father was there, too."

Neither of them said anything about Wayne Tindall. God would have had to work a miracle on him, to get him to forgive Robbie. Betty...well, who knew?

A quavering voice said, "Is it over?"

They both turned to see Joyce at the foot of the stairs. Acadia was shocked at her appearance. She'd aged so terribly since Acadia had seen her three or four years back. She was dressed for the day in her usual polyester slacks and crisp short-sleeved blouse, but her perm had long quit and her hair was gray and stringy.

She stared in equal astonishment. "Acadia?"

"Mrs. Owen." Acadia stepped toward her. "I came… I wanted to tell you…"

Joyce flinched. "Your father… I don't understand how Robbie could have done that…"

Acadia shook her head. "No, but the real Robbie wouldn't have. We all know that. He was…he was ill. And I wanted to say how sorry I am. You lost your son, too, and I know you loved him."

Joyce's face seemed to dissolve. Without sound, she began to cry. David moved swiftly to take her into his arms.

Feeling horrible, Acadia tried to sidle past them. "I should go," she whispered, but David's hand shot out and snagged her upper arm.

"No. Please don't go. Will you wait?"

His mother never looked at her again. She wept with silent hopelessness against her son's shoulder, and finally let him lead her upstairs. Acadia stood at the foot of those stairs wondering why David wanted her to stay. To thank her again, maybe, but she wished he wouldn't. She'd done what seemed right to her, and she'd rather he didn't make a big deal out of it.

She reached up and gently rubbed her upper arm, where his big hand had clasped her. She couldn't help remembering the feel of his hand on her back, too. Supporting her. Maybe, she reminded herself, only because *she* was supporting him.

Past the staircase railing she could see the yellow tape across the door to Mr. Owen's den. Acadia had never been in it. The kitchen, yes. They'd all been in and out of one another's houses. They'd get thirsty or hungry and raid the nearest kitchen, or someone would say, "Mom baked cookies today," and lead them all to a feast. But she'd never been upstairs, never seen David's bedroom—dream about it though she did once she'd developed that all-consuming crush on him. And she'd barely caught a glimpse into the den.

She knew from the news that Robbie had gotten his hands on his father's guns. Acadia could only imagine Mr. Owen's horror that his son had used his guns to kill people. Like most people around here, he'd had a hunting rifle or two, but she didn't remember him actually *going* hunting. Had he fought in Vietnam, maybe, or the Korean War? She'd really hardly known him at all.

"What are you thinking?"

Acadia started at the sound of David's voice. She hadn't heard him coming down the stairs.

"Oh, about your father." She gestured toward the hideous tape.

"He was almost as gentle a man as your dad." When she turned, it was to see him staring at the closed door. "I don't think he ever shot any living thing. He did teach Robbie and I to shoot, though. It was fun. He'd drive out to some godforsaken place, set up some bottles or cans, and we'd try to blast them into oblivion." His mouth twisted. "Rob was probably better than I was. Partly because Dad quit taking us when Rob first started getting weird, so he'd had a couple more years' practice."

Acadia winced.

"Mom says she hid the key. She doesn't know how he found it. I wish like hell she'd gotten rid of the guns," David said with sudden vehemence.

"You know not everyone even locks them up the way

they should. Rob could have broken in somewhere else and gotten his hands on a rifle."

His eyes met hers. "But would he have?"

When she didn't answer, he growled, "Probably. God." He bowed his head, kneading the back of his neck. "I don't know."

"Did he ever, well, threaten anything like this?"

"Mom says not that she knew of. You heard she'd thrown him out two weeks before?"

She nodded; it was common knowledge now that the crazy Owen man had been sleeping under bushes and stealing out of people's kitchens. He'd been filthy, his beard growing. People heard him muttering to himself. Sometimes he'd shout and gesticulate wildly. Everyone had been uneasy, but not scared the way they should have been. Why would they be? They'd known Robbie Owen his whole life.

Acadia wondered if her father had set food out on the porch for Robbie, as if he was one of the shy small folk—a brownie, maybe. She hoped Dad had done that.

I should be mad like everyone else is, it occurred to her. She didn't altogether understand why she wasn't. Sometimes in the E.R. she felt such rage as they fought to save the life of a gunshot victim. She wished the assailants to hell. She was not a saintly woman, given to forgiving all sins.

But Rob was different. Maybe it was because she'd known him for so long—known him when he was clear-eyed and sane. Maybe because he was David's brother, because he looked like David. Because he was part of her incredibly happy childhood.

One of her most vivid memories of Robbie was a time she'd fallen off her bike. She'd always been reckless, trying to keep up with the bigger kids. That day she'd been sailing down the steepest hill in town and suddenly she saw a car on a cross street and had to brake sharply. She'd skidded sideways and then tumbled end over end. She remembered sitting on the street, looking down at herself in astonishment a moment before the pain hit. She'd skinned elbows, knees, even a cheek. Her wounds, seeping blood, had been filled with grit. She'd started to cry, helplessly, mad because Acadia Henderson was too tough to cry.

It was Robbie who'd zipped to a stop beside her on his own bike. Who'd left that bike behind in someone's yard and walked her home, pushing hers with the wheel that wouldn't roll straight. He'd said admiringly, "Wow, you were really moving! Nothing stops you, does it, Acadia?" and thereby restored her self-esteem.

No, she couldn't hate Robbie Owen, not the way so many other people seemed able to do.

At least—not yet. Because she couldn't actually *picture* him doing what he did.

"I should get home," she told David.

"Mom said thank you. For saying what you did."

"You mean, out there?" She gestured toward the front door.

"No. To her."

"Oh." She frowned. "Other people must have said…"

"No." His jaw muscles flexed. "No one has."

"I think Lieutenant Sykes feels sorry for her."

"Yeah. Maybe. He's a decent guy. Ah…you want to go out the back door?"

"Are you kidding?" She started down the hall. "Yes, I'm going out the back."

"How'd you manage earlier?" he asked her. "Did you climb over the fence?"

Not all the backyards along the street were fenced, but the Tindalls' was. Of course.

She laughed. "I went in and out of gates with incredible

speed. Heaving myself over six-foot fences is not something my fitness regimen has prepared me for."

"What's your fitness regimen?" David asked her, sounding amused. Probably because she didn't possess a lot of noticeable muscle.

"Mostly I swim. But I take a once-a-week kickboxing class, too. The ability to kick butt is significant when you work in a big-city emergency room."

"I bet." He reached over her shoulder and opened the back door. He was so close, his breath ruffled her hair. "Acadia…"

"Don't you dare thank me again."

"Or you'll kick my butt?"

She didn't turn until she had gone down the three steps to the patio. "I'm not sure I could. But I'll get snippy. You don't want that to happen."

Laughing, he said, "No. God forbid."

"See you," she said, flipping a hand and heading toward the side of the house.

"Acadia."

She turned and narrowed her eyes.

"I missed you," he said, and his lean, dark face was entirely serious.

Her heart somersaulted. She took a step backward, then another. "My thirteen-year-old self would have melted into a puddle to hear you say that."

"I know," he said, flashing her a wicked grin, and went back into the house.

"Reeve!" his mom called. "Hurry! You have to see this."

She sounded so urgent he rolled off his bed and stumbled out into the living room. "What?"

"The news."

Dad sat in his recliner with a beer in his hand, but Mom was standing. Both stared at the television set.

"Look who's with David Owen." Mom sounded dazed.

"Who is it?" Reeve asked. He couldn't take his eyes off the TV, either. It made him sweat to see how much David looked like his brother. That face brought it all back—the terrible fear. Heart pounding, he made himself look at the classy redhead who stood beside David.

"Shh," his father said.

David Owen raised his hand, said he had a statement and then told everyone who the woman was.

"Acadia Henderson," his mother said at the exact same moment.

Reeve's mouth dropped open. What was *she* doing there, on the Owens' front porch?

He didn't move while David talked, and then Acadia spoke. His mother started crying when Acadia said her father would be waiting there just inside the pearly gates to take Rob Owen in his arms. Now it was her Reeve couldn't take his eyes from. How could she possibly mean what she was saying? Her dad was just killed. Reeve didn't buy all that shit about forgiveness and eternal love. How could she not hate Rob Owen's guts?

The scene went back to the studio, where a well-groomed man shook his head as if marveling. "That was a remarkable statement, Mary Beth."

The woman sitting beside him murmured, "I wonder how many dry eyes there'll be among our viewers."

"There are a lot of different kinds of courage," the newscaster said, then fixed a piercing gaze on the camera. "Next up, we'll be talking to folks who oppose having a sewer treatment plant built in their neighborhood. Stay with us." A commercial came on.

Reeve's dad clicked the remote and the television screen went blank. Reeve swallowed.

There are a lot of different kinds of courage. Reeve couldn't even look at his parents.

"Are they still bothering you?" his mother asked timidly. "Those reporters?"

Reeve shook his head. "Not so much." He hadn't been able to duck them since he was working at the Shell station, so his strategy had been to look dumb and sullen and say "no comment" over and over again.

When what he should have said was, "Walt Stenten gave his life for me. You hear about things like that, but that's not the same as having it happen right in front of you. Finding out that kind of courage is real." What he should have said was, *I didn't have any kind of courage that day. I don't understand why he'd die for* me.

If he had any guts at all, that's what he would have said. But he didn't.

"What you're doing for Anne Stenten is a good thing," his mom said. "I'm sure she needs the money, keeping the station open."

"That's what she said," he mumbled.

Dad shook his head. "I hope he had the sense to have life insurance."

"We never think it's going to happen to us." Mom sighed. "Reeve, you're not going back tonight, are you?"

"Only to close," he said.

"You need more help," she protested.

He shook his head. "It's nothing. It probably won't last that long anyway. Mrs. Stenten will have to sell the station." And then who knew if he'd even have a job?

"Maybe," Mom said doubtfully. "But who'll buy it?"

"If I could afford it, I would." Dad was looking at Reeve.

"Put you in charge, son. That's what you want, isn't it? To have a place of your own like that?"

That's what he used to want. Maybe. Except he'd never expected to stay in Tucannon. Like every other senior at the high school, he'd dreamed of escaping. Meeting girls he hadn't known his whole life. He'd thought of getting a job at a place like a big car dealership. He'd kept telling himself when his Bel Air was ready to roll, he'd go. Sometimes he'd imagined driving all the way across the country. Never mind that he didn't have any money, that he was spending most of what he made on parts.

Now he knew he couldn't go anywhere until Mrs. Stenten quit needing him. And he didn't know if he'd ever finish working on the car. He hadn't been out to the garage since he'd had to go out there to show that Lieutenant Sykes and a couple of other cops where he'd been, where Rob stood. They'd drawn chalk lines on the concrete of the garage floor and driveway while he stared at the dried blood until he couldn't stand it another second and then fixed his gaze on his creeper, askew against the garage wall where he'd left it when he fled into the house.

He knew Dad had hosed the blood away as soon as the police said it was okay. He'd closed the garage door, and nobody had opened it since. Eventually Dad would start grumbling again about not being able to park in his own goddamned garage, but probably not for a while.

Maybe, Reeve thought, *I can sell the car. I could put it up on Craigslist. Somebody might come with a trailer and haul it away.* Only everything in him fought that idea. Walt would be disappointed in him if he didn't finish what he started, after all the work they'd put in.

He turned without another word to his parents and blundered back down the hall to his bedroom, shutting the door quietly behind him.

Marge Perkins watched the news when David Owen gave his statement, too. She expected that tomorrow she'd be asked to comment on it and she had her back up from the minute he walked out onto his front porch dressed like the rich attorney he was, all set on impressing the reporters with how brokenhearted he and his mother were.

It gave her some satisfaction that Joyce Owen hadn't had the nerve to show her face. No surprise there! Why, she'd been hiding out for years, unable to explain to anyone why she was still coddling her son, who'd long since passed being a boy.

What Marge hadn't expected was Acadia Henderson. She remembered Acadia, who had run wild with the Owen boys and the Strauss twins and all the other hooligans back then. Of course, it made sense that she was in town to clear out her father's house. But to be so much as speaking to the Owens…!

Mouth agape, Marge listened as Acadia spouted some nonsense about her father feeling forgiving even after Robbie—*Robbie!* As if he was still a little boy!—murdered him. Charlie Henderson might be a meek man who'd let that brassy wife of his trample all over him, but Marge doubted even he'd think it was fine and dandy for dear little Robbie to spray bullets and soak the streets of Tucannon with blood.

She made a mental note of that line. Not that she'd necessarily be interviewed tomorrow; after all, she'd said what she had to say, and she knew those correspondents were trying to get a wide variety of opinions even though they'd thanked her for being brave enough to speak out. And John Nolan smiled and nodded at her every time he came into the café.

She snorted at the notion that Joyce and Pete had tried to get Rob committed to an institution. If that was true, why was this the first time anyone was hearing about it? It wasn't as if all sensible folks in this town wouldn't have spoken out in favor of putting him behind bars if a soul had ever come and asked for their opinions. If anybody had ever come asking, Marge felt sure she'd have heard.

"Joyce's trying to wash her hands of all responsibility, that's what she's doing," Marge told the empty apartment.

Was there any possibility Joyce would be arrested for making those guns available to her crazy, violent son? If he'd been a minor, his parents would most certainly be held accountable. Why shouldn't they still be? Marge considered herself a charitable woman, but she also believed in shouldering responsibility when it was yours to bear. And so she'd tell anyone who asked, she decided with a nod.

The respect in that news anchor's voice when he talked about all kinds of courage was enough to make her sniff and turn off the television, wishing she'd watched a different channel.

Most of the news vans had left after the statement was made. One stayed parked in front of the Owen house. A few of the reporters lingered in their cars, probably with their air-conditioning on. But by sunset, they were all gone.

She let herself out the front door, sneaked one horrified look at the bloodstain—*note to self: must clean it tomorrow*—and walked to the heap of flowers and more that had been growing all day long on the front lawn.

There had to be two dozen bouquets heaped on the mostly brown grass. Those at the bottom had dried up, but there were fresh ones on top. There was a new teddy bear holding a helium-filled balloon that said "Sympathy." A child's tattered purple Care Bear—Acadia hadn't seen one of those since she was a little girl herself. Who could have left that? Most disturbing to Acadia was the book about the

Vietnam War. She crouched on the sidewalk and opened it. On the title page someone had written, "You were right, Professor, history does repeat itself. One nightmare is pretty much like another. I owe you for helping me find the way out of mine. Wish I'd said that sooner."

Acadia pressed her hand over her mouth. "Oh, Daddy," she moaned.

There were other notes that said things like "Mr. H, you were the best," but it was the book she carried cradled to her heart when she found her way blindly back into the house.

She set the book on the end table next to her father's big chair, right where he would have laid it if he'd gotten up to fill his pipe or absentmindedly wander into the kitchen to make himself a bite to eat. If he was to be found anywhere in the house, it was here. She thought about leaving the book open, so that he could read the inscription, but knew how ridiculous that was.

"If you were here," she murmured, "I'd know, wouldn't I? I'd be able to feel you."

She wondered that her phone hadn't rung tonight. Guiltily she thought, *I have to call Mom.* And she would. Soon.

A knock on the back door made her start. Oh, God, who now?

Acadia made her way cautiously to the kitchen, wishing she'd turned the porch light on, but it wasn't so dark outside yet that she couldn't see David's face.

She opened the door, surprised and tongue-tied. "Hi."

"Hey," he said. "I, uh, happened to look out and saw you outside. I thought you might be feeling low."

"I am," she admitted, a lump in her throat. "Do you want to come in, or…?"

"It feels pretty good out here," he suggested, and she nodded. The house always held unpleasantly on to the day's heat, and she kept marveling that her father had never installed even a small window air-conditioning unit. She should be more used to the heat than she was, but in Sacramento at this time of year she went from air-conditioned apartment to car to hospital, barely stepping foot outside. With her fair skin, tipping her face up to the sun and dreaming of mai tais was as close as she got to being in the sun.

She didn't turn the light on. The night was descending fast, she realized, but she'd always liked these summer evenings. In Tucannon, it was the most neighborly time of day. In summers, even the kids were allowed to stay up late and enjoy the cool air. Acadia's mother used to go upstairs and throw open all the bedroom windows so the heat would escape before she'd go out to sit on the front porch to visit with some friend or other. The kids would keep playing in the street, calling to each other. The adults' voices would be soft, the murmurs blending up and down the street into a sound like the river low in summer. A laugh would carry, making other conversations pause. It was mostly the women who came out to talk, but Acadia remembered seeing a tiny flame when Daddy lit his pipe and stood at one end of the porch, maybe watching over her, maybe listening to his wife gossip.

Those were good times, she thought, with a sting in her eyes.

David sat on one of the Adirondack chairs Acadia's father repainted every couple of years. Two for the front porch, two for the back patio. The fierce Eastern Washington sun was hard on wood. She'd leave them with the house, she decided.

Acadia settled onto the concrete step, wrapping her arms around her knees.

"You okay?" David asked softly.

"I was curious what people were leaving. There were

notes from some of Daddy's students." She told him about the book.

"He was a good man."

"Yes, he was."

The silence felt so comfortable, so familiar, she felt tension leaving her like a long, relieved sigh. She wasn't in any hurry to break it, but finally she said, "Has your mother left the house yet?"

"She hardly leaves her bedroom. I'm not sure she'd do that if I didn't insist she come down for meals."

"I'm sorry, David."

He nodded.

"What's she going to do?" But what she was really asking was: *When will you be leaving?*

"I don't know. Move, I guess. With so much anger directed at her, how can she stay here? But so far I haven't been able to get her to talk about it." He leaned his head back and gazed up at the stars. "I called my boss today to ask for a leave of absence. God knows when I'll be able to go back to work."

Silly to feel such a rush of relief. "I did the same," Acadia said. "As long as I'm here, I might as well clear out Daddy's stuff and get the house ready for sale instead of having to come back." She hesitated, her thoughts reverting to Joyce. "I remember your mom having a sister. And you have cousins. They used to visit."

"Yeah, my aunt Jackie and her husband retired to a little town on the Oregon Coast. Yachats. It's a pretty place. But I don't know. Mom's always shaken her head and said she didn't understand how anyone could live with that much rain."

"She might find she likes it," Acadia suggested tentatively, wondering. Wouldn't he want his mother to move near him in Seattle? Of course, Seattle wasn't famous for its dry climate, either.

He grunted. She could barely make out his face now. "Aunt Jackie has cancer," he said abruptly. "She'd be here, except she's having chemotherapy. I don't know if this is a good time for Mom to go there or not."

"Wow. It never rains but it pours. Um. Bad pun?"

He laughed, but it wasn't a happy sound. "Good try, 'Cadia."

Her heart gave a little bump. "I forgot you used to do that. Drop the *A*. No one else ever did."

His head turned so that he was looking toward her. "I didn't remember that I did."

Don't be any more pathetic than you can help, okay? Don't let him know how desperate you were for the smallest hint of affection from him.

"It's weird being home," she said, looking toward the fence that separated Dad's backyard from the Tindalls'. Except Wayne and Betty were gone now. "How familiar everything is, in an unsettling way."

"I've been thinking that, too. The first night, I knew how long a step it took me to get from refrigerator to sink. What shelf the margarine would be on. The step that creaks. The exact way to jiggle my bedroom window open."

"The smells," Acadia said. "They're getting to me. Sacramento is dry, too, but…it's different here. Part of me keeps wishing it was spring, so the lilacs would be in bloom, but then I'm glad they're not." She was quiet for a minute. "Daddy started smoking his pipe inside after we left. That was a new smell. It made me wonder…" Her throat closed.

"Wonder what?" His voice was husky and still somehow soft.

"Whether a part of him was glad when we went. Whether he could relax."

"He might have been glad your mom was gone. I don't know, Acadia. But he talked about you all the time. He missed you."

Her arms tightened, and it occurred to her that she was darn near in a fetal position. "I wanted to stay with him. I didn't want to go."

"All things being equal, mothers still tend to get custody," David said gently. "You don't know what they talked about when you weren't there."

She shook her head. "You're wrong. I know. It would never have occurred to him. I was a girl. Of course I'd go with Mom. He never asked me. Neither of them did."

"You're still mad."

"I guess I am." She buried her laugh in her knees. "The joys of coming home. And then it hit me. This is the last time."

"Yeah," he said after a minute. "It might be mine, too."

"You *wanted* to leave."

"You would have, too, once you graduated from high school."

"Sure." Of course she would have, because David wouldn't have been here anymore. Given that newcomers were rare and she'd known every other boy in Tucannon, Acadia felt sure her crush would have continued unabated. Her heart would have broken when he left for college. She couldn't even imagine who she'd have gone to prom with.

Sometimes she thought she'd lived in two parallel universes—the real one, and the dream she'd clung to so stubbornly.

They both heard a car out on the street. He stirred. "I'd better go. I don't want something to happen and me not be home."

"I didn't say how crummy it was that someone threw that rock through your window."

"I expected it," he said flatly. "And I'll bet it won't be the last."

"And here I've been feeling sorry for myself," she muttered, glad he couldn't see her expression.

"You should be, Acadia. You lost your dad way before his time. You should hurt. You should be mad." He made an odd sound. "'Cadia Henderson always got mad. You fired up faster than the firecrackers we used to light on the Fourth."

"Yeah, well, redhead and all that. I didn't like people making fun of me."

"Little Orphan Annie." He was chuckling as he stood and started away into the darkness. "I'll never forget that haircut."

"Thanks for the reminder," she said to his back.

She heard his laugh when she could no longer see him.

CHAPTER SEVEN

ACADIA PROCRASTINATED HALF the morning, but the time came when she couldn't make a single other excuse to herself.

She had to stomp down into the basement to find a bucket. The mop stood in it instead of hanging on a hook on the wall. Oh, God, she thought. What do I need? Will a sponge be enough? Or maybe one of those scratchy things for the kitchen sink? Sandpaper?

Part of her wanted to call a decking company and have them come out and tear up the porch boards and replace them. That way she'd never have to look at the bloodstain again, much less touch it. But that was dumb; Dad would have kept the boards well sealed, and a good scrubbing should do the job. She could imagine his expression of bemusement if she wasted a thousand dollars or more replacing perfectly good boards because she was a coward.

"Fine," she snapped—to him, or anyone else who was listening. Acadia Henderson was *not* a coward, and no one was calling her one.

Upstairs she found a scour pad under the sink as well as a Brillo pad. She ran hot, soapy water into the bucket and, after peeking out the window to be sure no reporters were visible, carried it out to the front porch. Wouldn't she make a sight on tonight's news, she thought, on her hands and knees cleaning up her father's blood.

The stain was bigger than she'd been trying to picture

it all morning. The bullet tore open an artery, Lieutenant Sykes had told her. Dad had bled a lot.

She dumped the whole bucket of water on the stain, making sure it was thoroughly soaked. Then she went back in the house and refilled. Did it again, and again. Pinkish water washed away down the cracks between boards, but the stain seemed to darken. Her stomach was revolting. At last, wearing latex gloves, she made herself get down on her knees, dip the scour pad in the latest bucket of soapy water and start scrubbing.

She lifted the pad to rinse it out and stared in horror at the red coloring the bright yellow glove, dripping into the bucket. With a cry, she dropped the pad into the water, tore off the gloves and ran into the house. The screen door slammed behind her. She barely made it to the bathroom before she lost her breakfast.

Done, she rinsed out her mouth and marched back out onto the porch. Ignoring her revulsion, she put those damn gloves back on, rinsed out scouring pad and glove and went back to scrubbing.

But something happened to her while she was sponging up her father's blood.

She got mad. Grief was there, too, like molten lava deep inside, but the steam escaping was anger. She pictured the face she'd seen on television news—an unkempt Rob Owen she wouldn't have recognized if he'd come into her E.R. A man with the mad eyes of Rasputin. A man—*not* the boy she'd so sentimentally remembered—who knew what he was and refused to take his medication anyway. Beneath the steam, rage bubbled higher and higher as she scrubbed and scrubbed.

Still the water ran pink. Nausea boiled in her again, but she refused to quit. How many times would she have to wash her hands when she was done? Acadia thought fleetingly of Lady Macbeth, unable to wash away her sins. But no—what she was doing had more in common with ritual purification. If somehow she could clean away her father's blood, would her world be restored to normalcy? Sanity?

No. No, it wouldn't. Nothing would bring her father back. Oh, God, oh, God. Why had she held on to such petty resentment? When had she last said "I love you" to him?

Still the water ran pink. She was sobbing, even though her eyes were dry.

She heard footsteps. "Damn it, Acadia! I should be doing this for you," a deep voice groaned.

Light-headed, she swiveled and looked up, seeing the man standing there backlit by a scorching sun. It was as if Rob stood above her. Had he come onto the porch when he shot Daddy? Stood right *there?* Or fired from farther away? Had Daddy had even a moment of understanding?

She clamped a forearm against her mouth to hold back the rise of bile in her throat. "What are you doing here?" she cried. "I don't want you here! I lied! I lied! Maybe Daddy could forgive him, but I can't. Do you hear me?" she screamed.

She hadn't known how open David's face was to her until now, when it went utterly blank. The only reaction was the rise and fall of his Adam's apple.

"Yes," he said. "I hear you." He bent his head in a nod that was absurdly courteous, and he turned and left her alone on the porch with a stain that seemed to be spreading instead of shrinking.

HE PAUSED IN the door to his mother's bedroom and looked at her back, as he often did. She lay on top of the covers, dressed, and stared at the wall. Or perhaps her eyes were closed. David had no idea.

But she must have heard him coming, because she said, "Did you ask her to dinner?"

"No." He knew his voice was uninflected. He *knew* it. But something had seeped out, because his mother rolled over and looked at him.

"I thought you were going over there."

Walk away. Don't tell her. But it seemed he could withstand everything except the horror and fury he'd seen in Acadia's huge brown eyes. Aimed at *him.*

"I did," he heard himself say. Anger of his own was suddenly jagged in his chest. "She was out on the porch. Trying to clean up her father's blood. I don't know how long she'd been at it, but it was all over her gloves. On the knees of her jeans. Running down the sides of the bucket." He had to stop. "No, I didn't ask her to dinner."

He turned and blundered down the hall with no idea where he could go to hide from the expression he'd seen on Acadia's face. She wouldn't throw rocks through his mother's window, but at that moment when she saw him, she had wanted to. She'd wanted to hurt him and everyone else related to Rob. And he couldn't even blame her.

Downstairs he stood in the middle of the living room breathing like a bellows. His hands were balled into fists. There was nowhere to go. He couldn't get away. At this moment he didn't know if he could bear another minute in this house with his mother. She was a burden he would never be able to set down. He wasn't even sure he loved her. Or that she loved him.

He groaned and flattened his hands on the wall, bending to press his forehead against it. He was crying. Goddamn it, he was crying, huge racking sobs that hurt like nothing ever had.

Why had his mother never been able to see *him?* He was her son, too. *Rob, how could you? Why, Rob, why? 'Cadia,*

I need you. Stupid, stupid, stupid, I'm not a little kid anymore. For God's sake, get a grip.

But he couldn't seem to, not even when he knew his mother had come partway down the stairs and could see him. He was being turned inside out, and the process was incredibly painful. A self-sufficient man, he'd never known loneliness like this. He had never broken, but now the grief was so enormous he didn't know how he would ever stand straight again.

His legs folded beneath him. He fell, his hands sliding down the wall, and although the sobs had stopped the agony hadn't.

He heard her turn and go and was glad. He had nothing left for his mother. It was an enormous struggle to finally turn and sit, legs outstretched, back to the wall, all that kept him upright.

By the time he lifted the hem of his shirt to wipe his eyes dry, he had hardened inside. Little Acadia, all grown up, had made him feel vulnerable, but no more.

JOYCE STOOD IN the upstairs hall, out of sight of David, and thought her heart might beat its way out of her chest. This was almost as bad as the moment when she'd seen that Pete's gun cabinet stood open and *knew*.

She had never confessed even to Pete how often she had hated their oldest son even while loving him. Right now, all she could feel was the hate. He had damaged all of them, shredded their lives without offering anything in return. His self-absorption had been absolute. No matter what, she would probably have been angry; how could she not rail against fate? But it was the element of choice that had added this dark streak of rage to her heart. Robbie could have stayed on his medication. He said it made him feel dull. She had tried to convince herself over the years that, when he was medicated, he didn't understand what he was like when he quit and allowed the madness to grip him. If he'd been able to see himself… But a part of her had thought he *did* know, maybe even wanted the insanity in all its vivid colors and sharp edges, like an addict wanted to be stoned. And by the time he was twenty, the nice boy had lost the ability to empathize with other people. She doubted he had ever given a thought to what his illness did to his mother and father. To his brother.

Clutching the railing, she squeezed her eyes shut. *No. Don't lie to yourself. Robbie didn't do anything to David. Pete and I did that damage all by ourselves.* In their fear for Robbie, they'd quit seeing their younger son. Convinced themselves he was fine. Been blind to his every attempt to gain their attention.

Why had the sight of Acadia mopping up her father's blood hit Davey so hard? He certainly wasn't crying for his brother. Parents might love their children no matter what, but a brother was unlikely to. She supposed it was the realization of what Robbie had done. She knew perfectly well that she was hiding from that knowledge herself. If she walked outside, she'd have to see the blank windows in the Tindalls' next door, or the Hendersons' beyond it with that bloodstain.

Oh, Lord, she thought in horror—who would clean up Wayne's and Betty's blood? They'd never had children. Joyce had no idea who their heir would be. Who would see to it that they were buried? Choose something for each of them to wear? Once she'd been so close to Betty, and now she had no idea who either of them would consider best friends. If nobody came to care for the house, the way Acadia was her father's, the flowers would dry up on Wayne's prized rosebushes, his lawn would grow first brown and then shaggy. Grass would creep into flower beds. He had been such an insufferable perfectionist, but now her throat was clogged with misery because nobody would ever care for his yard the way he had. And he was such an awful man, she shouldn't care, but she did. She did.

Downstairs the hoarse sobs had stopped. Had Davey even moved? Was he reacting so powerfully to the sight of Charlie's blood? She knew he often went out to crime scenes; that was part of his job. Had Acadia said or done something? But if she had, why did he care so much?

She waited a long, long time, until she finally heard her son moving around downstairs, before she went on up to the bathroom. She could barely look at herself in the mirror. She had failed both her boys. Maybe, in the end, she couldn't have saved Rob, but why hadn't she let herself delight in her younger boy, who would have been any parent's pride and joy?

She knew, of course—she'd been afraid that any pleasure she showed in Davey's achievements would hurt Robbie, who knew he'd never equal them. She had been protecting her oldest. And so she'd chosen to hurt one son, to save the other from any sting.

That decision, she knew now, bleakly, was the worst she could have made.

Suddenly she realized she was staring at herself in the mirror. Meeting her own eyes.

A surprising thought crept into her head: David was still alive. Here, because she'd needed him. Was it too late to let him know she loved him, too? To tell him how very proud of him she'd always been?

Something grew lighter inside her. The difference was infinitesimal. It was likely that whatever she said wouldn't mean much to him, not like it would have when he was younger. But…what if she could mend even part of the rift? Hope he would understand? Hope that he still needed her, at least a little?

Why, that peculiar feeling must *be* hope, she thought in surprise. It wasn't much—one tiny shoot of grass in a sea of gravel. Fragile.

But it was enough to have her making her way back downstairs, instead of to her darkened bedroom.

ACADIA HAD SCRUBBED until the wood was raw and the last water she poured over the porch boards ran clear. And then she had stood in the shower scrubbing herself until her skin was fiery red and the hot-water tank had given up its last.

Exhausted, she tried to figure out how she could apologize to David, and whether he'd accept that apology with more than a cool nod and that thousand-yard distance in his eyes. Would he believe she hadn't meant what she said?

She lay on her bed staring at the ceiling, letting the fan she'd stolen from Daddy's bedroom create the illusion of cooler air. Eventually she must have slept, because she woke groggy and hollow feeling.

She splashed water on her face, brushed her hair and tamed it with an elastic, then decided she really had to eat. She stared unenthusiastically at the contents of her father's cupboards and refrigerator—an iceberg lettuce salad with no additions but a carrot and ranch dressing didn't inspire her. Tomorrow, maybe she should go shopping. Heavens, her father had probably quit bothering with vegetables and fruit when he was on his own. He seemed mainly to be stocked with frozen meals and canned goods. She settled on creamed corn—when had she last eaten that?—and a burrito she could nuke in the microwave.

As she sat to eat, she realized the silence was getting to her. Yes, she lived alone, but she wasn't actually alone all that much. If it weren't for David and her two brief conversations with Lieutenant Sykes, she would have gone days now without speaking at all.

I should call someone. Guilt, guilt. *Mom—she must be frantic by now. God. If I don't call her, she's going to show up on the newly scrubbed doorstep.*

And Acadia realized she very much did *not* want her mother here in Tucannon, for all kinds of complicated reasons.

In fact, there were all kinds of complicated reasons she didn't want to talk to her mother, even though she loved her. And, mostly, liked her, too.

But…some things you just gotta do.

With a sigh she went looking for her phone, and found it dead. No wonder it had quit ringing. She dug in her as-yet-unpacked suitcase for the charger, plugged it in and checked messages. There were twelve, five of which were from her persistent mother, the others from assorted friends and colleagues.

Her mother answered on the first ring. "Acadia! What's been *happening?* Why haven't you called?"

"I let my battery run down and didn't notice." Good explanation. Her mother's silence spoke for itself. "It's been upsetting," she admitted. "I guess I haven't felt like talking." Except to David Owen. "I'm sorry, Mom."

"I've been worried."

"I know." The guilt was almost as crippling as her grief had been earlier. "I haven't actually accomplished much yet. I mostly cleaned out Dad's bedroom."

"I don't suppose there was much worth keeping there."

Maybe that was a simple observation; Acadia, after all, had thought much the same. But she found she resented Mom's implication that Dad hadn't dressed well, whether it was true or not.

"I washed his blood off the porch today."

There was an appalled silence. Then, "Oh, honey. Why didn't you hire someone?"

She wanted to ask who she was supposed to have hired. A local teenager? Some maid-for-a-day service? Did they *do* blood? If so, they'd have done it impersonally. Or perhaps feeling disgust. *And it was my father's blood.* Yes, there were cleaning services that specialized in crime scenes, but probably not in Whitman County.

"It was something I thought I should do," she said.

"Do they know why he went outside when he could hear somebody shooting?"

On the news they'd talked about Rob's movements and the sequence of deaths. The Tindalls first, Acadia's father next, then Earl Kennedy. Robbie had done some shooting downtown then, wounding half a dozen people, including Wendi Rowe, the pharmacy assistant, and killing the as-yet-unnamed victim. Finally, he had gone to the Hadfields' house, no one seemed quite sure why, and he'd shot Walt Stenten there. Apparently nineteen-year-old Reeve Hadfield worked for Walt, who showed up to help Reeve rebuild an old car. Walt had thrown himself in front of Reeve, taking the bullet intended for the boy. He was the one clear hero to emerge from that day of horror. Whether Rob had gone to the Hadfields' intending to kill Reeve, or only happened to notice him in the open garage, nobody had said. Or, probably, knew. It was after shooting Walt that Rob had used the handgun for the first time, putting it in his own mouth and pulling the trigger.

"I suppose Dad was curious," Acadia said. "He wasn't coming or going. There was an open Pepsi next to his chair, and, um, he'd set down a lit pipe."

"Inside?" her mother said sharply.

"Let's not go there, Mom," she warned. *Like it's any of*

your business what Dad did in his own home. After you
walked out on him.

Hoo boy, Acadia thought in dismay. Did she still have
anger issues or what?

Acadia sighed. "Listen, I think I'm going to stay here
as long as it takes to clean Dad's house out and put it on
the market."

"And bury him."

Oh, God, yes. She had to plan a funeral for her father.
She'd been trying not to think about that.

She and her mother talked briefly about that, and then
she managed to end the call, although in doing so she was
pretty sure she'd hurt her mother's feelings.

That gave her a clean sweep for the day. Who else could
she call and offend?

Sighing, she turned on the television for the local news.
Watching had become a compulsion she hoped she could
break once the focus shifted from Tucannon.

The lead-in said, "Final victim in Tucannon massacre
identified." Acadia stiffened.

"Whitman County Sheriff's Department spokesman
Gerald Lester today identified the sixth fatality from the
shooting spree in tiny Tucannon, Washington." The scene
shifted to a middle-aged, uniformed man with bags under
his eyes who gripped each side of a podium as he spoke
into a microphone. "Also dead is Richard Baron, a teacher
at Tucannon High School. Mr. Baron, fifty-eight years old,
had taught English in Tucannon for his entire career and
was reputedly well liked. He is survived by one son."

They went on to recap a list of the other victims. Shocked
anew, Acadia turned off the TV. She didn't want to see that
same photo of her father.

Mr. Baron? Back before the move, she'd been so excited
about having him. The slackers hated him because he made

them work. The good students pretended to grumble, but loved his classes. She stared blindly at the dark screen. Why him?

Why Daddy? Why anyone?

Out of habit she waited until it was dark before she started to the Owens', even though she hadn't seen a TV van or anything like that for several hours. This time she didn't slip in and out of backyards. She marched down her front walk, turned right, passed the growing heap of flowers and signs and balloons in her yard and the somewhat more modest heap in the Tindalls' yard, and followed the sidewalk to David's front walk. She marched up it with the same determination that carried her all the way up onto the dark porch where she rang the bell.

Back doors were for friends. She'd thrown away that privilege.

Acadia hated being in the wrong. She hated even more having to admit that she was. But most of all, she hated knowing that no apology she could possibly make would ever be adequate.

The bell tolled inside. She squeezed her hands together as she waited, hearing the approaching footsteps. The porch light came on. After a pause, the dead bolt was turned and the door opened. Wearing the same jeans, T-shirt and utter lack of expression, David stood in the opening.

"Acadia."

Lord. If she was on trial for murder and he was prosecuting her, she'd probably throw herself in front of the jury and wail her guilt.

"I came to say I'm sorry." She kept her chin high. "I know you probably don't care what I have to say and that this doesn't mean a thing to you, but I want you to know I meant what I said only for half an hour while I was so upset. I'm not usually vindictive."

He stared at her, unblinking.

"Well, that's all." Her voice sounded scratchy. She nodded brusquely, turned around and started to leave. Her chest felt painfully compressed.

"Acadia."

She stopped halfway down the steps, her hand on the railing. She didn't turn back to face him.

"I've been saying you were entitled to feel angry."

"I'm not really," she said to the darkness. "Mostly I'm bewildered."

"Yeah." He sounded husky, hurt. "Me, too."

She nodded.

"Thank you."

"For?"

"Coming over here to say you're sorry."

Oh, she wanted to look back at him! But her eyes were filling with tears, which she didn't want him to see, so she only shrugged. "I meant it." Then, oh pitiful her, she added in an even smaller, gruffer voice, "I've liked talking to you."

This time she kept going, and he didn't follow her, although she was aware that he stood watching at least until the Tindalls' house blocked his view of her.

Sniffling now that he couldn't see, she swiped at her cheeks. Her only consolation was that she'd *mostly* kept her dignity.

CHAPTER EIGHT

"Who was that?" his mother asked worriedly, when he returned to the kitchen. She was wiping an already clean counter, which weirded him out.

Tonight, everything about her was weirding him out. She'd turned over a new leaf, which he should be glad to see, but he'd be happier if he had the slightest idea what had happened to make her decide to get up and offer to cook dinner and even try to make awkward conversation. Right now, he didn't know which was worse—the funereal silence in which they'd been living, or her unnatural stab at normalcy.

"Acadia."

"Oh?" Mom turned, sponge in her hand. "Why didn't you invite her in?"

"It's late, Mom. Acadia just wanted to tell me something quick."

"What?"

God, he wished she'd go to bed.

"That she was sorry to hear about Mr. Baron," he lied.

"Oh." His mother blanched. She wheeled around and kept scrubbing unnecessarily.

Watching her, David was unpleasantly reminded of earlier, when Acadia had been doing the same thing. What did his mother imagine she was cleaning up?

After a minute, she said, "That was a shock."

His head had felt like exploding ever since he'd heard.

Every movement since had been mechanical. He hadn't tasted a bite of dinner. Couldn't remember what he and his mother had talked about.

If there was one teacher in Tucannon he remembered with affection, it was Baron von Trapp. In those days, David had been so damn hungry for encouragement, even just to be noticed, he'd soaked up Mr. Baron's approval, his suggestions, his vision of a great future for David. Now David wished desperately he'd taken the time to visit the high school the last time he'd been home, if only to say, "Hey."

No, to say, *You really meant something to me. You made a difference in my life.*

Hindsight was a great thing.

And then there was Acadia and her edgy little speech. "He was the one who told us…"

David had momentarily forgotten his mother was still in the room. Pulling himself back into the present didn't help him decipher what she'd just said. He swiveled in his chair. "Who told you?"

The circles Mom was wiping on the counter grew tighter, faster. "Mr. Baron. He was the first one who noticed something was wrong with your brother."

"What?"

With what he guessed took an effort of will, she set the sponge on its little holder by the faucet and turned to face him. She wiped her hands absently on her dress, as though she thought she was wearing an apron. "He called me in for a conference. Robbie's sophomore year. He showed me some of Robbie's writings. And these strange pictures he was drawing in the margins. He was…kind. He suggested that we take Robbie for a psychiatric evaluation."

"I never knew that," David said numbly.

His mother seemed not to have heard him. Her eyes were fixed on a long-ago past. "Mr. Baron let me take the papers, so I could show them to the psychiatrist. Until then…well, I thought he was going through a phase. He was wilder than usual. Sometimes he'd just yell out for no reason, but then he'd laugh as if he'd done it to scare people."

God. She'd taken him to that past with her. "I remember."

"He wrote about whispers. About how there was another dimension no one else could see. Most of the times he couldn't see through the wall separating us, either, but he could always hear them. They were angry, he said."

David swore.

She shivered, and suddenly, with desperate fear, her eyes met his. "Your father and I did take him for the evaluation, and that's when we found out. I sat down with Robbie and we talked about what he'd written." She stopped, closed her eyes, swallowed. "Robbie yelled, 'Baron said we could write anything. He promised he'd never show it to anyone.'" She opened her eyes again, and pure misery looked out of them. "That's why he shot Mr. Baron. He always hated him after that. If I hadn't showed Robbie… It's my fault." She moaned. "My fault."

"No, Mom." David moved swiftly, sending the chair clattering away, taking her into his arms. "No, it's not your fault. Rob was sick. You know that."

She stayed stiff and said nothing.

He kept talking, telling her she'd done the right thing, as Mr. Baron had. He reminded her that Rob had also shot Wendi Rowe, of all people, and Charlie Henderson. He'd shot a bunch of people downtown. Mr. Baron just happened to be there. "There's no reason to think Rob went hunting for him in particular. If so, he'd have gone to his house, wouldn't he? It was chance, Mom. Bad luck he was there. And if he hadn't been, someone else might have died in his place."

Her stance gradually softened, thank God. She finally

nodded. "Yes. You might be right. Maybe…maybe Robbie had forgotten what Mr. Baron did. Maybe he didn't really even see him."

"No matter what," David gave her a small shake, "it wasn't your fault. You and Dad did everything you could."

She searched his face, and seemed to find what she needed, because she nodded again.

David relaxed. Inside, surprise bloomed at how certain he'd been when he said, *You and Dad did everything you could.* Yeah, they had. He was the one who couldn't be so easily absolved, who could have helped if he hadn't clung to hurt feelings. But that was something he had to deal with on his own. His priority now was helping his mother come to terms with a horror she couldn't hold back, any more than a seawall could hold back a tsunami.

"Well," his mother said uncertainly, "I suppose I'll head up to bed."

Please.

The depth of his longing pierced his shitty mood. "You okay?" he asked.

"Yes." Now she sounded surprised. "Yes. Thank you, Davey."

He smiled at her. "Good. Hitting the sack sounds like a plan. I'll probably head that way soon myself."

She kept standing there, while he felt more and more uncomfortable, until finally she said, "Good night" and, thank God, left the kitchen. Her steps on the stairs were so light he didn't hear them, but a minute later he did hear the toilet flush and then water running in the sink upstairs.

Oh, man. Elbows propped on the table, he buried his face in his hands.

Maybe because there was no profit in thinking about Mr. Baron, dead—*How is it that I didn't know he had a son? What happened to his wife? Did he read every word*

I wrote all the way through high school wondering if I carried the seeds of insanity, too?—David chose to think about Acadia instead.

I meant what I said only for half an hour.

Was that true? He couldn't decide.

He thought it was true that mostly she was bewildered. How could she not be? This whole thing was surreal. David had woken up that morning and, when he opened his eyes, stared at the poster of the Spanish Steps with a total lack of comprehension. For a second he might still have been in high school. His whole life since might have been a dream.

And then—*God*—he'd remembered. The faces of the dead had hit like hammer blows. Mom's utter hopelessness was another blow. As he'd lain there not wanting to get out of bed, he'd thought about Acadia. About sitting in the dark last night talking to her, as easily as if they were still fourteen and sixteen.

He heard her say softly, *I forgot you used to do that. Drop the* A. *No one else ever did.*

He'd thought so seldom about her in the intervening years, and yet with her he had this sense of time slipping, as if the *now* wasn't so far from the *then*.

Yeah, well, redhead and all that.

He'd smiled, and that smile was what had gotten him out of bed this morning. And now he remembered that little Acadia Henderson had detested having to apologize for anything. She would flush a fiery color and her eyes would shoot sparks as she spit to one neighbor or another, "I shouldn't have kicked the ball so close to your window and I'm sorry."

Groaning now, grinding the heels of his hands against his eyes, he discovered he was smiling again, despite everything. Only Acadia could look so bellicose when she was saying "I'm sorry" and yet leave you in no doubt she meant it.

He wondered if her cheeks had been flushed tonight. If not when she rang the bell, by the time she turned away?

He didn't know that he was going to be able to let himself feel as easy with her again. But, damn it, he was going to have to forgive her.

It was disconcerting to discover how much he would be willing to do for fiery 'Cadia.

Picturing again that god-awful haircut resulting in tight red curls, he chuckled. Later, he'd guessed she might end up beautiful, but that year? Nope, not a chance.

He'd have to ask her if she and her hair had ever come to an understanding.

"IT'S NICE you're doing this for Mrs. Stenten," Mr. Misner said, nodding to Reeve as he took his wallet from his back pocket.

Reeve, waiting to take his money, ducked his head and thought, *You're freakin' kidding me. Doesn't* anybody *get it?*

No. Nobody did. Not one person had asked, "So, how does it feel, knowing somebody died for you?" And no, not in that "all around the world, men and women in the armed forces are dying so you can live as a free American" way, but in a "he took a bullet meant for you" way. As in, "I saw him die" way.

"It's the least I can do," he mumbled to Mr. Misner, taking his three twenty-dollar bills. "Let me get you change."

Not very much change, not with gas prices being what they were. Especially here in the middle of nowhere. The Seattle-based reporters and cameramen bitched nonstop when they filled up their gas-guzzling vans, but it rolled right off Reeve. They were getting what *they* wanted out of being here. He could see the excitement in their eyes. Tragedy, human misery; they ate it up.

"Here you go, sir," he said, returning four dollars and twenty-three cents to Mr. Misner. "Have a good day."

Mr. Misner had no sooner left than old Mrs. Schweigert pulled in off the highway and maneuvered her boat of a Buick toward the full-service pumps. She was so tiny Reeve could barely see her white head over the steering wheel. He winced and took a step toward the emergency shutoff. One of these days, she was going to scrape that pump. Hey, what better time than now? He could hear it: *Another tragedy strikes the small town of Tucannon. Two people were killed today in an explosion at Tucannon's only gas station. Reeve Hadfield, who barely survived last week's massacre, was not so fortunate today.*

God. He almost wished.

But she made it.

He went to the driver's-side window and nodded. "Mrs. Schweigert."

"Fill 'er up," she ordered him in her creaky voice.

This was going to cost her, but she never bought gas when she was in Walla Walla even though she could have saved a few cents a gallon. This was her station, she always said. What he couldn't figure was why her daughter still let her mom behind the wheel of the car. Walt used to shake his head and say, "When I see her heading out onto the highway, I'm almost tempted to call the radio station and suggest they put out an advisory." For Walt, that was a speech.

Reeve reeled under the now-familiar pain even as he unscrewed her gas cap and set the gas to pumping. Only premium for Mrs. Schweigert and her 1992 Buick. Fortunately, the Schweigerts had always had money. They were wheat farmers, big enough to survive when smaller farms went under. The daughter's husband had taken over and was probably close to retiring now, too, but he had two sons to step into his place.

Out of the corner of his eye, he watched Mrs. Schweigert root through her purse while grumbling under her breath. Sometimes she couldn't find her wallet. She was the only customer Walt had been willing to run a tab for. She always paid.

Watching the numbers turn over on the pump, Reeve's thoughts reverted, as they did most often nowadays, to how people could not notice he was falling apart.

The only person he kind of thought might wonder was his mother. She looked worried a lot lately when she watched him. But even Dad had no idea. He wanted to buy the Shell station for Reeve? *So I can step right into Walt's life?* The idea repulsed Reeve.

All he knew was that he couldn't let Mrs. Stenten down. He owed her. He would die if that's what she asked of him. What scared the shit out of him was wondering what he'd do when she didn't need him anymore.

Why would Walt die for me? he asked himself in honest puzzlement.

Sometimes his own answer was: *it was instinct, that's all; he didn't sacrifice himself for me especially.* And sometimes—Reeve just didn't know.

WITH MORNING, Mom looked even more exhausted, if that was possible. She did shower, which David wasn't sure she'd been doing, and came down for breakfast. He let her eat, and then said, "We need to talk."

"Have you heard when Robbie's body will be released to us?" she asked eagerly.

Really?

This was *not* what he'd wanted to talk about, but okay, why not? "Maybe we should have him cremated," he said.

She shook her head, probably disappointed in him. "You know your father and I never liked the idea of being burned to a crisp."

If there was a God, David privately suspected his brother was burning to a crisp right now, although he hoped he was wrong. Depended, he supposed, on whether the Old Testament or the New Testament got it right. If God was merciful, He'd have been there with Charlie, arms open. If not… well, there were plenty of people in Tucannon whose vote would fall on the "if not" side of the ledger.

"You know there'll be a whole string of funerals coming up here." It had to be possible to make his mother see reason. "Those families aren't going to accept Rob being buried in the same ground as the fathers and mothers he gunned down."

She shriveled before his very eyes. A good thirty seconds passed while she stared at him. "But…he should rest with his father. I own a plot for him."

"That's yours, Mom," David said gently.

"No. No." She shook her head. "We—your father and I—bought another one. For Robbie. He kept threatening to kill himself, you know. We thought sooner or later he'd do it. Your father didn't want to leave me having to make too many decisions if I was alone when it happened. And this way the three of us would be together."

The three of them. He almost laughed, but could imagine how it would come out. But he couldn't keep his mouth shut. "The whole family, together again. How touching."

"Davey…" Her thin hand reached for his.

It was all he could do not to withdraw his, but he couldn't hurt her that way even though she didn't seem to have any consideration at all for his feelings.

"It's not like you're thinking." His mother was pleading. Tears shimmered in her eyes. "I just…I never thought you'd *want* to be here. You have a life. I hope you'll have a wife and family. Why would you want to be buried in Tucannon? It's not your home anymore."

He understood what she was saying, but the boy he'd been was still crying, *It always was the three of you, and me on the outside.* She was right, though. He didn't want to be buried here, beneath the dry, reddish, volcanic soil of Eastern Washington. He wanted... Damn it, yes! He did want a wife and children. He ached, suddenly, for a family where he belonged.

David swallowed. "It's all right, Mom. I know you didn't mean anything by it."

"I've always been so proud of you," she said timidly. "I thought you knew. I didn't say it often enough because... well, because the prouder I was of you, the harder it got to be proud at all of Robbie."

He stared at her. The contrast between him and his brother must have been painful. David had always known that. He'd even understood why she didn't hug him and say, *I'm so excited by your SAT scores* when Rob was around. It had never occurred to him that, even in her own mind, the heavier the scales got on his side, the lighter the weight on Rob's. Or maybe it was the other way around, he didn't know.

"It's all right, Mom," he said again.

She withdrew her hand and it disappeared beneath the table. "I hope someday you'll forgive me," she said, with an innate dignity that he realized he'd always admired in her.

"There's...nothing to forgive," he managed to get out, although his voice was scratchy.

He saw that she didn't believe him. He didn't believe himself, either. He had too many years of bitterness stored inside, kernels tucked away one at a time in empty corners that should, it occurred to him, have been filling with something else. Something warmer and more generous.

What he felt most then was regret.

"And no," he said, "Lieutenant Sykes hasn't said anything about releasing the body."

"All right." The lines in her face were carved deep. "Then what was it you wanted to talk about?"

"The lieutenant did knock on the door this morning. It was before you came down. He said we're cleared to go in the den and the basement." David hesitated. "Do you want to go through Rob's things, or shall I?"

His mother pressed a hand to her mouth, which almost made him groan. He felt like a bully, but, damn it, they had to start moving on! Couldn't she see that?

After a long moment, her hand descended to her lap again, and she said with that same dignity, "Thank you for offering. If you mean it, I'd be grateful. I don't think I could bear..." His mother's voice broke, and she stood up hastily, grabbing her cereal bowl and carrying it to the sink.

"Consider it done," he said, with as much gentleness as he could summon.

She nodded jerkily. "That rock. Did the policeman say anything about it?"

"The subject didn't come up." David hadn't expected it would. He couldn't imagine the sheriff's department had any interest in running fingerprints found on a note, however vicious. A rock through the front window didn't rise to being a major crime.

He hadn't told his mother that her house had been egged the night after the rock incident. He'd gone out in the dark, hosed it off and cleaned up the broken shells the best he could. It wasn't as if Mom was going outside these days where she'd see the mess, but he hadn't liked the idea of anyone else seeing it, either. He'd been so filled with rage while he trained a flashlight and the stream of water at the yellow, sticky streaks he'd almost sympathized with Rob for a minute. Almost.

"I'm going out to get the paper," he said, although he knew the news about Mr. Baron would be in it.

Going to the front door, he thought about ordering the *Seattle Times* as long as he was here. Clearly, he wouldn't be reading it or anything else online. The *Walla Walla Union-Bulletin* was a good newspaper, as far as it went, but he lived in Seattle. He needed to stay current.

He left the front door open behind him and had started down the porch steps when his eyes focused on…something, left on the brown grass by the mailbox. He almost called for his mother before caution told him to take a closer look first.

It was a bouquet of flowers. Vividly colored ones—orange daisylike flowers, fiery red roses, spikes of purple. Beautiful, in a garish way. Maybe like the colors of Rob's world.

David approached the bouquet as if it was a land mine. He wouldn't have been shocked if something with a flickering tongue wriggled out. He expected another nasty note at the very least.

There was a note, all right. Not even folded, just there to be read.

"You lost your son, too," it read. "In sympathy."

He picked the bouquet up and checked beneath it. No booby trap. His heart pounded and he looked around. The blinds two doors down, across the street, might have flickered. Otherwise, no one was out and about. When had this been left? Lieutenant Sykes hadn't mentioned it. So—it had arrived after he'd come and gone an hour ago.

A bouquet for Mom. His sinuses burned. He almost picked it up and carried it inside, but then he looked at the tributes in front of the two neighboring houses and thought, *No. It won't hurt if people are reminded we're mourning, too.*

Forgetting the newspaper, he took the steps back onto the porch two at a time, calling, "Mom! Mom, come here. There's something you've got to see."

ACADIA NOTICED THE solitary bouquet lying on the Owens' lawn and felt both delight and shame—shame that it hadn't occurred to *her* to make that kind of gesture. In fact…

She grabbed the local phone book and her phone, and called a florist in Walla Walla.

When she gave the address, the woman said, "But isn't that…?"

"Yes," Acadia said. "It is. But Rob Owen's mother is a nice woman. I want to do something for her."

"Oh," the florist said. "Well, all right."

They discussed what flowers Acadia wanted in the bouquet, and what the note card should say. She felt…not satisfied, when she hung up, but a little less ashamed.

Lieutenant Sykes had personally delivered a huge pile of flattened packing boxes that morning, clearly purchased brand-new from a shipping business, but refused payment when she offered it. He'd even included a giant roll of Bubble Wrap and half a dozen rolls of heavy-duty packing tape.

Which left her no more excuses.

She hauled the bags filled with Dad's clothes downstairs and set them near the front door, then took several boxes into the dining room. Mom had taken some of their nicer china and glassware when they separated, but Acadia knew that most of what was left had come down to Dad from his parents and grandparents.

The interior of the buffet was so dusty she suspected Dad hadn't once opened it after Mom was gone. Acadia armed herself with dust clothes and set to work. She was grateful to discover, as she started lifting one piece out at a time, that somebody, probably long in the past, had put stickers on the bottoms of some, saying in a tiny, crabbed hand things like "probably came from Aunt Sally circa 1850." She knew that somewhere her father had a family tree, so she'd be able to figure out who Aunt Sally was.

Most of the items in the buffet got dusted, carefully wrapped and placed in one of the boxes she boldly labeled with black marker as KEEP—DINING ROOM. Finally, she rocked back on her heels and frowned, studying the buffet itself. It was huge and of a very dark wood that she suspected had never been refinished, which was a good thing if the piece was as old as she thought it was. A dim memory told her the style was Eastlake. For now, it was certainly a KEEP, too. She hoped when movers tipped the enormous sideboard away from the wall she'd find a sticker on the back of it, too.

For now, she'd dust it and make a mental note to pick up some furniture oil. The wood looked awfully dry to her.

She was smoothing her hand over stylized flower carvings when the doorbell rang.

Please not reporters. *And—Lord, are you listening?— please not my mother.*

It was neither. David stood on her doorstep.

He inspected her, amusement in his gray eyes. "Cleaning house?"

"And packing." She probably wore a gray film of dust like pancake makeup.

"Ah…I'm heading out for groceries. You need me to pick anything up for you?"

"Are you going to Walla Walla?" Wow. If so, she'd beg to go with him. The idea of getting out of town made her feel giddy.

"No." The muscles in his jaw flexed. "I refuse to slink

around the way my mother has been. There's not a reason in the world I can't buy my groceries at the Food Emporium."

She thought about pointing out that, at the very least, everyone would stare at him, but refrained. He knew that. Even when they were teenagers, his refusal to back away from a challenge was one of the things she'd admired in him.

On impulse, she said, "I'll come with you if you'll give me a minute to clean up."

"You're sure?"

Acadia knew why he was asking. This would be David's first public appearance in Tucannon, save for the press conference. It might not be a pleasant experience. And that, she discovered, was exactly why she wanted to be at his side.

As if David Owen needed *her* to protect him.

"That I need cleaning up?" She offered him her best saucy grin. "Well, I haven't looked in a mirror yet, but…"

He laughed, and her heart squeezed. "I'll wait."

"Come on in," she said, stepping back.

She left him looking around the living room, probably bemused by the step back in time. Upstairs, one peek in the mirror and she squeaked in alarm. She took a record-quick shower, French-braided wet hair and dressed in clean, capri-length chinos and a snug-fitting, peach-colored T-shirt with cap sleeves. Sandals, and she was ready to go.

David turned from the photos on the mantel he'd been studying. His expression warmed at the sight of her. "Still a redhead, I see."

She made a face at him. "You have no idea how many times I've considered changing that. Trouble is, freckles don't go so well with blond hair, or even plain brown hair."

He laughed. "In the good old days, you could blister the air talking about your hair."

"It's so unjust. Neither of my parents is—" she jolted at a stab of pain "—*was* a redhead."

His eyes flickered. He'd noticed the quick catch. "Anyone else in your family?"

She sighed, locking the front door. "Apparently a great-grandmother on Dad's side. She was white haired by the time he was a little boy, but he remembered asking why she had those spots all over her hands and even her face. Of course, that killed my hope the freckles would fade away with age so that by the time I was a grown-up, I'd have glorious Titian hair and *no freckles*."

She did love the sound of David's laugh.

He led her down the sidewalk to where he was parked at the curb. "Well, you have the hair."

"I eventually looked 'Titian' up in the dictionary and learned that it describes a reddish-brown color." She wrinkled her nose. "Not copper-red."

Over the roof of his Lexus, he looked at her. "Your hair *is* glorious, 'Cadia. You know that, don't you?"

She blushed. Of course she did. "Um…thank you?"

Another laugh. She was storing them up like pretty pebbles collected on the beach. Later, she could look at them collected in a clear glass jar and remember.

The drive to the Food Emporium was a mere ten blocks. Acadia was sorry to see, when they pulled into the parking lot, that the store appeared to be doing a bustling business this afternoon.

"Good timing," David muttered, finding a slot near the back of the small lot.

She nodded. In the silence after he turned off the engine, she said, "Are you *sure* you don't want to go to Walla Walla?"

At the same moment, they both noticed a young woman

and her two children standing stock-still, staring at him with obvious shock.

"Too late," he growled, and opened his door.

The girl screamed, "Mommy, it's the bad man!" and jumped behind the full grocery cart her mother was pushing.

David nodded politely and waited for Acadia.

When she joined him, he bent to murmur in her ear, "A sensible woman would have accepted my offer to pick up some groceries for her."

"Now, when was I ever sensible?"

They were both smiling as the glass doors obligingly slid open for them.

CHAPTER NINE

THE SHOPPING EXPEDITION was every bit as god-awful as
David had anticipated. It was saved from being worse only
by Acadia's presence.

From the moment they walked into the store, confused
gazes darted from one to the other of them and back again.
It wasn't hard to read the thoughts: *there's the monster's
brother, how dare he walk in here as though nothing has
changed, but...isn't that Charlie's daughter? Why is* she
with the Owen man?

He felt guilty for accepting her offer to accompany him
on this outing, but not so guilty he didn't tailgate her with
his cart so as to stick close. Real close. And, hell, his admiration for her grew by the aisle. She stared down the
gapers, nodded to the mutterers as imperially as Queen
Elizabeth II confronted by impertinence and greeted semi-
friendly faces with warmth. And she didn't let the fact that
they were running the gauntlet stop her from comparing
prices as they shopped.

"Do you really care whether the house-brand tomato
sauce is fifteen cents cheaper?" he asked her, pretending
not to notice the cluster of townspeople gathered by a display of Coca-Cola products at the end of the aisle.

She grinned at him. "We're not all rich lawyers."

David snorted. "You do know what prosecutors get paid,
right?"

"Is it something like what nurses earn versus doctors?"

"Pretty close," he agreed.

He added some tomato sauce and canned tomatoes to his own cart, then looked up to see disaster oncoming in the form of a bullnecked man with a choleric face. Well, they'd made it halfway through the store, better than he could have hoped for.

"Mr. Rossi," he said with a nod. He had worked for Mr. Rossi in the city Public Works Department—such as it was—between his freshman and sophomore years in high school. The summer was the only time in his life he'd been fired from a job.

"So you've finally showed your face in Tucannon," Mr. Rossi said in disgust. "Are you enjoying giving all these good people nightmares?"

"I'm home to bury my brother and take care of my mother, as a good son should," he said levelly. He wouldn't let this asshole get to him.

Acadia turned slowly, her astonished gaze surveying Rossi. "I take it you know this guy?"

"You might recall Mr. Rossi, Acadia. He's the one who decided kids were trespassing if they stepped foot on the baseball or soccer fields unaccompanied by an officially designated coach."

"Oh." Her eyebrows rose. "Then it was you who tried to get me arrested."

Rossi's face was turning an alarming shade of purple. "It's my job to care for the fields! You kids were damaging them."

"By playing ball," David said.

"You Owen boys were the worst," he said bitterly. "And you." He pinioned Acadia with a glare. "I remember you. The redhead. You rode right out onto the baseball field and did wheelies."

She chuckled. "So I did. Surely I wasn't the only kid in Tucannon who ever did anything like that."

He ignored her and turned his glower onto David. "I'd have thought you'd have the decency to stay out of sight as long as you have to be in town. I'm not the only person asking myself how different from that brother of yours you are."

Acadia's cart rattled as she bumped it, taking a pugnacious step forward. "What a terrible thing to say! If you had any decency, you'd welcome David home and tell him how sorry you are for his family's tragedy. He's a good man who—"

"He looks just like the cold-blooded killer who stained the streets of this town red."

Other shoppers had drawn near. David tensed, seeing Marge Perkins from the Bluebird Café with her self-righteous nose high in the air.

"Rob Owen did a terrible thing," Acadia said, sweeping the crowd with her eyes. "But he was mentally ill."

"He shouldn't have been allowed to run loose and get his hands on guns," someone said.

And I thought this was a good idea? David thought. "My parents fought to get him committed. What else do you think they should have done? Taken their troubles elsewhere, so *you* were safe?"

"Now you claim they tried to get him committed," Marge declared. "Why didn't *we* know anything about it if they tried so all-fired hard?"

He unclenched his jaw. "Maybe because none of you asked. Maybe because the friends my parents had depended on all their lives faded away when Mom and Dad really needed them. Maybe because no one in this town was really looking."

He saw a few flushed faces. Gazes slid away from his and the crowd began to break up.

"Shall we finish shopping?" Acadia ignored everyone else as if they weren't there. "Or maybe we ought to take our business to another town."

"Let's finish since we're already here." David's stare challenged Mr. Rossi. "If you'll excuse us?"

Making huffing sounds, the asshole pushed his cart the opposite direction from them. Looking down her nose, Marge Perkins wheeled her cart in a U-turn and followed.

Acadia dropped two boxes of spaghetti noodles and one of rotini on top of the canned goods she'd already selected. "This lends new meaning to hating to grocery shop," she muttered.

He actually laughed. "You volunteered."

"Jerks." She sounded furious.

A display of cereals teetered when she brushed it. He reached past her to steady the pyramid. "Somebody put flowers on our front lawn this morning."

She turned her head and smiled. "I saw."

His eyes narrowed. "It was you, wasn't it?"

"No. I wish it had been. Those flowers made me ashamed I hadn't thought of it."

After a moment he nodded. "Mom cried."

Acadia stopped although they were in full view of the checkout lines and cashiers. "There wasn't an awful note or something like that, was there?"

"We must both have suspicious minds. I poked them expecting a flag to pop out saying 'Boom, you're dead' or something. But no." He told her what the note had said, and she nodded solemnly.

"That's nice. I wonder who put them there."

There was something in her voice that made him wonder if she didn't have her suspicions, but when he asked she only shook her head. "I have no idea, David." She looked at her cart. "I need ice cream. Lots of ice cream. And vegetables."

They got on with their shopping.

Bruce Ritchie stopped him in frozen foods to tell David he hoped God smote anyone with the name of Owen. David tried to remember if that was the actual past tense of smite. "Owen is a pretty common last name, Mr. Ritchie," he said mildly. "I'd like to think God distinguishes who he smites a little better than that."

Acadia was picking out some peaches when Marvella Hatcher, the old witch, declared it would be a blessing when his mother packed up and moved. And what was Acadia doing, keeping company with one of the Owen boys after the other had murdered her father?

She looked Marvella in the eye and said, "I'm supporting a childhood friend who doesn't seem to have much of anyone else he can count on. And I'm supporting Joyce, too. Do you know how many cookies I ate in the Owens' kitchen? How many times Joyce bandaged my skinned knees? Shooed me home when my mother was worried, hugged me when someone made fun of me? If she needs a hug now, in turn, I'm here for her." And then she went back to putting peaches, one at a time, in a bag, and gave the nasty witch no more never-mind, as David's mother would have put it. Marvella turned an ugly shade of red and made herself scarce.

David was tapping watermelons to test for ripeness when he heard a friendly voice call his name.

"Damn, if it isn't David Owen!"

He turned to see a tall, lanky guy with shaggy, dishwater-blond hair and a genuine grin. "Alan? What in hell are you doing here?"

They clasped hands and shook. "My dad died a couple of years ago. Don't know if your mom told you. I try to get home three or four times a year to keep up the house for Mom. She's got a teenager mowing her lawn, but you know what these old houses are like." His smile faded. "Man, I'm sorry about what happened. I'll bet your mother is taking it hard."

"Yeah, she's, uh, not so good." He turned to Acadia. "'Cadia, do you remember Alan Finley? We were teammates all the way through high school."

"Of course I do." She smiled and held out a hand, too. "You sank that shot from darn near halfway down the court to win the game with Othello the year before I moved away."

He looked like a guy who grinned often. "My moment of glory. Acadia Henderson, if I live and breathe." Once again solemnity replaced his smile. "Oh, damn. Your father. I was real sorry to hear."

"Me, too." She smiled with more difficulty. "How is your mother?"

"Hanging in there. Dating, believe it or not. Chief Bolton, who'd have thunk?"

"Beats being lonely." David shook his head.

"That's what I tell myself."

They exchanged further news. Alan lived in Portland, was married and had two kids. The second was only six weeks old. He was a photographer for the *Oregonian,* the Portland newspaper, and sold occasional photos to national and regional magazines. Still played basketball, he said, in an adult league. David admitted he did, too, in a league primarily made up of prosecutors, judges, defense attorneys and cops.

Even Acadia laughed at that. "I bet that gets a little rough now and again."

"Yeah, it's tempting to apply an elbow sometimes when

the action on the court doesn't totally justify it." He looked at Alan. "Your wife and kids with you?"

"Not this time. I'm only here for a couple days."

"Any chance you'd come over for dinner tonight?" David smiled at Acadia. "I was already planning to invite you. Mom would be glad to see both of you. It would be good for her."

He held his breath until both agreed.

"Better get Mom's groceries," Alan said. "But I had to say hello first."

The clerk who waited on first Acadia then David wasn't anyone either recognized. Not more than twenty-two, twenty-three, she obviously knew who they were, but went about her business efficiently, only sneaking alarmed looks at David.

Crossing the parking lot, they were the target of more glares, but two more people also stopped to shake their hands and express regret about Rob and Acadia's dad. One was Mrs. Kastner, who, now graying and growing stout, still taught fourth grade at the elementary school. The other was Lyman Engle, a good friend of David's father. He owned a real estate firm in Walla Walla that specialized in farms.

He cleared his throat. "We'd be glad of your listing, though, if you decide to sell your dad's house, Acadia."

She smiled wryly at him. "I will be. If you want to send someone out to look it over and talk listing price, I'd appreciate it."

He assured her she would have his personal attention and they made an appointment.

Once David's and Acadia's groceries were stowed in the trunk, Acadia said, "Well, that could have been worse."

"Yeah," David admitted, "it could have been. I'm a little surprised anyone was friendly. I half expected to get lynched."

"Because you look like Rob?"

Putting the key in the ignition, he grimaced. "I always have. That's why Rossi fired me from my job that summer, you know. He saw Rob pissing on the pitcher's mound on the high school field. Rossi and I had tangled that day, and he decided it was me. Wouldn't listen to reason. I don't think he cared which of us it was."

"The 'Owen boys' did get lumped, didn't you?"

"I didn't mind when Rob was my big, cool brother, but later…" He moved his shoulders as if to relieve tension. "You might say it got inconvenient."

"I'm sorry." Acadia reached out and covered the hand he'd let lie on his thigh. She gave it a squeeze, as if it was the most natural thing in the world.

David looked at her. "Thank you for coming, 'Cadia. I'd girded my loins, but it really helped having you with me."

Her cheeks turned a little pink, but she shook her head. "It was nothing. Besides, I wasn't looking forward to sticking my head out in public, either, and it was easier with company."

He let it go at that, although if there was an obligation, it sure as hell wasn't on her side. He also insisted on helping carry her groceries into her house. "Six o'clock," he reminded her, and she said, "Wouldn't think of forgetting."

Carrying his own groceries in, David thought about the way she'd fired up in his defense. If somebody had slugged him, he suspected Acadia wouldn't have hesitated to wade right in. In all the meaningful ways, she hadn't changed at all from the skinny girl she'd been the last two summers he knew her.

The girl who, he had always known, had a gigantic thing for him.

It was a small step to wondering whether there was any chance it would be possible to revive that crush. If Acadia Henderson loved a man, he'd never have to doubt how wholehearted her feelings were or whether she'd always be in his corner.

Standing in the driveway, the last grocery bags in his hands, he looked toward her house. He couldn't forget the huge divide between them: his brother had murdered her father. Rage still burned in her, even if she was trying to dismiss it now.

But he felt something completely unfamiliar at the idea of the all-grown-up Acadia loving him.

It scared him, and tempted him both.

And underneath, something else stirred: unease at all the self-reflection he'd been doing. What would Acadia think if she *really* got to know the man he'd become?

ACADIA WALKED IN the front door and went straight to Joyce, hugging her. Joyce put her arms around the young woman and hugged back.

"I'm so sorry," she said.

Acadia offered a sad, crooked smile and said, "I know you are, and I'm sorry about Robbie. There's no reason you'd have ever expected it to come to anything like this."

Astonished, Joyce thought she might burst into tears. She had to draw several deep breaths before she could say, "No. I had begun to be afraid of him, but it's true I never thought…" She couldn't finish, and could tell she didn't have to.

Acadia bent forward and kissed her cheek. "I know," she said softly.

Well. So this was Charlie's daughter, grown up. Joyce had been fond of the skinny, freckled girl with a daredevil streak and the awful temper. Some of the other children who were part of the neighborhood gang had faded from her memory even though they'd stayed around long enough for her to see them in caps and gowns, but Acadia wasn't the kind of child you could ever apply the word *fade* to. Of course, Charlie had proudly showed her school pictures and, on her occasional later visits, Joyce had seen that she was growing into a pretty young woman, but she was still astonished when she looked at the Acadia standing here now.

Why, she'd become beautiful! She was still slender, but not like those women who starved themselves. With that sharp chin, beautiful cheekbones and high, curving forehead, as well as her coloring, she brought to mind an illustration in a book of fairy tales. If she let down her mane of red curls and wrapped a crown of fragrant white blooms around her head, she might be the queen of the fairies. Yes, Titania.

"There are three bouquets out there now," Acadia announced, and Joyce blinked. Three! She hadn't been able to imagine who had left the first one, never mind three! Well.

Joyce hadn't seen Alan Finley in many years, either, but he looked much the same except for the length of his hair and perhaps a few laugh lines beside his eyes. He had a folder tucked under his arm but said vaguely, "After dinner," when David asked about it.

David had insisted on cooking, a gourmet meal of teriyaki tenderloins on a nutty brown rice. Even the salad was fancy, with fresh wild greens, Walla Walla sweet onions, hazelnuts, slices of pear and a balsamic vinaigrette dressing. Dessert was more pears, drowned in a brandy sauce. Joyce noticed that Acadia and Alan ate the meal as though it was everyday to them; well, they were both urbanites, like David. Their lives were such worlds away from the one Joyce had always known.

Their conversation mostly went over her head, too—

movies, books, concerts, politics. But they were all such nice young people, one or the other regularly remembered her and commented on local events or someone Joyce knew, just to include her.

It warmed her to hear that Lyman had spoken to David. He was one of those people who'd tried to stay in touch with her after Pete died, but she hadn't encouraged him and he had eventually given up. Perhaps she'd been wrong to push friends like him away. She didn't know now whether she'd done it for them, as she'd told herself, or whether she'd been entirely selfish, unable to *care* about anyone else.

Right in the middle of the dessert course, she asked, "Was everyone civil today, at the grocery store?"

Alan, bless his soul, looked surprised at her question, but David's eyes briefly met Acadia's.

"No," he said after a minute. "We ran into Mr. Rossi. Remember him? He never liked Rob or me. And, uh, Marvella Hatcher was there, too."

Heart pounding, Joyce still said, "It would be like her to be hateful."

Acadia laughed. "There are people like that everywhere. I didn't remember her at all."

"I believe she had a son about your age." She tried to think. "John...no, Joseph?"

Acadia's eyes widened. "Joey? Joey Hatcher? Oh, no! I hated him. He always called me names. That was his *mother?*"

David chuckled. "What did Joey call you?"

Giving him a disgruntled look, she mumbled, "It doesn't matter. Never anything nice."

"Give the kid a break. With a mother like that, he was doomed to be a jackass," David suggested.

Fifteen years ago, Joyce would have chided him for his language, but that was silly now, wasn't it? She could imagine the kind of language the criminals he prosecuted used. If she weren't here, he probably would have said something much worse.

She noticed that he and Acadia were quick to steer the conversation in another direction altogether. She wondered how many other people had said cruel things to her Davey, today at the store. What would they have said if she had been at his side?

She was sorry when it was obvious the evening was breaking up.

Alan cleared his throat, however, and said, "I don't know whether this is the right time, but I brought you some pictures I took with my first camera."

They all hovered around when he opened the file. Right on top was an eight-by-ten black and white of Robbie. He might have been a junior or senior, already troubled by the voices, perhaps, but looking so normal. He was shooting a basketball and laughing at the same time.

Joyce's throat closed up and she reached for the picture.

Below it were others—mostly of Robbie, but some of David, too, and even one of her and Pete in the bleachers at a basketball game. In contrast to the people around them, they were sharply in focus, both leaning forward in apparent suspense.

"You were talented even then," Acadia said. "That one is so...David." She stared at another photograph, this one also black-and-white, of David in the midst of a jump shot. He'd spent hours a day there, behind the middle school, doing layups, outside shots, dunks, his dedication astonishing for a boy his age. Most of the time there wasn't even a net in the hoop, which had been rusting.

Joyce saw the look on Acadia's face, the yearning her young self had felt for the boy in the picture. David was looking at her, too, not at the photo of himself, and Joyce saw the moment Acadia realized it and donned a mask.

"Boy, do these take me back!" she said with a laugh.

Alan said, "I have a few of you, too, Acadia. I should have known you'd be here. If you'd like, I'll print you some copies and send them."

"That would be really kind," she said simply. "My parents didn't take all that many pictures."

He nodded, and left shortly after. He surprised Joyce with a hug and promised to look in the next time he was in Tucannon—he told her he came every two or three months for at least a few days. A good son, she thought approvingly, and didn't say, *I doubt I'll be here the next time you come*.

It frightened her, to think of having to move to Seattle, but she couldn't think what else to do. Davey was all she had now. But he hadn't yet made any such suggestion, and she was afraid he didn't want her near. Why would he, as little as she'd given him over the years? And even if he did—she'd still be on her own much of the time, which made her realize how much she liked the known. The same stores, her mail arriving at nearly the same time every day, the road to Walla Walla she knew like the back of her hand. She didn't want to move anywhere, if truth be told, but she was going to have to, wasn't she?

This time, instead of thinking, *my fault,* she felt a renewed surge of anger at Robbie. Most often she could recall him as a little boy, or the teenager who'd been a wide receiver on the football team and a forward on the basketball team two years ahead of his brother. Tonight, she saw only that strange, expressionless face he'd worn as he pressed her hand toward the hot burner.

David disappeared for some time when Acadia departed in Alan's wake, presumably walking her home, which Joyce was glad to see.

There had been something in his eyes tonight when he looked at Acadia. His voice was different when he spoke her name, too—softer. Joyce wished with all her heart that he would find happiness. If it weren't for what Robbie had done, she could have wished that Acadia might become her daughter-in-law, but really, what were the chances now?

Charlie, she asked silently, *is Acadia right? Could you really have forgiven my boy? Oh, I wish you were here, to rejoice in having your daughter home. I wish...*

But she wished for so much, she couldn't find words for all of it.

AT HER FRONT door, David kissed Acadia on the cheek.

It was, of course, entirely casual, she told herself, keeping her smile steady as she said, "Thanks for a fabulous dinner, David."

He hadn't yet stepped back. With one hand he held open the screen door. They were, of course, in plain sight of neighbors who might be—and probably were—watching them out their front windows. She wouldn't have cared, had he shown any desire to kiss her again. Really kiss her.

"Thanks. Maybe I have a new career path as a chef, in case the prosecutor's office decides I'm a liability."

Indignation parted her lips. "You're kidding! They wouldn't...?"

He laughed, although something dark resonated in it. "I have no reason to think I'm going to get fired. But the thought crossed my mind. Seemed like when I asked for the leave, my boss agreed with suspicious alacrity. The Owen name has become notorious in this state, in case you hadn't noticed."

"You could move," she suggested. *Say, to Sacramento.* "Take your mother with you."

"Maybe." His lashes briefly veiled his eyes. "What about you, Acadia? Are you going to be glad to get home?"

She blinked owlishly at him for a moment. "To Sacramento?"

His head tilted. "Isn't that home?"

"For a minute, all I could think was…"

"That *this* is home." His mouth twisted. "Yeah, I've had the same bizarre thought. Despite all the years away, when someone mentions home, half the time I get this quick picture of Mom and Dad's, not my condo."

"Yes." Her voice was faint. "Mom never bought a house after she left Daddy. We were always moving. I've even moved a couple of times since I started working in Sacramento. The lease expired, I'd find something better." She shrugged. "I was mad at my father, so I wouldn't come home, but…" She realized what she'd just said. *Home.*

David's gaze stayed on her face. "I notice you call your mother Mom, but your father Daddy."

"People have made fun of me a few times, but I couldn't seem to change how I think of him."

"Because you were still a child when you moved away."

She had a feeling all the complexity of her emotions was in her smile. "Yeah. I think that's it. I got major rebellious after we moved, and I wouldn't have been caught dead calling my mother 'Mommy.' But…somehow my relationship with my father never matured." She bit her lip, then added very quietly, "I wish it had. I wish I'd given us the chance."

David tucked his knuckles beneath her chin and lifted it. "He loved you, Acadia. I think he understood better than you realize."

"Maybe." She drew a shuddery breath, shaken by what he'd said and by the feel of his touch. "That doesn't say much about me, though, does it? I'm thirty years old, and I never forgave my daddy for letting Mom take me away."

His hand dropped to his side, where it stayed fisted. His eyes, intense an instant ago, grew opaque and he finally took that step back. "I never forgave either of my parents for putting Rob first. What does *that* say about me?"

"Maybe," she said, "none of us ever entirely grow up."

"Maybe not." David gave her a crooked smile, but it was obvious he was distancing himself.

And she had to let him go.

"Good night, David. I'm glad we did this."

He nodded and released the screen door. Halfway down her porch steps, he said, "Good luck with that real estate agent," and then kept going.

Acadia closed the door, leaned back against it and touched her cheek with her fingertips.

David Owen kissed me.

She had to laugh at herself as she pushed away from the door. Even her thirteen-year-old self would have considered *that* kiss to be tame stuff. She'd dreamed about something considerably more passionate.

How disconcerting to discover that she was still clinging to the same dream.

CHAPTER TEN

SHORTLY AFTER BREAKFAST the following morning, the door-bell rang. David, who had been about to make himself check out the basement, thought immediately of Acadia. Maybe she wanted a second opinion on pricing the house.

Sometime in the past day or so, he'd quit peering through the blinds like a nervous old lady before answering the door. He'd slam it if it was a reporter. But to his surprise, he found Alice Simmons waiting on the porch. She'd always been a dumpy, sweet-faced little woman, older than Mom by five or ten years, at a guess. Never married, as far as he knew. Growing up, David had considered her to be his mother's best friend. He didn't know what had happened between them, but assumed that, like everything else around here, it had something to do with Rob. Mom's friends had deserted her as completely as a politician's when he'd lost an election.

"Ms. Simmons," he said coolly.

"David. How good to see you."

"And you," he said, sticking to his policy of civility unless all else failed.

"This may be too soon, but I was wondering if your mother is up to having visitors yet."

His gaze dropped to her hands, which he saw were clenched rather tightly at her waist. Was she nervous?

"I think that depends on whether they're friendly."

She looked startled. "Why would you expect me to be anything but friendly?"

David hesitated. "Tucannon isn't exactly a homey place these days for anyone named Owen."

Her expression held compassion. "Joyce brought some of that on herself, you know. If she hadn't isolated herself, people would have been more inclined to think of her as part of the community."

"I assumed her friends dropped her."

She sighed. "No, it was the other way around. I don't know if it was pure determination to solve her problems alone, or if it was depression or what, but she drove us all away. I was stubborn the longest, but when she quit returning phone calls or accepting invitations, I'm ashamed to say I got miffed and gave up."

Well, damn. David stepped back and opened the door wider. "I misunderstood. Please, come in. Mom could use a friend."

"Thank you," she said with dignity.

"Who is it?" his mother called from the kitchen. She did this every time, stayed out of sight like a turtle with its head in its shell, but too nosy in the end to wait until he reappeared to find out who'd come by.

"A friend to see you," he said, and led the way.

Mom had dressed to clean house today. She'd clucked when he admitted that no, he hadn't run the vacuum cleaner since he'd come, or mopped the kitchen floor, either.

"Alice?" she whispered.

"Oh, Joyce. I'm so sorry."

The two women fell into each other's arms. They wept and kept saying they were sorry and things like "I should have known." David hovered until they separated and looked at each other, their eyes damp.

"Oh, I've missed you so much!" Alice exclaimed.

"Will you have a cup of coffee?" Mom was already reaching into the cupboard. She saw him and said, "Weren't

you going to start downstairs?" as if she was surprised to
see him standing there.

"As long as you don't need me."

"Of course I don't," she said sharply.

Raising his eyebrows, David accepted this dismissal, but
reluctantly. He'd have rather done anything else than finally
open that basement door and find out how his brother had
lived these past ten years. Even listen to two middle-aged
women cluck at each other.

Well, crap, he thought, opened the damn door and, despite the smell that hit him immediately, descended into
hell.

Standing at the foot of the stairs, he looked around in
disbelief. Hadn't his mother ever *looked* down here? How
could she have let Rob live like this?

Yeah, and where were you? his conscience asked.

He couldn't decide which was worse, the writing and drawings scrawled on every surface, or the filth. His stomach's
reaction to the stench made the decision for him. Swearing,
he waded to the outside door, unbolted it—it had no less
than three dead bolt locks on it as well as two chains—and
flung it open, then forced open the window set high on the
back wall, too.

One thing you could say was that it was cooler down
here than in the rest of the house, but apparently not cool
enough to keep food from rotting. God Almighty! Why
hadn't Lieutenant Sykes said something? He could have
started shoveling this out days ago.

He held his breath until he made it to the top of the
stairs again, where he saw that this door, too, had several
dead bolts that locked from the inside. It would appear Rob
hadn't wanted his mother or father to see how he lived.

Without compunction, he interrupted the women, sitting
at the kitchen table. "Garbage bags?"

"Kitchen trash bags are under the sink. There's a box of the big black garbage bags in the pantry."

He nodded and went to get them. He grabbed some rubber gloves, too. His mother watched apprehensively as he passed back through the kitchen. He'd have liked a face mask, too.

Too bad. He went back down into his brother's corner of hell.

ACADIA SAT OUT on the front porch that evening, determined to reclaim it. So, okay, she still hadn't actually stepped on any spot where the boards were bleached a paler shade than the rest since her all-out assault on them. But she did settle at the top of the steps, tugging her T-shirt away from her sweaty body to let the marginally cooler air in on her skin.

This was the first night since she'd arrived that she heard people out and about, it occurred to her. None were right here on this block, but they weren't so far away. Kids out playing, she thought. A mother calling to them. Life was stirring again in Tucannon.

She felt less grief tonight and more melancholy. She'd signed the papers today to list her father's house for sale. Soon, home would no longer be here.

She saw David the minute he started down the sidewalk toward her house, moving under the streetlamp. Acadia wasn't sure he saw *her* until he reached the foot of the porch steps. Then he asked, "Mind company?"

"I would love company," she told him.

With his long legs, he made taking the steps two at a time look easy. He sat at the top, like she did, directly across from her, and stretched out those legs. "Cooling off?"

"You know it's probably still eighty degrees, right?"

"Feels like the inside of a refrigerator compared to this afternoon."

"Sadly, that's true." She ducked her head and took a surreptitious sniff in the vicinity of her underarm. Not good.

"I don't remember the heat bothering me when I was a kid," David commented.

"We were used to it. Now you're coming from Seattle. I'm coming from an air-conditioned world."

He laughed.

They sat in companionable silence for a long time. David was the one to break it.

"Lyman make it by?"

"Yes, and I signed the papers. He's going to put up a for-sale sign tomorrow."

"Feel weird?"

"Horribly," she admitted.

He nodded. She couldn't see his expression well, but knew he wasn't looking at her.

"How did your day go?" she asked at last.

"Did you know Rob lived in the basement? Mom and Dad had fixed it up for him as kind of an apartment."

"I think you said something."

"Yeah, well, I figured it was time to start packing, cleaning. You know." His voice held a thread of something unfamiliar. Horror?

"And?" she whispered.

"It was like walking into one of his nightmares." David shook himself. "You should have seen it. No. I wouldn't wish that on anyone."

She straightened. "What do you mean?"

"To start with, it was filthy." Now he sounded harsh. "Unbelievable. The floor was literally ankle-deep in papers, books, drawings, dirty dishes, food that had rotted God knows when. Dirty clothes. I swear, everything he owned was dirty. The sheets on the bed…" He shook himself, and Acadia thought maybe it was a shudder.

"Did your mother know?"

"I don't think so. I don't think she'd been down there in years." He paused. "I hadn't been, either. Even when I was home, Rob made it clear I wasn't welcome. He had three dead bolts on the outside door to the basement and a couple on the door at the top of the stairs into the house."

"He needed a space of his own."

"Maybe, but…" He muttered an obscenity. "How could living like that do anything but make him worse?"

"I don't know." She watched him worriedly. "Did you start cleaning?"

David grunted. "If you can call throwing a whole hell of a lot away, yeah. I didn't even ask my mother. I scooped up clothes, rotten food, even some of the dishes, and dumped it all in garbage bags. I could use a Dumpster."

"You can get one, you know."

"Yeah, I may call tomorrow and ask for one. Even the furniture doesn't look salvageable to me. I think I'll break most of it up and get rid of it. No one will ever want to sleep on that mattress again, I can tell you."

"Poor Rob," she murmured.

"Yeah." He was quiet for a minute. "Once I get it cleaned up some, you can take a look if you want. I've never seen anything like it. He was artistic. I don't know if you remember that."

She nodded, then realized he might not be able to see her. "Yes. He was the star of the annual student art show. Mrs. Sanderlin loved him. He had a style that was psychedelic. Back then, I'd never seen a Fillmore poster, but that's what she said his work was like."

"He's drawn and painted all over the basement walls and ceiling. It's like there are these layers. I think when he first moved down there he must have decorated like I did my bedroom. You know, posters, pictures. Then at some point he drew or painted on them. Classic. He gave people beards and horns, and painted flames around them."

"Hell."

"Yeah." David lifted his arms above his head, stretched and groaned. "Then it got worse. He painted scenes all over the walls, right over the top of the posters as if they weren't even there. Definitely psychedelic, and grim. Swirling scenes of skeletons rising from graves, worms crawling out of their mouths, crap like that. And then there are places where other scenes are superimposed on top of the first. You have to see it to believe it."

"You should take pictures," she heard herself say.

"What?"

"It might help if people could see through his eyes. It doesn't make what he did any less awful, but…it's important that people don't think of him as some kind of cold-blooded killer. He was mentally ill, and that's different. Not…not accountable in the same way."

David didn't answer for long enough, and she wondered if she should have kept her mouth shut. But at last he said slowly, "Maybe. And, you know, as horrific as it is down there, I kept thinking he had such a gift. Some of what he painted is really beautiful, even though his vision was so ugly."

"Do you suppose Alan would come and take pictures?" Acadia suggested. "He could see that they get shown on the news. In magazines. You know we're on the cover of *People* magazine this week, don't you?"

"I saw it in the checkout," he said grimly.

"I don't think most mentally ill people also have the ability to let people see their distorted view of the world." She felt awkward, even presumptuous, but she said it anyway. "It might be a way to…I don't know, bring something good out of this."

Air escaped him in a rush and he bent forward, curling as if in pain. She watched anxiously, until he sat up again. Even in the dark, she could see how ravaged his face was.

"I don't know, 'Cadia. But I'll think about it. Okay?"

"It's your decision, not mine."

"It should probably be Mom's, but I'm not sure I want her to see, either."

"Maybe she needs to," Acadia said gently.

"Maybe," he said, voice low.

A car passed on the street, finally turning into a driveway a block and a half up. The sound of a laugh drifted to them, a woman's. Acadia could almost close her eyes and remember other nights, when the children playing included her and David, when her mother or his might have been laughing, when her father would have sat out here, not talking but contented. Tucannon, she thought, would recover and go on, not so different from what it had been, although she suspected the tragedy would always be a watershed. Perhaps parents wouldn't be as relaxed about their kids being out of sight as they'd once been. Teenagers who were a little strange might not be accepted as long as Robbie had been.

"A friend of Mom's came to see her today." David's tone had changed, become bemused. "Ms. Simmons."

Acadia tried to summon a face to go with the name and had to shake her head. "I don't remember her."

"She didn't have any children."

"I mostly remember the other kids, some of the parents, the teachers. And some adults we saw a lot, like Miss Rowe."

"You'd know Ms. Simmons if you saw her. Alice." He still had that odd tone in his voice.

Acadia thought about the way they both referred to most adults in town as Mr. and Mrs. and Ms., the marks of respect their parents had drilled into them. The children in this town had never been encouraged to call adults, even close friends of the family, by their first names.

"I bet you didn't call her that to her face."

He chuckled. "Good God, no. You know, I think growing up here had us at least a generation behind kids in most of the rest of the country."

Acadia smiled. "I was just thinking that. San Francisco was such a culture shock."

"I bet. The University of Washington was a big enough one for me, and Seattle is probably still conservative compared to San Francisco."

Some instinct had her drawing her knees up tight to her body, so she could wrap her arms around them. "That first year was really hard." Funny, it had been a long time since she'd thought about how miserable she'd been. "I didn't fit at all. I wanted so desperately to come home."

"I'm sorry, 'Cadia." He was watching her, and his voice was a low rumble that was still somehow…tender, or perhaps she only wanted to think so. "I wish I'd paid more attention to you when you were here."

Acadia laughed at that. "You know I had a terrible crush on you that last year or so."

"I knew."

And she'd so prayed then that he didn't know. She felt sorry now for her thirteen-year-old self.

"Having to move would have been worse if you'd given even the slightest sign of noticing me," she informed him. "As it was, I knew my grand passion was hopeless anyway. You had a girlfriend. I can't remember her name."

"Ah…Kristy. Kristy Nordahl." He was amused now, but something else, too. "Big tits, no brains."

"Right. Kristy." Smiling, Acadia loosened her grip on her knees. "Oh, how I hated her. She had everything I wanted."

"Except brains." David was definitely laughing at her now. "She was lucky to graduate from high school."

"Really? Did you stay in touch?"

"No, she wasn't my girlfriend for very long. I didn't exactly have a girlfriend that next summer, when you came home."

Exactly? What did that mean? "Really? You never said."

"I think," he said, "*you* were my girlfriend that summer."

She lifted her chin to gape. "What? No. You never so much as touched me."

"Well, you still didn't have much in the way of tits." He sounded apologetic.

She blew a raspberry his way.

He laughed. "But I liked you, Acadia." He paused. "I still like you."

She quit breathing. *I'm dreaming. David Owen did* not *just say that.*

He rose to his feet. "I'd better get home before I get mushy. Thanks for listening to me tonight."

She gulped, swallowed and *almost* managed to sound normal. "Anytime."

"Good night, 'Cadia," he murmured, and went down the steps. At the bottom, he paused. "I can't help noticing you do have tits now." And while he sounded amused, that *something* was in his voice again.

Under the streetlight, she could see him until he had almost reached his own front porch. Stunned, she didn't move. Had he been telling her he was *attracted* to her? That he had been the summer she was fourteen, too?

Oh, my God. David Owen likes me, *skinny Acadia Henderson.*

Joy forked through her, and she said aloud, "Daddy, can you believe it?"

THERE WERE FEWER outsiders in town now, although Marge knew that there would be a resurgence for the funerals. Nobody had been interested in a quote from her for days now. Which certainly didn't bother her—she'd said what she had to say.

She grabbed a couple of laminated menus when she saw the Wardells come in the door, but without even looking at her they headed for the only booth that was vacant on that nitwit Hailey's side of the café. Half of Marge's booths were empty. It had been like that for at least two days. Pretending she hadn't noticed the Wardells at all, she dropped the menus back in their slot and went to see if Jim Crawford's BLT was up yet.

Some people didn't like what she'd said. If they thought they were hurting her feelings by refusing to sit at one of her tables, they were wrong. Let them be waited on a few times by Hailey, silly, careless and now five months pregnant besides, which made her slow. The regular diners would change their tune soon enough. And Marge was not a person to back away from her opinions, even if having expressed them did result in fewer tips for a few days. *Somebody* had to speak out.

She was disgusted by the recent television coverage, which had turned to fluff. All the major news channels had settled on a theme of "healing." The cameras filmed children on the school playground, people shopping on Main Street, "survivor" Reeve Hadfield pumping gas at the Shell station. Wendi Rowe's status had been changed from critical to serious; her niece insisted her spirits were good. Last night there had been a short interview with Anne Stenten, who talked about how proud she was of her husband, who had thought of Reeve as a son. Nobody was interested anymore in whose fault all this had been.

"Order up," Arnold called, and she reached for it only to see that it was a burger and fries and not the BLT she was waiting for. Normally, to be helpful, Marge might have taken the plate to the table, but she saw that it was for Table Six, which was Kirk Merfeld, and what *he* was doing here without Marie and sitting with Genie Fanning from his office, Marge didn't know. The Merfelds always sat at one of Marge's tables. Let his burger get cold, she thought, vengefully.

Oh, yes, people would change their tune soon enough, but she wouldn't forget who was really a friend and who wasn't.

A pair of strangers came in, and she grabbed menus and led them to the best booth, right in the front window.

DAVID COULD HARDLY believe it when his mother announced that she intended to go to Earl Kennedy's funeral.

To give himself a moment, he said, "His body has been released?"

"Alice says it has, and the rest will be in the next day or two. Earl's son has already arranged to bury his father on Saturday."

"Was Earl a friend of yours?"

"His son, George, has worked on our furnace."

David shook his head. If he had to be brutal, he would be. "What makes you think you'd be welcome, Mom?"

She stared back at him, her mouth all pinched, her eyes fierce. "What would it look like if I didn't go?"

Oh, God help them. "You're not planning to go to *all* the funerals?"

"Yes, I am." Her back was so straight she had to have gained a couple of inches on her usual stature. "Alice agrees it's the right thing for me to do."

He groaned.

"You certainly don't have to attend with me."

"I assumed we'd go to Charlie's." For Acadia's sake. "And maybe the Tindalls'," he allowed, when her expression didn't soften. "But you haven't so much as set foot out of doors yet. This first funeral may be the worst, with the cameras rolling. Do you really think it's the place to show your face?"

She kept saying it was the right thing to do. She ended up walking out of the kitchen while he was midargument. He heaved a box of macaroni and cheese across the room to relieve his frustration and rejoiced in the small explosion, even though now he'd have to sweep up the damn macaroni.

How could he have forgotten how mule-stubborn his mother was capable of being? He and Rob had known to ask Dad first for permission to go camping with the Strausses, or to drive all the way to the Tri-Cities, or to buy something they absolutely *had* to have. Dad had ways around Mom's decrees. But once she put her foot down, they all knew better than to keep arguing.

Crap, he thought. He'd been washing the same few clothes and getting by, but he hadn't brought anything suitable for funerals. And it appeared he'd be attending a whole string of them.

God. Had Acadia heard from Lieutenant Sykes? Had she made any plans for burying her father?

It might be midday, but he stalked out of the house anyway and went down the block to Acadia's. His stride checked when he saw the for-sale sign that had been installed out front, the soil around the post freshly turned. Lyman hadn't wasted any time.

Acadia's eyes were red and swollen when she came to the door. "David?" She sounded surprised.

He stepped over the threshold, shouldered the door closed and did what he'd been wanting to do all week: he gathered her into his arms.

She made a muffled sound, pressed her face to his chest and began to cry.

David cradled the back of her head in one hand while he held her close with his other arm. "I'm sorry," he murmured. "I'm sorry, 'Cadia. You should have called me. You know I'd have come."

She didn't cry long. He doubted she ever did. Her shoulders quit shaking, and for maybe thirty seconds she rested quietly against him. He closed his eyes, rubbed his cheek against the top of her head and thought, *Acadia*. Only that.

Sniffing, she drew back and swiped at her eyes. "Ugh. Let me go wash my face."

He barely got a look at her face before she fled. Although her tears had made his chest ache, he still smiled a little at the tomato-red blotches. Freckle-faced redheads weren't pretty criers.

She didn't look a whole lot better when she returned. She grimaced and said, "Not what you expected when you rang the bell, was it?"

"Actually, I thought you might need a comforting shoulder."

"Really?" She frowned at him. "You're psychic?"

Huh? "I assumed you'd heard from Sykes."

"What do you mean? He hasn't called today." Her expression changed. "What could he possibly have to say now that would upset me more than I already am?"

"Only that they're starting to release the bodies." Seeing her blank stare, he said, "Not your dad's, I guess."

"No. Whose?"

"Earl Kennedy. Funeral is Saturday."

"Oh." She turned that over in her mind. "I didn't know him. Did you?"

"No, and as far as I can tell, neither did my mother. But she's decided she's going to the funeral," David said grimly.

"Really?"

"Oh, yeah." He touched Acadia's cheek. "Why were you crying?"

"My dad's dead."

"Your dad died a week ago."

What had to be half a dozen emotions passed across her expressive face. Finally, she said, "You want something to drink?"

He wanted an excuse to stay, so sure. "Yeah, that would be good." He smiled. "Make it a Pepsi."

"Did I tell you how many thirty-six packs he had in the basement?"

"Yes, and I'm glad to help you use some up."

She handed him a can from the refrigerator and took out another for herself. They both popped them open, not bothering with ice. "I'll show you what upset me," Acadia said abruptly, and turned and led the way to Charlie's den.

On the way, David noticed that she'd emptied the big old buffet that dominated the dining room. Several packed and labeled boxes were stacked beside it. Seeing that gave him a pang. Except for the basement, he hadn't started packing up his mother's things yet. He wasn't going to like seeing those rooms empty, either.

No matter what, Acadia will never be back, he thought, with what he knew was grief. On its heels, he felt determination. He wasn't going to let her disappear from his life again. He wasn't sure yet what he felt for her, but he knew he needed at least to stay in touch. To know she was okay.

She'd started in on her father's books, although she

hadn't gotten very far. A few boxes were packed. The outline of where the books had been was clear in the dust. As long as Charlie had lived alone, he probably wasn't much on housecleaning. If Acadia hadn't fallen apart when he'd put his arms around her, David might suspect the red eyes had been a reaction to her stirring up the mites.

"Look at this." Sounding indignant, she toed a shoe box. No, one of those lidded photo boxes, covered in a maroon paisley design.

David bent and picked it up. It was completely full of envelopes. Letters, he realized. All from Acadia.

Staring into the box, she said, "I think he kept every letter I wrote him. And look how few there are."

"I wouldn't say this is a few."

"We're talking seventeen years here." She swiped the back of her hand angrily at her cheeks again, and David saw she was once again leaking. "Damn it. I never knew!"

David set the box on the end table and reached for her hand, still soggy. "I'll bet you started emailing at some point instead, didn't you?"

"Yes, but…"

"And you called."

"Yes, but…"

"But what?" he asked.

"Not often enough!" she wailed.

He laughed and tugged her into his arms again. "Acadia," he said against her hair, "that's one hell of a lot of letters considering you were a teenager who was mad at your father. Teenagers are famous for being jerks to their parents. I sure as hell was. And you came home, too. You spent several summers here, didn't you? Maybe a few Christmases?"

Her head bobbed.

"You should be happy to know he treasured your letters."

"The box wasn't even dusty!" This was a wail, too, and he laughed again.

"Of course he loved you. You knew that, didn't you?"

"Oh, damn," she mumbled, and tugged herself free. "What is *wrong* with me?"

"Not one single thing. You lost your father and you're grieving. Give yourself a break."

After an indignant snuffle, she treated him to a grouchy look. "I haven't seen you cry yet. That minor leak doesn't count."

He froze. Inside and out. It was a minute before he said, "I have," and couldn't help how clipped it came out. Nothing on earth would have made him tell her he'd cried when she'd turned on him. That not until then had he let himself feel the overwhelming horror of what Rob had done—and of what Rob's death meant to his mother and to David himself.

"Oh, well, then," Acadia mumbled, so ungraciously he unfroze and realized he was smiling.

"Why suffer alone when you can ensure other people suffer with you?" he said.

"Right." Suddenly she laughed. "I'm an awful person."

"No, you're not. Don't try that one on me." He nodded toward the hall. "Go wash your face again."

When she came back, he'd put the lid on the photo box and set it in a carton she'd labeled in black marker DEN—KEEP. "Someday you can take these out and read what you wrote to your father," he said, when she saw what he'd done with it. "But don't do it now, Acadia. Now is too soon. There's enough to make you hurt without doing that."

She bit her lip, but nodded. "Fine. You're right, oh wise one." Then she said, "Did you get that Dumpster?" and they were talking about other things. None that were pleasant, but what was these days?

And yet he felt a hell of a lot better when he left her than he had when he arrived. Not so alone. He'd spent a lot of years satisfied to be alone, but he was changing in ways he hadn't yet identified. How he thought about Rob had shifted, his understanding of what his parents had endured and how they felt about both their sons. His memory of that last summer Acadia came home to stay with her dad. He was unsettled by all the changes, and yet… he felt better about himself than he had in longer than he could remember.

Which made no sense at all, he thought, letting himself back in the house where he'd grown up.

CHAPTER ELEVEN

FOURTH OF JULY, and David had expected to be watching the fireworks with some babe. He'd have his arm around her, right? And after the grand finale he'd kiss her and, if they weren't already in a spot where he knew they would stay private, he'd take her somewhere they could have their own grand finale. But, no—here he was, the Fourth of July, and he hadn't hooked up with anyone yet this summer. Instead, he was watching the fireworks with a girl. Not quite a kid, but close.

Leaning on his elbows, his head tipped back so he could see the multicolored starburst against a velvet black background of sky, he realized he didn't regret being part of the crowd at the park, or the fact that he was with Acadia instead of the hot babe he probably could have had. A couple of the girls he worked with at the vineyard had seemed interested—one of them was even a college girl. But he spent the days either sweating between rows of grapevines or making nice for tourists, and by the time he got home all he wanted was a shower, dinner and some conversation before he went to bed, so he could get up in the morning and do it again.

And it was weird but true that he was enjoying Acadia Henderson's company and her conversation. It wasn't like this thing they had going was girlfriend/boyfriend. She was only fourteen. Yeah, she'd shot up several inches since last summer, and her figure wasn't totally board-

like anymore, if you could call the two little buds she had going tits. He thought it was funny how self-conscious she was of them. She wore sacky T-shirts, and hunched except when she forgot.

Right now, she was forgetting. She lay flat on her back on the grass in the middle of the park and stared up, her mouth forming a wondering O as another firework rocketed into the night and exploded in a glittering wheel of red and blue. The night was still warm, even though it was past ten o'clock. For some reason his gaze went to those baby tits. Had she thought the thin material of her T-shirt hid them? He didn't even know why he was bothering to look. If he wanted tits, he should have stuck with Kristy and her size-C rack. But Acadia's fascinated him for some reason. He kept trying to imagine what she'd look like without the tee. Probably like she'd puffed up from a pair of mosquito bites, he thought with a suppressed snort. But of course there'd be nipples. Small pink ones? Bigger brown ones? He knew her chest was freckled, but that might only be where her skin was exposed to sun, above the collar of her shirts. Was she freckled down lower, too?

Oh, man. He forced himself to stare upward again. What was he thinking? Repeat to self: she's fourteen. *Still mostly a little girl, sulky when she was pissed at her dad, grumbly talking about her mom, riding her bike during the day because she wasn't old enough to get a summer job except for occasional babysitting and lawn mowing. No way should he be imagining what she looked like naked, or how it would feel to put his mouth on those small breasts. And it was sick that he was getting a hard-on thinking about it.*

A part of him thought maybe he should still try to hook up with some girl his own age. But the truth was...he didn't really want to. He was actually enjoying the summer the way it was—hot, sweaty work, and spending about half his evenings sitting on Acadia's porch talking, or sometimes going for a walk. A few times they'd gone to the bridge and she'd made a big production out of crossing all the way over, because her dad had always forbidden her to do that. She'd jump up and down on the other side and yell, "I am a rebel!"—which he thought was pretty funny.

She sighed in pleasure at the fireworks, which looked about like they did every year—Mr. Cotton, who was in charge, did not have very much imagination. David tilted his head again to look at her rapt face and found himself smiling. Yeah, this was like taking a little kid to see the fireworks. Fun.

The grand finale came in a huge, multiple explosion— bang, crackle, bang. The whole crowd, including Acadia, let out oohs and aahs.

David bounced to his feet and held out a hand for her. She let him boost her up.

"Maybe I should look for Dad," she said, although her nose wrinkled.

"In this crowd? Do you even know where he was?"

"No. I think he was sitting with the Reardons, but I'm not sure."

"Let's just walk home," David suggested. "He'll show up."

She tried to hide it, but he could tell she was pleased. "Okay."

He hoped they didn't see Rob, who'd been in one of his freakish moods earlier. It was like he was nuts or something, but Mom and Dad weren't saying, and David couldn't even hold a normal conversation with him anymore. Who knew what he'd say to Acadia?

Cutting across the field, he didn't see Rob, but they did run into some of David's friends from high school and he exchanged high fives and "hey, how's it going"s. Shy, Aca-

dia hovered, keeping enough distance he could pretend he wasn't with her if he wanted. But a couple of the guys greeted her, Alan with a "Wow, you're back?"

"Only for the summer," she told him.

"You moved to San Francisco, right? I'll bet you hate having to spend the summer in Tucannon."

Acadia shrugged. "San Francisco is cool, but sometimes I miss it here."

After David and she broke away from the crowd, he asked, "Do you wish you didn't have to come stay with your dad this summer?"

She was quiet for a minute, then said, "No. I've made friends, but...it's not the same. And, you know, it's a city. Mom didn't want me on my own all day while she was at work. So..." Another shrug.

God, what he'd give to be on his own in San Francisco. It was like some mirage, as glorious and exotic as the Taj Mahal, floating on the horizon. He wanted to get out of Tucannon so bad.

If I could be anywhere, *he thought.* Fourth of July, and I could be anywhere, with anyone... *Weirdly, his mind stayed blank. He nudged it.* Anywhere, with anyone...

His bare arm brushed Acadia's and he looked down at her. She was getting tall enough and leggy enough to almost match his stride. He actually liked walking with her. He didn't usually, with girls.

They turned the corner onto their street. Their houses lay just ahead.

On impulse he said, "Let's keep walking."

Somebody let off a small backyard rocket a couple of yards away. The Meaghers must have driven home, because their kids were already out in the front yard running around waving sparklers.

"I want sparklers," Acadia declared, flinging her arms

*out and twirling in a circle in front of him. "I wish I'd
bought some."*

*"Let's see if the Meaghers have extras." He jogged
across the street and asked. Mrs. Meagher laughed and
handed him a box and some matches. He pulled out two
of the long, skinny sparklers, shoved the box in his back
pocket and lit the first two.*

*As crazy as those little kids, he and 'Cadia danced
down the sidewalk, waving glittering patterns in the air
and laughing like maniacs. He loved her laugh, belly deep,
unselfconscious.*

Anywhere, with anyone…

FRIDAY NIGHT, he sat beside Acadia on her porch. They each
had their usual places. His mind drifted back to that long-
ago summer, and he realized she had always gone straight
to that same spot, top of the stairs, her feet on a tread a couple of steps lower, her arm sometimes hooked around the
railing post, her shoulder sometimes resting against it. And
he had always sat on the opposite side of the porch steps,
same level, comfortable with the space that separated them.

"You came home that summer you were fifteen, too,
didn't you?" He knew she had.

"Yeah." As usual, he couldn't see her face well. The
living room light was on behind him, and there was a
streetlamp half a block away, but she was in the shadow of
the overhang. "It was…different."

"I wasn't here."

She was staring off into the darkness. "And Chloe was
spending the summer with *her* dad. Her parents got a divorce that year. So she wasn't here, either."

She'd had two best friends in middle school, he knew.
He'd never paid much attention to either; they were kind of

giggly and not very interesting. Chloe and…who was the other one? "What about…Holly? Was that it?"

"You went to high school with her, and you don't remember her?"

"Give me a break," he said. "Unless she was really hot, I'd have never noticed her." David was embarrassed to know how true that was. Her friend Holly could have been smart, funny, quirky, and she'd have probably stayed invisible to him and his jock friends. They went for the girls with great bodies and shiny blond hair they tossed when they flirted. He'd preferred blondes.

Now…he didn't so much have a type anymore. Attractive, yeah, but when he let himself get involved he liked a woman with brains, too. Mostly attorneys, a cop once. She had been working on an MBA and wanted to become an FBI agent.

"Holly had new friends and I didn't really like them." Acadia laughed at herself. "It was my fault, no surprise. Everything here was supposed to stop. Flash freeze. I could come back the next summer, and motion would start again."

"Me, too?"

She laughed again. "Definitely you, too." But she went quiet, broody. "But you'd gone to Nicaragua, and instead, Rob kept following me around."

David's head snapped around. "What?"

"Yeah, it was…" She spoke softly. "Strange" was the word she finally settled on. "I couldn't tell if he had a thing for me, which I couldn't *imagine* because I was, wow, fifteen and not exactly a beauty queen."

Jaw tense, David didn't argue even though he could have. He thought that at fifteen she might have been beautiful. She'd been coming close the year before.

"What—he stalked you?" David said, disturbed.

"Sort of. But he never really scared me. Mostly he kept

his distance. It was more as if he wanted to stare at me. Sometimes he even used binoculars. I told Daddy, and he talked to your father, who said I worried Rob because he wasn't totally sure I was supposed to be there. He thought maybe somebody had sent me to spy on him."

David let out a heartfelt profanity.

"He talked to me once in a while. Sometimes he seemed like Rob. You know?"

"Yeah." He swallowed. "I know."

He remembered how disturbing they were, those moments when he realized it was the brother he'd known and idolized who was sitting next to him, talking as if nothing had changed. Those times made his heart hurt. He wanted to hold on to them, because even by then—that year when he was seventeen, a senior in high school, and Rob was nineteen and living in the apartment their parents had made for him in the basement—David had known that Rob wasn't going to get better.

Mom and Dad still thought so, but David knew, and Rob did, too. His eyes had become hopeless when they weren't suspicious and crazy.

"The next summer," Acadia said quietly, "I got a job and didn't come to Tucannon. After that, I was never here for more than a couple of weeks at a time."

"Why was it we never overlapped?"

"I think maybe we did a few times," she said even more quietly, "but you were busy with friends and…there was one Thanksgiving you brought a girlfriend home."

He looked at her in surprise. Had he? Then it came back to him. Yeah, what was her name? Shari Snider. Her mother had just remarried and Shari hadn't wanted to go home.

"I didn't know you were here," David said.

Acadia made a noise, sort of an "uh-huh." Noncommital. He'd wasted his time with Shari, when he could have been hanging out with Acadia. That was his sophomore year in college, so she'd have been seventeen. A senior in high school.

"Did you have a boyfriend by then?" he asked.

"Yeah, kinda. More a friend. We were both gawky and social misfits." Her voice now was relaxed, amused. She didn't mind the memory. "I'll bet you never went through a geeky phase."

"I was a jock," he said with mock outrage. "I was way too cool to be geeky."

They sat in silence for a long time after that. David liked talking with Acadia, but he liked these stretches, too, when they were comfortable enough with each other not to feel they had to talk only to be talking. This time, though, it freed him to think about tomorrow, and he groaned.

"So, I can't persuade you to put on a dress tomorrow."

"Not a chance," she told him firmly.

"Friends stick by friends."

Her head turned and she looked at him. "Is that what we are?"

He didn't know what they were. "Best friends," he insisted, deliberately extravagant. *Don't take me seriously.*

"If you really want, I'll go to Walt's funeral," Acadia offered.

This was the week to top all weeks. Mark your calendar. One funeral after another. Tomorrow—Saturday—Earl's. Wayne and Betty's Tuesday, Walt's Wednesday. Charlie Henderson's a week from tomorrow, thus on Saturday. Mr. Baron's was the only one not yet on the schedule. Even Rob's was set now. Once Mom and David had gotten word his body was being released, Mom had, thank God, agreed they needed to wait to bury him until all the other funerals were over. And they'd do it quietly. David wanted to think they could sneak him into the ground without igniting an uproar, but wasn't real optimistic it would be that easy. No matter what, he was being buried that following Wednesday.

Acadia had talked to the funeral home director yesterday and the pastor today. Earlier, she'd told him the outcome of the two conversations, but she hadn't wanted to go into detail. The one thing she'd said, which broke his heart, was that she'd forgotten to leave out clothes to bury her father in.

"I'll have to dig in the boxes." She'd drawn a shuddery breath. "Except he didn't have a really nice suit. Maybe I should go buy him something."

"Would he want to be buried in a fancy suit?" David had asked, and she'd moaned and clunked her head against the porch post a few times.

"I don't know. Maybe not."

"Don't worry about what people will think," he had suggested. "Think about what *he'd* want."

And—shit—David wondered if Mom had yet realized they'd have to produce something for Rob to be wearing, too.

He stretched, groaned and said, "Crap. I'd better get moving."

As if she was still brooding about appropriate funeral attire, she asked, "Did you bring a suit to wear to funerals?"

"No, but I had a friend go by my place and pack a suitcase. He couriered it to me. You didn't see the truck this morning?"

"Nope. Ugh. I know what I have to do tomorrow. Go shopping. I didn't bring anything suitable, either. Especially given the heat."

"I think my suits are all wool." And black. Oh, yeah. He was going to be sweating like a stuck pig by the time he got home tomorrow. Thank God he'd had the foresight to request two suits; there wouldn't be time to dry-clean one often enough to accommodate this week's schedule.

And yes, he knew he was thinking about the superficial—about clothes—to keep himself from dwelling on the reality. He and his mother would be spending the next week attending the funerals of six people his brother had murdered. Six people, some of whom had meant a hell of a lot to David.

And yes, he also knew there was an excellent chance that he and Mom would get run out of the cemetery. Probably not lynched, but only because the cops were bound to be in attendance. He couldn't understand her insistence on doing this.

Acadia stood when he did. "It's funny," she said, voice dreamy, "when I think of Tucannon, in my mind it's always summer. Hot days, warm nights, voices up and down the street. Bats darting at twilight, just at the right moment to give you a scare. It's not that I hated the school year, but…"

When she drifted to a stop, he finished for her. "Summer was when you were happiest. Maybe we all were. That's what I most often remember, too."

They stood there for a moment, unmoving. And then she let out a breath that was also a half laugh. "Of course, the miserable winters might have something to do with it. I have to admit, I don't mind not having to own a down parka anymore."

"You're not a skier?"

"Can't afford to be," she said briskly. "Good night, David."

"Good night." He said it, but he didn't move. Neither did she. They were alone. The night had fallen quiet some time back. He could see her better now, the light from the living room window touching her face, that fey chin and big, startled eyes. Her expression…he didn't know what it

meant, but tonight he didn't seem to have the willpower
to up and go.

"'Cadia?" he whispered. She was on the porch proper;
he stood a step below her, which meant their faces were
almost on a level.

Her lips formed the word *what,* but it was soundless.

He had one of those thoughts—*this is what I wanted
that summer. To kiss her.* He hadn't been able to admit it
to himself. He was too cool, a junior in high school, she
was a gawky beanpole. But, yeah, he realized, only now, *I
had a major thing for her that summer.*

And he'd let her go.

He didn't know if he really had a chance or not now. In
the shock and grief and confusion of this past week and a
half, what he felt was probably wrong.

Tonight, he didn't care.

"Acadia," he repeated, and with one move crossed the di-
vide that had always separated them, these summer nights.
He stroked her cheek with the back of his hand. So soft.
She closed her eyes and rubbed her face against his hand.
David groaned, lifted her chin and kissed her.

It started out gentle, even hesitant, as if he *was* sixteen
again and she an innocent fourteen. Their lips brushed;
hers quivered. He nibbled, and she nibbled back. He'd quit
breathing. Except for his hand, which had come to wrap
the back of her neck, only their mouths touched. He licked
the seam of her lips, which parted.

Suddenly, it wasn't enough. A sound tore its way from
his chest. He dragged in a breath, braced his hip against the
porch railing to prevent them both from crashing down the
steps, tugged her against him, thigh to thigh, pelvis to pelvis, and he plundered her mouth. Her arms twined around
his neck and they kissed, deeply, desperately, like he'd never
kissed a woman before. It was all sensation, need. God, his

fingers were kneading her buttock, pressing her closer. He was rocking against her. He wanted to get a hand on one of her breasts, plump and so damned sexy, but then he'd have to let go of her firm, perfectly rounded ass or her delicate nape, and he couldn't make himself do either. Occasionally one or the other pulled back to gasp for air, but then they went back to kissing as if anything else was unthinkable.

He wanted to pull her deeper in the shadows of her porch and lay her down, but then—*hell*—he had the vision of her kneeling there scrubbing, scrubbing, and he groaned and finally lifted his head.

"Oh, damn. 'Cadia." He held himself utterly still, but his body was seized by tension.

She rested her forehead against his chest. Cheek against her springy hair, leached of fiery color by the night, he breathed in her scent. Tart, maybe lemon, mixed with pure woman.

Acadia was the one to finally straighten, slowly, deliberately, separating herself from him with gentle finality. "Oh, boy," she murmured.

Because she seemed to want it, he removed his hands from her. "That was a long time coming." His voice was hoarse.

"For which one of us?"

"Both, I think."

"I never thought…"

He cleared his throat. "I didn't, either." He smiled crookedly. "We were both wrong."

"Well. Wow." She blinked up at him.

Now he was able to laugh, the sound low and husky. "I can second that. I liked kissing you, 'Cadia Henderson. I hope it was mutual."

"It was mutual." But he heard an uncertainty he didn't like. Nerves? Or disbelief?

"My timing might be a little off."

She laughed, too, now. "How about if we try 'good-night' again?"

"Yeah. Damn." Smiling, he cupped her face, bent forward and kissed her lightly. He hoped she couldn't tell how close to wrenching it was for him to let her go and turn away.

She wished him luck tomorrow, told him to take care of his mother. He had to walk home, dazed, his body aching with need. He'd had his share of women, but he had no idea what had just happened there.

His mind went to work on the problem. It had to be the product of the extraordinary stresses they were both under. The barrage of powerful emotions that covered the gamut of human experience.

The memories.

It couldn't possibly be…what it felt like.

He swore, and made himself think instead about what time he and his mother should leave in the morning to make the service, yet be late enough arriving to ensure they were at the back.

Reality check.

"I THOUGHT it was supposed to always rain at funerals," David murmured out of one side of his mouth, lips barely moving.

Joyce had read that—supposedly the heavens wept, or some such thing—but this was Tucannon. It rarely rained at all in this arid corner of the state. All she had to do was lift her gaze to see the dry landscape beyond the irrigated boundaries of the cemetery. Shades of tan and brown and hints of raw, charcoal basalt thrusting out of the soil. Even the foliage was brown in August.

The service was being held at graveside rather than in

the church or funeral home. Rows of folding chairs had been set up facing the casket, suspended over the grave itself, hidden by drapes. Canopies provided shade to some of the seating, all taken before she and David had arrived. The television cameras were here, but kept at a decent distance.

Only a few heads turned when they had walked quietly across the lawn and taken seats in the last row. Alice had been waiting for them there, and her smile was somber but approving. Joyce saw vague surprise on Carl Lange's face, and something closer to shock and disapproval on…oh, what was that woman's name? Joyce struggled to place her. She closed her eyes, and the context appeared to her. She was a hairdresser, that was it. Never Joyce's, but she'd had the next chair at Clip 'N Curl. Joyce, of course, had taken her business to a salon in Walla Walla years ago. Mary… Well, no reason ever to have known her last name. Joyce did remember her gossiping incessantly. One reason she'd quit going to Clip 'N Curl was the never-ending exchange of whispers and news and innuendoes. She'd been afraid customers in other chairs might start talking about Rob or his irresponsible parents without noticing she was there.

I shouldn't have run away, she reflected. *I should have faced them all down. How much better off we all would have been if I'd had the courage to do that.*

Truthfully, she couldn't understand how or why she'd found the courage to insist on attending today. Joyce knew David thought she should have stayed home. Invisible. Or perhaps, it occurred to her, he was only surprised, because she'd been such a coward for so long.

She remembered, as she began listening, why the service was being held at graveside. Earl Kennedy's son had wanted him buried in Tucannon, but his father had been Catholic and there was no Catholic church in town. She tried very hard to pay attention, but the sonorous phrases floated like the distant hum of bees in a garden. And, after all, she hadn't known Earl. She was here out of respect.

Newfound respect for herself as well as for the deceased, she thought. She was trying very hard to believe it was not her fault that Earl Kennedy was being laid to rest today, on this hot August day. Any more than it was her fault that Wayne and Betty and Charlie would be buried in turn this week; that Walt had had to sacrifice his life to save that boy's.

She sat stiffly, her hands folded on her lap, but inside she cried, *What else could I have done? Tell me. What else?*

She had been convinced for so long that there had to be something—some way she, or she and Pete together, had failed. But hadn't they tried everything they knew to do to help their poor, tormented son live a life of some dignity? Hadn't they tried to protect him and everyone around him? Hadn't she, in the end, made him leave the house to protect herself? Didn't she have that right?

Out of the corner of her eye she saw Davey's quick, concerned glance. In automatic reassurance, she patted one of his big hands, lying loose on his thighs. Surprise flickered on his face, but he was well practiced at hiding emotions and it didn't last long. Joyce kept her own gaze straight ahead.

Her thoughts drifted. Davey had always had those enormous hands and feet. Both boys had surprised her, the way they shot up. But Robbie had stopped at six foot, while Davey kept growing through college. He wore a size-thirteen shoe, last she knew. And those hands... From the time he could toddle, he'd had a ball of some kind gripped in his hands most of the time. She was still amazed that after college he had turned down an offer to play professional basketball in favor of law school. Pete had been less surprised.

"Boy's too smart to make a career out of a game," he'd insisted. "Too determined to straighten out the world."

He had been intensely focused in a way the other boys weren't on the court and playing field. But she had seen the same focus when he studied. The same unwillingness to settle for anything but the best from himself.

She had wondered, sometimes, if that was why her son hadn't yet married or seemed to have a serious relationship. Either he was so driven he didn't make time, or he demanded too much.

But perhaps she'd been wrong. Something was happening to him that paralleled what was happening to her yet was quite different. He was so difficult to read! But he had become gentler in recent days, and she'd heard him laugh more often. Not with her, but with Acadia. He went over to her house every single evening and the two of them sat on her porch talking by the hour. Joyce herself had taken to sitting out on her own porch, as she once had, though then she'd rarely been alone. The house had begun to feel so stifling, so confining. Of course she couldn't hear what Davey and Acadia were saying—she wouldn't have wanted to even if she could! But the low bass of his laugh came more often as the days passed. Instead of returning home looking grim, he often bounded up the front porch steps like the boy he'd once been. She had begun to have a secret hope: that he had found happiness with Charlie's girl.

You would have liked that, too, wouldn't you, Charlie?

Her thoughts had meandered so that she hadn't realized they were going in a circle until she arrived back where she'd started. It was Davey who had lent her courage. No, David, she reminded herself. He wasn't close to being the little boy she called Davey. It was *David* who had begun to convince her that she needn't bear the entire burden of responsibility for what Robbie had done. For all the distance he still maintained with her, he did *not* blame her, a fact that still astonished her. For all his anger at her, he had been just. He had given her support far beyond what she had any right to.

Others had helped, too, Joyce thought. Alice, so eager to renew their friendship. And those multiplying flower bouquets on the front lawn. What an absurd thing, to matter so much! The first to arrive were now brown and withered, but it didn't seem to matter. There still weren't so many—David and she pretended not to count, but she knew they both did. Nine people had now offered a wordless message: *I am sorry for your loss.* A few had signed cards. She was still stunned by those names. Kurt and Renee Jurgen, Alice—Alice's had been the third, the Sonnenbergs and of all people, Jonah Bolton, the police chief. Well, he had known better than almost anyone the struggle Pete and she had undergone. Still, Joyce would never have suspected he was capable of any sensitivity.

She had begun to realize more people had cared than she knew. More yet might have cared if she had let them.

Including David, if only she'd given him the chance. And, perhaps, quit seeing him as a boy and accepted that he was a man.

He nudged her, and she saw that people were beginning to stand.

"Shall we leave?" he murmured. "You've made your appearance."

"No," Joyce said firmly. "I need to pay my respects to George."

David muttered something under his breath she suspected was blasphemous, but he only rose to his feet when she did and shook his head. "If you're prepared to walk into the lion's den," he said, "I guess I can go with you."

Was it possible that there was a glint of admiration in his usually so cool gray eyes?

Wishing it was not so terribly hot, she joined what had become a line of mourners waiting a turn to express their regrets to the family.

And really, it wasn't so bad after all. Perhaps it was the solemnity of the occasion that blunted people's tongues. Joyce did hear a few scandalized murmurs, all saying, in essence, "How dare she appear here today?" But only a few people directly approached her, and those pressed her hand and said, "I'm so glad to see you out, Joyce," and "You must be brokenhearted."

When she squeezed George Kennedy's hand and told him how terribly sorry she was, he only shook his head, tears in his eyes, and said, "It means so much to me that you came. And for saying that. Thank you, Mrs. Owen."

She felt such relief her feet scarcely touched the grass as David steered her away from the gathering and back to their car.

CHAPTER TWELVE

ACADIA INSISTED TO herself that she hadn't been watching for the Owens' return, but the sound of car doors did lure her to peek out the front window. She could just see their driveway, where David had parked.

They both got out, apparently unscathed. Over the roof of his Lexus, Acadia saw that he wore a dark suit coat, white shirt and red tie. She had a vision of him in court, similarly dressed, strolling toward the jury box, then back to face the witness. Nobody would be able to look away from him.

Not fifteen minutes later, he appeared at her door.

"I was beginning to think you were a vampire," she said, letting him in.

"The idea of coming awake only after nightfall is starting to hold a whole lot of appeal." He had changed—so quickly, he'd likely started ripping the tie and jacket off before he got in his front door. He now wore a distinctly faded T-shirt, cargo shorts and sandals. His hair was wet, leading her to assume he'd showered, but his face was still flushed. "God, it was hot out there."

"It's hot in here."

"Not quite as bad."

"Maybe that's only the lack of tie." She nodded at him. "Your wardrobe has expanded."

He looked down at his ensemble. "Yeah, I needed something besides jeans. Mom is just old-fashioned enough not

to approve of me wandering around the house in my box-
ers."

Acadia suspected he would be a fine sight indeed wearing only boxer shorts. A voice inside her suggested he might
look finer, even, without them.

No argument there, she decided, trying to blank out the
picture that had come to mind. Remembering last night's
kiss had her flustered enough.

"How did it go?" she asked, pretending a casualness she
didn't feel. She handed him a cold Pepsi without asking.

He opened it and took a long swallow. "My mother surprised me."

"Because she decided to go?"

"And refused to duck and run when people noticed her.
She insisted on staying long enough to shake Kennedy's
son's hand and tell him how sorry she was. People were
staring and whispering, and she held her head high."

"Maybe you don't know her as well as you thought you
did," Acadia suggested. She opened her own can of soda
and concentrated on it instead of looking at David. "I guess
I didn't know my father as well as I thought I did, either. I
wish I'd known how much he loved me."

"Would it have made any difference?" David asked
gently. His eyes were unnervingly penetrating.

On a jerk of anger, she lifted her head at that. "What
do you mean?"

"No matter what, he couldn't give you what you really
wanted—the security of your childhood back again. Mom
and Dad, together the way they belonged. Tucannon, never
changing. The same friends." His mouth quirked, although
his eyes remained watchful. "The chance to realize how
desperately you wanted to escape, just like the rest of us."

"You think I shouldn't have been mad at him."

"I think you were mad for unrealistic reasons," he corrected. "Would your mother really have handed over custody to him? Would you have wanted them in court warring over you? You were a teenage girl. It seems to me reasonable that both of them assumed you were better off living with your mother."

She backed away from David, coming up against the kitchen counter. "He could have fought for both of us." The misery she'd thought herself over had risen to choke her voice.

He set down his drink on the table, his forehead creasing. "'Cadia, I'm sorry. I'm talking about things I don't know anything about."

She shook her head hard. "The irony is, you know as much as I do. Even when I screamed at her back then, she wouldn't talk to me about what had gone wrong. I didn't even try to ask him."

She was appalled at herself—at the unhappiness in her voice, the old resentment and hurt balling in her chest. What was wrong with her? Why did all these emotions feel as sharp edged as when they were new, the summer her parents sat her down to tell her they were getting a divorce?

"From what I remember, they were an unlikely pairing from the beginning. She was something of a flower child, wasn't she? And your dad…" He hesitated. "He always seemed so steady and, I don't know, staid. He might have been politically liberal, but I doubt he was a man who liked change of any kind."

"No." Acadia had to press her lips together to contain grief. "No. Do you know, he ate the same breakfast every single morning of his life, as far as I know? Two poached eggs on two pieces of whole-wheat bread. A slice of cantaloupe. That's it. Day in and day out."

"Maybe the miracle was that their marriage lasted as

long as it did. Long enough to let you grow up in a stable home."

She gave a strangled laugh. "Until they decided to shock me when I was at the absolute worst age. A couple of years earlier would have been better. A couple of years later..." *After you had gone away to college anyway.* "But I was thirteen. Do you know what a mess thirteen-year-old girls are?"

He laughed and picked up his soda again. "Not really. I've never spent much time with one."

"Hormones are berserk. You want to be beautiful, mature, independent, but deep down inside you are absolutely certain your nose or ears or bony knees are objects of ridicule, the pimple that sprouted on your chin flashes like a neon beer sign, you will *never* get breasts, and if you do they won't look like fill-in-the-blank's anyway."

"Fill in the blanks?" he repeated, his amusement obvious.

Some of her own humor restored, Acadia made a face at him. "Oh, whatever TV star you currently think epitomizes feminine beauty. Or, in my case, Kristy Whatever's."

David's laugh carved deeper lines in his cheeks. "She did have particularly gorgeous..."

"Oh, shush. My mood was improving. I don't want to think about Kristy."

"I don't, either. I hadn't thought of her in years until I came home this time." He pulled out a chair, turned it around and straddled it. "There's a hell of a lot I'd blacked out, I'm coming to realize."

"Me, too." She braced her hands on the counter and jumped up. Ironic, given that she was taller now, but it had been harder getting up here than when she was a kid. "You look better," Acadia said, lightly bumping her heels on the cabinet below her.

"Better?"

"Than when you came. Your color has improved."

"A drink, and your company."

"I was as sulky as a thirteen-year-old girl."

That amused him, she could tell. She took ridiculous pleasure in making him laugh, as if her ability to do so made her special. Which was silly—his current grimness was easily explained. For all she knew, he was known as the comic of the King County Prosecuting Attorney's Office.

He asked what she'd been up to so far today, and she admitted to how slowly she was progressing at packing up her father's library.

"It's awful. Part of me wants to keep every single book because he treasured all of them. The sensible part of me knows I'm never going to open a tome about the Dutch in the seventeenth century or…or the Dred Scott case."

"The Dred Scott case was actually really interesting," he began.

She wrinkled her nose. "You would think so."

"You know, there are undoubtedly books on your father's shelves that he thought were wrong-minded or just plain lousy. He was a teacher—he'd use them as examples of historical biases or inadequate research or pedantic writing. Anything that looks dull to you—hey! That's probably a lousy one anyway."

Now he'd made her laugh, and feel better about some of her decisions.

"How goes the basement?" she asked, and he grimaced.

"I'm plunging back down there this afternoon. Knee-deep has become ankle-deep, and don't think I'm kidding. The airing out isn't going so well, either, given that even with window and door open, the air doesn't so much as stir."

She commiserated and cautiously agreed to come and take a look in another day or two.

David tossed his soda can in the open recycling bin she'd

started—despite the fact that the local garbage service offered no recycling. He rose to his feet, restored the chair to its place tucked under the table and said, "You look cute sitting up there. About ten years old."

"My mother chewed me out every time she caught me." Acadia bumped her heels a few more times just because she could, proving again that she'd never grown up, then hopped down. "And I seriously doubt I look ten years old."

"Well, no. You do have..." The words were teasing, but his gaze flicked lower, to where her T-shirt fit snugly over her breasts. A vee of sweat emphasized her cleavage. The flash of heat she saw in his eyes didn't match his tone.

She, of course, blushed, tripped over her feet and all but sprinted to get out the kitchen door ahead of him. *I am capable of being cool, sophisticated, even seductive. I am.* She sighed. Oh, sure. This was Tucannon, where she still thought of her father as "Daddy," where she was taking secret pleasure in defying her mother's rules. This was David Owen, the most passionate love of her entire love. And wasn't all of that pathetic, given that she was thirty years old?

At the front door, before she could reach for the doorknob David caught her arms, turned her around and tugged her up against him. "I *really* liked kissing you, Acadia," he murmured, then did it again. She rose on tiptoe and kissed him back with a woman's confidence that existed side by side with the astonished awe her inner teenager felt.

The kiss might have gone on considerably longer if they hadn't both become aware sweat had them sticking together.

"Can I come back this evening, 'Cadia?" he asked, the door open. "Let me know if you're getting tired of me."

Fat chance.

"I would love it if you came back tonight," she admitted. It wasn't until David flashed a wicked grin and departed that it occurred to her to wonder whether he'd been asking for more than the chance to lounge on her front porch and while away an hour or two talking.

If so—was she ready to take the next step with David?

She almost snorted. Yes, she was usually somewhere between slow and foot-dragging about getting naked with a man, which might be why she'd let it happen with so few guys. But really—David Owen? *And you'd say* no?

She might be sorry a few weeks from now, when they both went back to their lives. She might get her heart broken. But *no* was not a word she'd be saying to David.

And—*face it*—her heart would crack when they went their separate ways, whether she'd slept with him or not.

Reeve had called ahead, but he was sweating when he rang Mrs. Stenten's doorbell. This was so freakin' stupid. What was he *doing* here?

But it was too late. He heard footsteps coming, and then the sound of a chain rattling and the dead bolt being turned. People didn't used to lock. Now, he bet everyone in town did. Almost every night now, he waited until his parents had gone to bed, then got up and slid ghostlike through the house to check window and door locks both. The fear he couldn't shake kept making him face his cowardice over and over again.

The door opened. "Reeve, come in," Mrs. Stenten said.

He'd only seen her a couple of times since that day, and he hadn't been all that eager to meet her eyes. He saw now that she didn't look so good. Reeve thought she'd lost some weight, but not enough to explain why her cheeks seemed sunken and her eyes too deep set. They were dull, too, and her skin had lost something. She used to be plump, pink cheeked and always smiling. He thought of her as a Betty Crocker kind of lady.

He followed her silently into the living room, where she invited him to sit down. Feeling totally dorky, he looked around and chose one end of the sofa. That recliner over there—God, that had to be Walt's. The fabric was worn and there were imprints where his head, butt and elbows had rested.

Reeve wrenched his gaze away, hunting desperately for something else to look at.

Mostly the room wasn't that different from his own living room. There was a TV—plasma, he thought, and bigger screened than Reeve's parents'. Mrs. Stenten must not like recliners, because the other chair in the room had a floral print and was sort of stiff and upright looking. When his gaze crept back to Walt's place, it settled on the rings coffee cups or beer cans had made in the finish on the end table that would have been at his right hand. A coaster sat there, and Reeve bet Mrs. Stenten had always been nagging her husband to use it.

"I don't want you to feel guilty, Reeve." Her voice was soft. "Walt thought a lot of you."

"I thought a lot of him, too," Reeve blurted. He rubbed his hands on his thighs. "He was really great to me. Giving me the job and helping me with my car and all." He forced himself to meet her eyes. "I really miss him."

"Yes." Her expression didn't change at all, but suddenly tears were running down her cheeks. She didn't even seem to react to them, except her tongue snaked out to catch some. "I wasn't sure I would." She struggled visibly for a smile that was so not successful. "That's a terrible thing to say, isn't it? But when you're married long enough, sometimes you start to wonder."

He didn't have to say anything, which was a good thing because she kept talking.

"Not that long ago I was thinking that I might as well

live alone, for all the company he was. Some days I swear he didn't do more than grunt when I brought him his beer or served dinner."

Oh, man, he didn't want to hear this. Why was she telling *him?* he wondered frantically.

"At least the two of you had something to talk *about*." That should have sounded bitter, but that's not how it had come out. It was more like she was talking to herself. "He and I had probably finished saying everything ten years ago."

But then, taking Reeve by surprise, she focused on him, and there was something almost fierce in her eyes.

"But what he did for you, Reeve, reminded me who he really was. Why I loved him, even though he was frustratingly quiet when I needed him to talk to me. You may not understand, but I'm grateful for that."

She was wrong; he *did* understand. He could tell it hadn't occurred to her, though, that what her husband did had made him, Reeve, feel worthless. Part of him hoped nobody ever noticed, while another part wanted to yell, *I'm grateful, okay? And I don't want to have to be. I wish I'd taken a bullet, too, because I'd rushed Rob Owen or thrown my body over Walt's, or...something. Something a* man *would have done.*

"Well," she said, wiping her cheeks. "Enough out of me. You must have wanted to ask me something."

"I just...uh, hoped you'd tell me more about him. I didn't even know he'd been a marine. He never said."

"He had that tattoo."

He had noticed the eagle gripping an anchor on Walt's biceps but never thought anything of it. Remembering how dismissive he'd been of anyone Walt's age, Reeve winced.

"He'd intended to be career Marine Corps," Mrs. Stenten said, "but he was wounded in Somalia and after that his

knee tended to give out unpredictably. He was always good
with engines, so…" She shrugged. "We moved to Tucannon because my parents were here. He was going to open
an automotive repair shop, but then he found out the station was for sale so he bought it instead. We had one son…
did you know that?"

Wordless, Reeve shook his head.

"He was born with a heart defect, and he only lived nine
months. Neither of us had the heart to try again after that."
She sighed. "I wish we had. It was one of those things we
didn't really talk about. We just…" She made a helpless
gesture.

They sat in silence for a minute. Reeve wanted to escape. These weren't the kinds of things he'd hoped to learn
about Walt. He'd wanted…he didn't know, maybe to find
out Walt *wasn't* always such a hero. That he'd done bad or
mean or stupid things sometimes.

Well, maybe he had, Reeve realized. He hadn't noticed
that Mrs. Stenten wasn't very happy. Or else he'd noticed
but hadn't cared enough to do anything about it.

"He won medals," she said suddenly. "He kept them
shoved in a drawer, as if they didn't matter, but I knew
they did even if I let myself forget." She stood. "I'll get
them to show you."

She came back a minute later with a flat box, which she
handed to him. He opened it and stared at the two medals
pinned inside: a Purple Heart and a Bronze Star. One for
being wounded, one for heroism.

"I have pictures, too," she said, and disappeared again,
returning with a couple of photo albums. She sat beside him
on the sofa and opened the first album on the coffee table.

It made Reeve feel funny to see Walt so young. *Maybe
my age.* But wearing a uniform, and looking really proud.
His hair was buzz cut; he might as well have been skinned.

Walt wasn't handsome, even then; he'd always been short and stocky and his ears kind of stuck out. But he bulged with muscles, and he was smiling. For his parents? His girlfriend?

"Did you know him then?" Reeve asked.

"We met later when he was on leave." She turned the pages, and Reeve saw the progression of the proud young man into a serious guy. You could tell he'd seen things he'd never forget. The wedding photos were in there, Mrs. Stenten a little plump then, too, but also…pretty. *I might have asked her out, too,* he thought, and was alarmed by the idea. Eventually there were photos of Walt after he'd been wounded, on crutches, lines of pain on his face. Those lines had never totally gone away, Reeve thought, and was bothered by his memory of the way Walt would grunt when he got up and down. God, had he never quit hurting? If so, nothing would have made him say so, not to anyone except his wife. And maybe not even to her, Reeve realized, thinking about what she'd said.

There were photos of them with a baby who was kind of homely and looked like Walt, with those same ears, but Mrs. Stenten hurried past them.

There was one of Walt posing in front of the Shell station, taken a long time ago. He couldn't have been more than thirty. He looked proud in this picture, too.

"That was the day he took over ownership." She gently touched the picture, then closed the album.

Reeve sat there feeling as if he'd been dragged behind a car down a gravel road. His skin was raw. He swallowed and pushed to his feet. "Thank you, Mrs. Stenten. I really appreciate you showing me…" His voice cracked, horrifying him.

Her eyes were damp when she looked at him. "I'm glad you came, Reeve." She closed the box that held the two medals. "I want you to have these. You're the right person to keep them."

"What...?" He lurched back a step. "No!"

"Let me give you one of these pictures, too," she said, opening the album again. She chose that first one, of the young Walt Stenten in his Marine Corps uniform. Taking the box back from Reeve, she opened it and tucked the photo partly beneath the Purple Heart. "There," she said, handing it back. "So you don't forget him."

He opened his mouth and nothing came out. Closed it and gulped. When he was finally able to speak, he had a bad feeling it wouldn't sound anything like him.

"I wouldn't anyway." He'd been right. He swallowed again. "I won't. I promise."

She nodded, as if accepting a vow. At the front door, she hugged him, quickly and awkwardly, letting him go before he could reciprocate. He mumbled, "Thanks," and she smiled—sort of, with so much sadness in her eyes he could hardly stand it. And a moment later the door closed and he was on the other side of it, holding in his hand more proof of what kind of man Walt Stenten had been.

Embarrassed by his tears, Reeve slung his leg over his motorcycle, gripped the handlebars and hung on. He had to sit there for a long time before he felt confident he could drive safely.

THAT EVENING, Acadia called her mother again. She picked a time late enough to catch Mom after work, but earlier than Acadia expected David.

She'd thought all afternoon about what he'd said about her parents, and about why she hadn't been given any choice about which parent she'd be living with. It made her ashamed of how much anger she'd clung to, aimed at both her parents. Her reaction when she'd first arrived here in the wake of the horrible news was typical. She had been determined to shut her mother out entirely. Mom couldn't be allowed to share any of what Acadia felt for her father. *She* was the one who'd abandoned him. With stomach-churning bitterness, Acadia had been certain her mother had no right even to pretend to feel grief for Daddy.

The adult Acadia knew her parents had once upon a time loved each other, even if it all went bad eventually. Maybe that kind of love never entirely disappeared. Mom had sounded distraught when she'd called Acadia at the hospital with the news about the awful happenings in Tucannon.

Tonight, her mother answered on the first ring and Acadia updated her. "I don't know if you want to come to Dad's funeral…"

"I do," her mother said quietly, "if you want me."

"I'd like to have you here."

As simple as that.

"I can only come for the weekend," Mom said. "I'll book a Friday afternoon flight. Is it as hot there as ever?"

"It's August. What do you think?"

"Lord." There was a pause, during which her mother shifted gears. "I don't like to think of you alone so much, honey. I don't suppose anybody your age who you knew is around."

Sneaky, Acadia thought. "Mostly David Owen," she said, hoping her mother bought the casual tone. "Well, you knew that because of the statement to the press. Oh, and I spent some time with Alan Finley. I think he was David's age, but it was still nice to catch up. By the way, I listed the house with Lyman Engle."

"David Owen." Not being dumb, Mom ignored the camouflage. "Does he still look as much like his brother as ever?"

"I never saw Rob as an adult, but…yeah. I think so."

"You were so crazy in love with him, and he'd never in a million years have noticed you." Mom clucked.

"Gee, thanks, Mom."

"You know what I mean. He was just enough older, he wasn't likely to pay attention to a girl your age. Especially one who hadn't hit puberty."

Acadia made a face at the reminder of her bean sprout figure.

"Didn't your dad say that David is an attorney now?"

"A prosecuting attorney. He was probably skinny back then, too, but he's filled out very nicely. He's here in town to help his mom."

"Poor Joyce." Her mother was silent for a moment. "I knew that was the worst part of moving for you. Leaving him behind."

"And Dad."

"Well, that goes without saying. Does David have a wife with him?"

"No wife. We've been getting together evenings, talking. You know. Sitting out on the porch."

"Where your father was gunned down." Mom sounded incredulous. "That porch?"

"I used the back door for the first week." She didn't mention the crime-scene tape. "Since then I've been remembering all the nights you sat out there talking to one of the neighbors. And Daddy would lean against a pillar, so quiet you'd forget he was there unless you happened to notice the glow of his pipe."

"Those are good memories," her mother conceded after a minute.

"Maybe it's dumb, but I wanted to, I don't know, reclaim the house. Including the porch." This mattered to Acadia, a whole lot. "I'll never have reason to be back here, and even if I were, someone else will be living in this house.

So I want to leave holding on to the happy times, not the way Daddy died. Does that make sense?"

"Yes." Mom's voice was soft. "Of course it does. It's smart. You usually are, though. I don't think I told you how proud I was of you for supporting the Owens. I don't envy Joyce all those years of trying to deal with Rob. The things that bitch Marge Perkins said about Joyce and Pete made me sick. I cried when you said that about your father waiting for Rob."

Acadia found herself clutching the phone like a life buoy. "Was I wrong, Mom?" she begged. "Would Daddy have forgiven Rob?"

"You know he would have. Even when he was looking down the barrel of the gun, he'd have felt sorry for Rob. Your father didn't have a mean bone in his body."

Acadia's fingers relaxed, and then she thought, *Why not?*

"What went wrong between you and Daddy? I don't re-member you even arguing."

It was a minute before her mother spoke. "We did argue, but we tried to be careful not to do it in front of you. It was my fault, Acadia. It wasn't your father so much—I loved him, but I was miserable in Tucannon. It wasn't the life I'd ever wanted. That flush of first love, you think you'll be happy anywhere, but it's not true. I hadn't even finished college, and jobs were scarce. Charlie would have been happy if we'd had two or three more kids and I'd been a housewife just like Betty Tindall and Joyce Owen and three-quarters of the other women in town. My restlessness grew and grew until sometimes I felt as if I was bouncing off the walls of that house. I wanted out so bad. And finally I couldn't stand it anymore."

"Did you ever suggest we all move?"

"Of course I did! In the end he said he would, but it was too late. His resistance, his refusal to understand how

I felt, undermined our relationship until there wasn't anything left but how we felt about you. I held on for years because of you."

"I'm sorry," Acadia whispered.

"No, I'm sorry." Mom's voice was thick. "You *were* happy there." She gave a funny little laugh. "And I killed all possibility of you getting together with David."

Now, finally, Acadia was able to smile even though her eyes had been stinging. "No, Mom, I don't think you did kill all possibility."

"You've been doing more than talking when you sit out on the porch?" Her tone said, *Aha!*

"Maybe." She grinned, even though her mother couldn't see her. "And that's all I'm telling you."

"Well," Mom said, as only a mother could. "I am definitely showing up on your doorstep Friday evening. Count on it."

CHAPTER THIRTEEN

FROM SUNDAY LETTING-out-of-church-time on, old acquaintances had started coming to call on Acadia. A few showed up to see David's mom, too, and even him. He wasn't quite sure what had opened the gates, so to speak; why was it not correct last week, but now it was? Where Mom and he were concerned, their appearance at the funeral was probably explanation enough. But Acadia?

The arrivals who took him completely by surprise were Aunt Jackie and Uncle Warren. When he'd talked to her a few days ago, she'd reluctantly admitted to feeling "puny." The chemo treatments were hitting her harder than she'd anticipated. "I should be there for Joyce," she fretted, but he had thought he'd convinced his aunt that he and his mother were doing fine.

Apparently not. Because Monday afternoon, there they were.

Mom and her sister were already hugging when Uncle Warren climbed out of the car on his side and stretched. Tall, skinny and balding, he was a quiet guy who mostly let his wife do his talking for him. It would have been easy to assume Jackie was the dominant partner in that marriage, but David had seen her turn to her husband often enough to know better.

"I wasn't sure my stomach would tolerate the drive," Aunt Jackie announced, "but I'd been having a good few days so we threw the suitcases in the car and came straight from my treatment. I hope that's all right."

"Well, of course it's all right!" David's mother exclaimed. "Although I hate to think of you going to all that effort because you were worried about me."

"Nonsense," Aunt Joyce declared. "We're determined not to make more work for you. We've already made reservations at a hotel in Walla Walla—now, don't you argue—but we decided to drive on through to see you first."

David's eyes met his uncle's over the roof of the car. Uncle Warren's held a twinkle. They both knew those hotel reservations were a token. There was no way Mom would allow her own sister to stay anywhere but in this house. The two women had a brief, vigorous tussle over the issue, but Warren had already popped the trunk and David was starting to carry suitcases in before they were done.

"You're family," Mom insisted. "For goodness' sakes, I can't have you driving back and forth every day, especially with you not feeling up to par!"

And that was that.

In one way, having Aunt Jackie here would be great. The only downside was that David felt able to slip away for only a few minutes that evening to see Acadia. The few minutes stretched into half an hour, and he did kiss her good-night, but he still felt disgruntled when he had to leave her sitting on the porch. He told himself he was imagining that she looked forlorn; he had invited her to come back to the house with him and say hi to his aunt and uncle, but she'd politely declined.

"They must be exhausted, especially your aunt with her in the middle of chemotherapy. The last thing they need is to be polite to a near-stranger."

Aunt Jackie did look like hell. It had shaken him up a little, when he got a first good look at her. To start with, she wore some kind of turban, which he supposed meant her hair was falling out. But she'd also lost weight and her skin tone was on the gray scale, especially disquieting to see in August. And no, the Oregon Coast didn't have the kind of sun they had in Eastern Washington, but there were enough sunny days she should have picked up some tan.

When he got back to the house, Uncle Warren was just coming down the stairs. The two women were chattering in the kitchen.

David asked, "Would you like a drink? I've got a decent Scotch."

His uncle offered a rare smile. "I would."

He proved willing to talk about his wife's condition. He verified what she'd told David—the prognosis was excellent, but the treatment was causing more wear and tear than her optimistic nature had allowed for.

Relaxing in Dad's recliner, Warren said comfortably, "She'll be fine. Jackie's a tough nut to crack. She was determined to get here, and stay until Rob's funeral, and nobody says no to Jackie when she's determined."

"The body still hasn't been released. Doesn't she have to be back home for the next round of chemotherapy?"

He shook his head. "They arranged for her to get it at the hospital in Walla Walla. We're set for next Monday."

David nodded thoughtfully.

They all said their good-nights shortly thereafter. He went to bed and lay thinking about the changed dynamics. His mother would need him less. He could concentrate on getting the basement reamed out. He'd put a bug in Aunt Jackie's ear about Mom's future plans, too. Maybe *she* could get somewhere persuading Mom to think about her options so he'd know whether he should start packing or what.

Having a moment of optimism himself, it occurred to

him that having backup might mean he'd be able to spend some extra time with Acadia, too.

TUESDAY MORNING, he waved goodbye when Jackie and Warren carried his mother away for the thrills and chills of lunch in Walla Walla. Her first real outing. David prayed her face wasn't so memorable everyone would recognize her from the never-ending newscasts.

He was going back to the house when he saw a woman pull up in front of the Hendersons'. It took him a minute to place her—he couldn't remember seeing her since he'd graduated—but after a moment's thought the name came to him. Jennie Merfeld. She'd been…a year behind him in school, he thought, which meant she'd been a year ahead of Acadia. Probably they hadn't been close friends, then.

She was one of those people he'd never really known. Recognized, sure. If they'd happened on each other in Seattle, he might have stopped and said hi, because they had Tucannon in common. Otherwise, he didn't have any real recollection of her personality.

Resolutely heading down into the basement to continue cleaning, he wondered what Jennie Merfeld was saying to Acadia right now.

The Dumpster he'd asked the garbage company for sat out at the curb, and he was filling it fast. His mother's spirits might be improving, but she hadn't yet stuck her head down in the basement. He was just as glad. She had enough nightmare memories to haunt her, without adding one more. He figured Jackie, at least, would want to take a look, but not yet. That gave him a few more hours to reduce the horror factor.

He managed to wrestle first the mattress, then the bedsprings, up the stairs and into the yard. Sweating although it was still only midmorning, he was groaning at the thought of dragging them all the way to the street when a car stopped and a man got out. David waited, wary even after he recognized his high school upper-level math teacher, Mr. Montalvo, striding around the house to him. Montalvo's courses hadn't been David's favorites, but they'd gotten along okay.

"David." Montalvo had gotten paunchy and gray now threaded his dark hair.

"Mr. Montalvo."

"Let me give you a hand with those."

Man, that would be such a relief. "Thanks," he said briefly, "but I'd better find you some gloves. These are, uh, pretty disgusting."

"I have canvas gloves in the trunk." Montalvo reversed direction and came back a minute later pulling on the gloves. "Out by the curb?"

"Yep. I figure I'll lean 'em against the container for now."

They exchanged only a few words while they hauled the two awkward pieces out.

"Anything else you could use help with?"

David hesitated. It was still a sty down there, but who was he protecting? "Thanks," he said. "I could use a hand getting some of the furniture up the stairs."

Mr. Montalvo followed him in, then stared in obvious shock. "My God. I knew, but…"

"Nobody but Mom and Dad really knew. Even I didn't."

"Damn." He frowned, turning in place to take in the walls, tipping his head back to study the ceiling. "Your brother was gifted."

"And crazy."

"Yeah." The teacher sighed. "Hard to miss that." He shook himself. "The dresser?"

"Yeah, I'm going to get out an ax and break up the furniture that's left. None of it is salvable." And David wasn't sure he would have if he could. He was half tempted to bring in a Catholic priest to perform an exorcism of the basement when he was done. He didn't exactly feel evil hovering, but he'd catch himself looking over his shoulder a lot, as if he wasn't alone. Something was still here; something restless.

Like my imagination.

Montalvo labored alongside David until they had all the furniture standing in the middle of the back lawn, which was burned by the summer sun to a crackling brown. Mom hadn't done any watering this year, that was for sure. The furniture, stained and broken, wasn't any prettier a sight.

David stripped off a glove and held out his hand. "Thanks. I really appreciate your help."

"You're very welcome." They shook solemnly.

"I take the *Seattle Times,*" Montalvo surprised him by saying. "I've seen your name a few times. Looks like you've done well for yourself."

"Thanks." David walked him to his car, talking on the way about his job and a few memories of high school. "Hearing about Mr. Baron…" He shook his head. "That might have been the worst. He encouraged me a lot. Do you know if a funeral has been scheduled for him?"

"His daughter isn't burying him here. She lives in Denver and decided to have him closer to her."

The news came as a jolt. David had never been a fan of the ceremonies surrounding death, but he realized he had wanted to say goodbye to Mr. Baron.

He wondered if the daughter had really wanted her father buried near her, or if it was more a matter of *not* wanting him to spend eternity in the same cemetery as his killer. If so, he couldn't say he blamed her.

"If you have her address," he said, "I'd like to write to

her." Maybe putting into words on paper how much Mr. Baron had meant to him would serve as his own goodbye.

"Sure, I'll give you a call." Mr. Montalvo clapped him on the back. "It was good to see you, David. We'd all like it if you'd come by the high school the next time you're home."

"If Mom stays here in Tucannon, I'll do that," he promised. He'd had some damn good times at the old high school. He wished again that he hadn't stayed away so long.

The two of them were still talking when Acadia saw Jennie Merfeld out. Jennie gave David one hostile, direct look, then marched to her car, got in and drove away.

"Her parents aren't so bad," Mr. Montalvo observed dispassionately. Then, "It was a brave thing, what Charlie's daughter did standing up beside you. I wish I'd had the chance to teach her."

"She wishes so, too." Unfazed by Jennie Merfeld's dislike, David grinned. "Acadia is still bitter about getting dragged away by her mom. I mean, Tucannon? San Francisco? Why wouldn't she be?" Montalvo laughed, and David said, "Hey, would you like to meet her?"

She walked out to the sidewalk when she saw them coming. "Mr. Montalvo," she said, holding out a hand and smiling. "Unlike David here, I *liked* math and the sciences. I was really looking forward to taking calculus from you."

When both men laughed, she made them explain why. She coaxed them in for a glass of lemonade, and when Mr. Montalvo paused in the door of Charlie's den, she said, "I don't suppose you'd like any of his books? Wow. I didn't think. Do you know anyone else who might want some of them?" She peered doubtfully past him into the room. "I wonder if some would be useful in the high school library. That might be a good memorial for him."

"I wouldn't mind taking one to remember him by," Mr. Montalvo said gently. "And I'm betting the librarian would be delighted to take some of these off your hands. Do you want me to give her a call?"

"Please," she said gratefully, then went to get the lemonade while the two men browsed the shelves she hadn't yet gotten to.

Mr. Montalvo had picked out a book on local history by the time she returned with a pitcher of lemonade and glasses on a tray. No, not a tray, David saw with amusement—a cookie sheet.

"So Jennie Merfeld came by," he observed, half sitting on Charlie's big old oak desk.

Acadia snorted. "Ostensibly to say how sorry she was about my father, but really to inform me that I'd been taken in by you and that she hoped Rob burned in hell for what he did." She glanced at Mr. Montalvo. "I'm sorry, I hope the Merfelds aren't friends of yours."

"Kirk is a good man, not the kind to hold Joyce or David responsible for Rob's sins. I'm not sure about Marie. I never had the daughter in any of my classes."

Which meant she hadn't been on an advanced placement track in high school.

"She wasn't a friend of yours?" David asked Acadia. "I was surprised to see her."

"I knew her." She scowled. "We played softball together for several seasons. She was scared of the ball, but the coach worked for her dad so he always put her in anyway."

David's mouth curved at her disgust. He couldn't picture Acadia afraid of much.

After Mr. Montalvo made his excuses and left, David said, "You want to work out some aggression?"

Her eyes lit with interest. "How?"

When he told her what he had in mind, she agreed with enthusiasm. She went to fetch her father's gardening gloves, which were ridiculously big on her hands but would do to keep her from getting blisters, and followed him to his backyard. There they took turns with the ax, swinging until two dressers, a bookcase and a cedar chest splintered and fell into pieces he could toss into the Dumpster.

They'd both worked up a major sweat by then. And—crap—it was time to start getting ready for the second funeral of the week, Betty and Wayne Tindall's.

"You're welcome to come with us if you want to be stared at," he said. "If you'd rather drive yourself, I won't be insulted."

"Of course I'll come with you," Acadia said stoutly. "Lord. Why is it being held at the hottest time of day?"

"At a guess, because Betty's sister, who planned it, isn't a local. At least the service is in the church."

Acadia thanked God and seemed to mean it, a sentiment with which he wholeheartedly concurred. They parted ways to shower and dress. David groaned at the thought of donning tie and suit coat. Socks and shoes were bad enough. Had to be a hundred degrees today.

He found his family had returned and were ahead of him in getting ready—a good thing, considering there was only one shower in the house.

He'd once again planned a late arrival, but was less successful today. A fair number of people were still streaming into the church when their small group arrived. He discovered quickly that Acadia's narrow-eyed glare worked better to silence his mother's opponents than his own icy stare did. Despite the wretched occasion, she made him want to laugh.

And, while the big stone church wasn't cool, the interior was a good twenty degrees lower than the outdoor temp. His mother had worn a dress that he hadn't seen in years. It looked like something from the 1940s, navy blue with white polka dots, a white collar and white belt. She'd even fastened a small navy blue hat to her head.

"Nice dress," he murmured to her as he edged past, and she folded her hands on her lap.

"Betty liked it."

He'd let himself forget what good friends she and Betty had been. Wayne was such an asshole, he tended to over-shadow his wife to the two Owen boys. But Betty had always been good to them, softening her husband's harsh-ness with an apologetic smile and some of the best cook-ies he'd ever eaten.

Acadia, who had already taken a seat, blushed and started to rise again. "Sorry. I miscounted. You'll want to be next to your mom."

"No, you're fine." He settled at the end of the pew, an-choring one side as his uncle was the other.

Remembering Betty and Wayne, he concentrated more on the eulogies than he had at Earl Kennedy's service and less on the reaction of other people sitting around them. The focus, he discovered, was more on Betty than her husband, probably because it was her sister sitting in the position of chief mourner, but maybe because more people stood up to speak about Betty than about Wayne.

When one person after another rose to speak a few words, David keep an uneasy eye on his mother, but she stayed put. Maybe common sense, maybe shame, and maybe she wasn't sure she'd be able to speak through the tears that streaked her face. She produced a hankie from her small white purse and mopped her cheeks. Jackie kept shooting her anxious glances. Acadia, who had sat on her other side, took her hand and held it through much of the service.

David looked as much at those linked hands as he did at the faces of the people talking. He already knew Acadia's hands were as small and slender as his mother's, which were marred by the beginnings of arthritis that made her joints knobby. He'd looked at Acadia's hands before; he had no trouble remembering how they felt touching him. But it struck him that, while they were long-fingered and graceful, they also had a practical look to them with nails that were short and unpainted. Something twisted in his chest at the sight of those two hands holding each other. Maybe it was Acadia's readiness to offer comfort, maybe his mom's willingness to receive it from her. Or maybe it was how he felt about these two women.

And no, he wasn't going to put that in words.

He and Acadia flanked his mom on the way out of the church, and then on the walk to the grave site, Aunt Jackie and Uncle Warren bringing up the rear. There were fewer whispers today, he thought. Probably no one was surprised Joyce and David Owen had showed their faces. And maybe people remembered what good friends Joyce and Betty had been.

Betty's sister hugged his mother and whispered a few words in her ear. She shook David's hand and then Acadia's, and told Acadia how sorry she was about her father. All in all, it was civilized—and harrowing beyond belief.

Blown-up photographs of Wayne and Betty had been set on easels here at graveside. David guessed both had been taken ten or fifteen years ago. They looked as they had in his memory of them. Betty's smile was timid and sweet. Wayne had been caught pruning his roses, his hands careful and his expression intent. He'd loved those roses. Oh, hell—none of the neighbor kids had ever given him a break. Yeah, he'd been a grumpy old man, but they'd gone out of their way to get his goat, too.

Wayne and Betty were almost as big a part of the landscape of David's past as his own parents. He hadn't expected to feel so much grief. Saturday's funeral hadn't been an adequate warm-up for this one.

Head bowed, he stumbled as they turned away from Betty's sister. Acadia caught his arm, giving him momentary support. All the way to the car, she walked between him and his mother, who clung to her. David kept a hand on the small of Acadia's back. Touching her steadied him, kept his eyes from misting over.

I've never leaned on a woman before, it occurred to him. *Not physically, not emotionally.*

He'd been doing a lot of leaning on Acadia these past ten days. Knowing that might bother him, but she'd leaned, too. He was reminded of his unconscious awareness of his aunt and uncle's marriage. From the time he was a boy, David had noticed the way they kept an eye out for each other. Always knowing where the other one was. Caring for each other, in quiet ways. He didn't know many marriages like that, not even his parents' for all that David was sure they'd loved each other.

Once they were all in the car, Acadia sitting in the back between him and his mother, he said, "Walt Stenten's funeral tomorrow morning. Hell of a week. Aren't you glad you came, Aunt Jackie?"

She turned her head to look at him over the seat. "Yes, I am. I knew Betty well, too, you know."

Chastened, he didn't say anything more during the short drive.

When they got out of the car at his house, he stopped Acadia with a hand on her arm. "Are you planning to go tomorrow?"

She hesitated. "I didn't know Walt. I mean, I'd have recognized him, but…I said I'd go, but that was when I thought you and Joyce were on your own. Now that you're not, you don't need me."

Something tore inside him. "I need you," he said, voice guttural.

Her eyes widened. In the direct sun, they were the most extraordinary color, a rich brown flecked with gold and with striations of other colors he couldn't have named. "You mean…tomorrow?" she whispered.

They started down the sidewalk toward her house. They'd passed the Tindalls' before he found words. "Not tomorrow if you don't want to come." He sucked in a breath. "There've been a few days when I think you're all that got me through them."

"Oh." She brushed his hand with hers. "Ditto."

On her porch, she fumbled with the key and finally got it in the lock. David felt tangled up inside. He didn't want to let her go inside alone, but knew that probably she intended to go straight upstairs for a shower and a chance to get out of the dress-up clothes. At the thought he yanked to loosen his tie.

"Uh…tonight?"

Door open, Acadia looked at him. "Of course. Oh, I didn't tell you my mother is coming Friday. For Dad's funeral, you know."

"You okay with that?"

She smiled. "After thinking about what you said the other day, I'm the one who called and invited her. Thank you for that."

"You're welcome." He smiled, too, but for some reason nothing either had said had eased the strange sensation in his chest, as if he'd swallowed something wrong. He had the impulse to thump his breastbone.

"See you tonight," she said, and he found himself alone on the porch, the door having been firmly closed in his face.

The heat felt especially oppressive right now as he walked back. He glanced at Wayne and Betty's place, which had a desolate, too-long-empty look even though two weeks shouldn't have had that result. The sister apparently wasn't staying here. If she'd come by, David hadn't seen her. The lawn, which Wayne had always watered on a regular schedule, was already ragged and turning brown in spots. A few rose blossoms showed bright on his bushes, but most had dried to a crumpled brown, too. Wayne would have been deadheading, deep watering, fertilizing and pampering. David wished with sudden passion that Wayne was standing in the living room right now glaring at the Owen boy walking past, suspicious he might decide to do something like cut across the corner of his yard.

"Shit," David muttered, looking away from that blank front window.

He glanced back, but there was no sign Acadia was hovering in her own front window watching him go, either, not the way she would have when she was thirteen.

It came to him then that some of his discomfort came from his fear that he felt something for Acadia that wasn't reciprocated. This gut-deep *need,* this hunger just to see her, to feel the passing brush of her fingers on the back of his hand, to see her smile or hear her laugh, was out of his experience. He'd always known that sometime in his teenage years he'd screwed a lid down tight on his emotions. He hoped he was a compassionate man on the job and a good friend. He sure as hell enjoyed sex. But he'd never felt anything as wrenching as this.

It had to be a consequence of what Rob had done, he told himself again, frowning at the backwash of guilt and grief and misery Rob had so unknowingly sentenced his mother and brother to when he blew his brains out. No wonder all this had freed up every emotion David had buried for all these years.

He wanted to be convinced that was it. Because otherwise? Otherwise, he'd fallen in love for the first time in his life. With a woman who laughed about her teenage infatuation with him, who certainly seemed to like him and be glad of his companionship, who'd kissed him with enthusiasm, but who also didn't seem anywhere near as messed up as he was. As much as she could while also grieving for her father, Acadia, he feared, was enjoying David's interest in the spirit of it being a dream come true. The raw emotion she'd displayed all had to do with her father, her mother, her memories. Her pain.

Not him.

God. Had she noticed that since leaving Tucannon he'd turned into a cold-blooded bastard? He knew he wouldn't be an easy man to love.

She was burying her father on Saturday. How much longer would it take her to pack up his stuff? David believed she would stay for Rob's funeral, but then she'd have no reason not to get on a plane and fly back to California and a life she was probably missing.

"I need you," he'd said.

"Ditto" was the rejoinder a friend made, not the passionate cry of a woman in love.

He didn't have much longer to get a read on her. To say something, if he was going to.

His common sense said that a smart man would let her go, wait and see how he felt later. Maybe, if nothing changed, give her a call a month or so from now and say, *Hey, I'm going to be in San Francisco, can we have dinner?*

He'd always been a smart man. But, damn, his chest hurt.

CHAPTER FOURTEEN

DAVID WAS ODDLY quiet that evening. Acadia didn't mind the silences that often settled between them; some nights, she too liked to do nothing but sit, tip her head back and soak in the atmosphere. She savored more than David's presence. There was her father's, too. Acadia wasn't delusional enough to believe it was real; probably her sense that he wasn't far away had to do with subtle cues that triggered unpredictable memories. But those were okay, too—she was eager to grab at every remembrance of her father she could lay her hands on. Tucannon had made him live for her again, even though she'd come home to bury him.

"Have you noticed," she murmured, not looking at the brooding man sitting a few feet from her, "that Tucannon has its own smell?"

He stayed quiet for a minute. "Yeah. I hadn't thought about it, but I always roll down the car window when I get close."

"Mmm," Acadia said dreamily. "I can't even put my finger on what it is. The soil? But it's the quality of the air."

"You mean, the lack of gasoline fumes?" David suggested drily.

She laughed. "Okay, maybe."

He apparently brooded some more. She didn't push, only waited. "Will you miss it?" he asked eventually.

Acadia drew her knees up, wrapped her arms around them and sighed. "Yes."

"What did you and your mom talk about?"

"I asked her about their marriage. You were right. It wasn't so much Dad as having to live here. I was so happy, until that last summer I didn't guess how much she hated it here." She told him what Mom had said about not having finished college, about no good jobs, about Dad thinking she ought to be nothing but a housewife and mother. "Maybe in the end it wasn't Tucannon at all. It was the fact that he didn't try to understand until too late."

"I can see that," David said after a minute. "I was thinking today about my parents' marriage and my aunt and uncle's. No good reason, I guess, except I don't see Aunt Jackie and Uncle Warren very often. Every couple of years, maybe."

"And what were your conclusions?"

Once again some time passed before he spoke. Maybe he had to shape what he'd been thinking into a coherent explanation. "Mom and Dad were solid," he said at last. "Don't get me wrong. I don't think they argued any more than most couples do." He gave a half laugh. "Dad never spent nights on the sofa."

Acadia chuckled, sensing he was trying to add a light note to what he had to say.

"But they were focused outward. A lot of their attention was on Rob and me, I guess, but later so intensely on Rob, I wonder if they ever thought any more about, I don't know, their relationship or each other as individuals."

She said softly, "It could be that always happens when you have a gravely ill child."

"Maybe."

She waited, aware he wasn't done.

"Mom has a sharp tongue. She hurt Dad sometimes without even noticing."

Acadia could see his face well enough to know furrows

had formed on his brow. He was doing the same thing she'd been doing, it seemed—taking another look at his parents. Seeing through adult eyes rather than the eyes of a child.

"Aunt Jackie and Uncle Warren are different," he continued in that same low, meditative voice. "They watch out for each other. They have kids, too—you probably remember my cousins. Seemed like every summer they came for a few weeks."

His cousins had been Rob's age and older, so she hadn't gotten to know them well, but she nodded. Whether he noticed or not, she couldn't tell. He was remembering, set on making a point.

"They're careful with each other's feelings. I guess that's the best way to put it. Even now, with her sick, I see her watching out for him, not only him for her. Maybe that's not a good description…"

When he didn't finish, Acadia said, "No, it is. I know what you mean. I haven't seen it often, but I envy couples like that."

"There's still some spark there, too. He doesn't say much, but he looks at her sometimes like she's everything."

"She's All That."

"God." He laughed in surprise. "I saw that movie. Don't remember it, but I saw it. And yeah, that's what I mean."

Acadia bumped her chin on her knees. "They're lucky."

"Yeah." His voice had roughened. "They are that."

He was looking at her now. "'Cadia."

She shivered at the way he said her name.

"Come here." He held out a hand.

She blinked at his outstretched hand. He wanted *her* to cross the divide this time? Was there some symbolism in it?

If her heart hadn't been break-dancing, she'd have laughed at herself. He wanted to cuddle, was comfortable, thought she might as well move her butt as he moved his. And she was okay with that.

Without standing up, she scooted over close enough for his arm to wrap around her and bring her snugly up against him. Her hip pressed against his; when she in turn wrapped an arm around his waist, her head rested perfectly beneath his collarbone. She felt him nuzzle her hair.

"It's springy," he murmured.

"You just noticed?"

His chuckle rumbled beneath her ear. "Nobody could *not* notice your hair."

"It's a pain."

"It's beautiful."

She snorted.

"Come on." Humor threaded his voice. "Guys have to have told you that before."

"Call me a skeptic."

"Yeah, that does go with your personality." David sounded thoughtful.

She tried to straighten. He kept her firmly tucked against him. "What's that supposed to mean?" she demanded, indignant.

"You're a fearsome woman, Acadia Henderson. And yes, that's a good thing."

She smiled and rubbed her cheek against him, inhaling the scent that was David. "I can accept that."

"Good." She heard his smile. It was a while before he said, with a strange lack of intonation, "I'm not much like the boy I was at sixteen."

Huh? His point? She thought about it, and said tentatively, "I'm not much like my fourteen-year-old self, either."

"Yeah, I think maybe you are." There was something in his voice, but no more helpful in reading where he was going with this than his former no-emotion-at-all had been.

"I catch glimpses of that Acadia all the time. Me…" His shoulders moved, as if uneasily, and that loosened his arms enough so she was able to sit up and twist to look at him. "I got angry at my parents. I felt abandoned. Back when you knew me, I was unbelievably cocky. Thought I was king of the world. I could do anything. Change the world. Sometime since then, I quit wanting to. I got harder. Distanced myself from people."

"And yet you decided to be a prosecutor instead of going into, oh, corporate law or private practice where the bucks are."

"Maybe," he suggested, "it's my way of punishing people like my brother."

"Is it?" Acadia asked softly.

He was silent for a long time. This close, she could tell how turned inward his expression was. "I truly don't know," he said at last.

"I think," she said, "that you're trying to make the world a safer place. Isn't that important?"

"You're trying to see the best in me."

She kissed his cheek, loving the rasp of stubble. "And that's so un-Acadia-like. Fearsome women do *not* lightly ascribe undeserved goodness to anyone."

The darkness in his eyes cleared and his mouth relaxed into a grin. "You're right. What was I thinking?"

She kissed his jaw, right where a muscle flexed, then his neck. "What I believe is that there's more of the boy in you than you think. Let him out and he may surprise you."

"So there's two of us inhabiting this body?" Apparently she'd driven all humor out. "I'm kind of hoping that's not the case."

She cringed at her tactlessness. "You know I didn't mean…"

"Yeah. I know." David cupped her cheek. His hand was

so big her chin rested on it and his fingertips moved lightly on her temple. One smoothed her eyebrow. "I want to know you're seeing me as the man I am."

Her heart cramped at the intensity she saw on his lean, dark face. "I see you," she whispered.

"Good," he said hoarsely, and his mouth claimed hers.

SHE HADN'T GOTTEN what he was trying to say, and he couldn't blame her. It was probably idiotic of him to worry about whether she was acting on a teenage crush when she came into his arms. How could the two of them separate past and present? God knew, the past was all around them. His immediate reaction to her, the minute he saw her getting out of her car that day, probably had to do with his memories of the spitfire little girl who'd lived two doors down as well as the gawky, funny, fascinating almost-woman she'd been that last summer. If they'd encountered each other in Seattle or San Francisco, it would have been different, but here they were, on her daddy's front porch on a hot summer night like so many others they both remembered.

And his brother had killed her father. Yeah, on this same porch.

He couldn't forget that there was another funeral tomorrow, too.

No, there was no getting away from the past.

He felt so much desperation he tried to consume her. He couldn't summon any finesse, any tenderness.

I need you.

He was blind, deaf and dumb with the power of the emotions ripping through him. God, he hoped she'd meant it when she said, "Ditto."

Her arms came around him, hard, and the next thing he knew she was straining against him, sucking his tongue, biting at his mouth. When he momentarily tore his lips away so he could nip at her neck, she made a frantic little sound that spelled the end of his self-control.

She wanted him. Thank God, thank God.

David surged to his feet, bringing her with him. "Not here."

Acadia turned her head blindly, as if she'd forgotten where they were. "No. Oh, no. Inside."

"Yes." He all but dragged her in. The screen door slammed behind them. David pushed her up against the wall and went back to kissing her with all the aching need that had been driving him since he first set eyes on her ten days ago. He pressed his erection against her belly, squeezed a hand between their bodies to rub her full breast. Her hard nipple stabbed his sensitized palm in the most erotic contact he ever remembered having. And, damn, they were both still fully clothed.

He could have taken her right there, against the wall, or borne her down to the floor and begun stripping her. A remnant of civility had him growl, "Upstairs."

Her hips arched against him and he came close to losing the newfound scrap of resolve. But, "Yes," she whispered.

He felt primitive enough to carry her, but she started ahead of him, tugging him along with one hand in his. He stayed just far enough behind her to admire the sway of her lush ass. Mesmerized, he'd quit giving a damn for past, present, future. *Now* was what counted.

He'd never seen her bedroom. Not in all the years he'd known her. As violently turned-on as he was, he stopped in dismay at the sight of it. The whole damn room was… virginal, but it was the bed that made him groan. It was a twin, like his. Unlike his, it had a ruffly bed skirt and a white eyelet coverlet. It was pretty. And he was planning to have carnal sex on that bed?

In a small voice, Acadia said, "Mom was trying to make me be a girl."

"What?" He wrenched his attention from the bed.

She was studying the room with equal dismay. "I didn't think…"

"It's all right."

"Dad's bed is full-size, but…"

Repulsed, David said, "No."

"No," she echoed.

The mood was being lost. He wouldn't let it go. "I wasn't surprised by the twin bed," he told her. "Mine at Mom's house is, too."

"No." Acadia looked at him in astonishment. "You've never replaced it? Don't your feet stick out?"

"Feet?" he said ruefully. "Try shins on down. And no, I've never spent enough time there to bother." He paused. "Rob's old bedroom has a double bed."

"That's not a lot better for you, is it?"

"At least I can sleep crisscross. But…" Oh, hell. "I don't want to sleep in Rob's room."

"Ghosts."

"Something like that." He thought about his earlier uncomfortable sense that some restless part of Rob lingered. "Singular, anyway."

"I keep thinking my father…"

"Charlie, haunting you? Come on."

She relaxed. Even smiled a little. "Watching over me, maybe."

"There you go." He tugged her to his side. "Your bedroom is girlie. I never would have expected that."

"I hated it," she said gloomily. "Mom insisted on redoing it when I was, oh, eleven, I think. I had a hodgepodge of whatever on the walls. A poster of some girl band. Sports stuff. A really cool poster of an African lion that Mom said had a cold stare. She shuddered every time she looked at it."

He stifled a laugh. "You and your mom must have something in common."

"Weirdly enough, we're both nurses. She went back to school after the divorce. She's a floor nurse at Group Health, the kind that wakes you up the minute you finally drop off to sleep so she can take your temp. Me, I like a little more excitement."

"You are exciting, 'Cadia." His voice came out as a rough purr, not intentional, but he'd abruptly lost interest in reminiscences. He turned her to face him. "What say we mess up that bed?"

She wriggled against him. "If you fall off, I take no responsibility."

"Oh, I think I can stay on top of you, sweetheart."

That's all it took—the vivid picture of her splayed beneath him—and he had to kiss her.

Their clothes flew. She had the prettiest breasts he'd ever seen, and no, they weren't freckled. The freckles sort of petered out as they reached her bra line, and the ripe flesh beneath was pure cream. Her belly and hips were the same delicious shade, and the triangle of hair that covered her mound was as fiery and springy as the hair on her head.

He had to stop just to look at her, long legged, long waisted, with slim hips. Skinny Acadia, all grown up. "Beautiful," he muttered thickly.

She'd been appraising him, too. "Lovely," she agreed, and brushed her hand lightly over the dark hair on his chest.

David groaned, lifted her and laid her on her bed. Sprawled there, not trying to hide anything, she looked wanton, a courtesan from a nineteenth-century oil painting of a nude. It was that wild hair, he realized, that somehow wasn't modern. He planted a knee on the bed and bent over her, his mouth closing without warning over her breast. Acadia moaned, arched and threaded her fingers in his hair.

He suckled, kissed, explored, but not for as long as he'd have liked. Next time, he told himself. Right now, he had to have her. He felt clumsy, hasty and desperate.

"Forgot to grab the condom." He rolled, and half fell from the bed.

Acadia grabbed his arm but giggled. "Told you it would happen."

Shit. He saw that he'd shed his shorts by the door.

"I'm on the pill," she said.

He rolled back toward her. "You're okay with me not using a condom?"

"Yes." Her eyes searched his. "If you are. I mean, I want…*you*."

He totally lost it. In one move, he was on top of her, between her legs, thrusting deep. Her hips surged up to meet him. She felt unbelievable—tight, slick, hot. He braced his weight on one elbow, kissed her voraciously and used his free hand to grip her thigh and drag it up around his waist. Her knees squeezed his waist and her hands dug into his back and butt.

She wasn't a quiet lover. She made all kinds of sounds, and every one arrowed straight to his groin. When she came, she said his name as if he'd taken her by surprise. And then she said it again, with such exultation he went off like one of those Fourth of July fireworks, his entire body bucking as pleasure seized him.

He sagged onto her, mumbled, "I'll crush you" and tried to lever off her instead. But her arms closed around him almost fiercely and she said, "Not yet."

No. Didn't want to leave Acadia's body. His brain was ticking slowly; he was all sensation. Incredible satisfaction. Such utter slackening of any motor control, he might be drooling for all he knew. Her hair tickled his face, a curl lying over his eyelid. Didn't want to open his eyes anyway. Didn't want to move. This was what happiness felt like. Maybe he could stay here forever.

But the ability to reason returned, if slowly, and he thought about the fact that he probably outweighed Acadia by a good sixty, seventy pounds, at least. Reluctantly, he heaved himself to one side, taking care not to shoot over the side of the narrow bed and end up in an ignominious heap on the floor.

He opened an eye cautiously and saw nothing but copper hair. "You in there?"

"Um…" She still sounded insensible. "I think so," she finally decided, and lifted a hand to brush her hair back from her face. "Wow."

"No shit. Or should I say holy shit?"

"That was…really good." Her voice was still dopey, but amazement colored it.

"Good," he agreed, closing his eye even though he liked looking at her. Right now, all he wanted was to hold her close, breathe her scent in and *feel*. He wondered if anyone at home would notice if he didn't appear until morning.

Yeah. Of course they would. He didn't want to embarrass Acadia. No, he couldn't stay the night.

A grin tugged at his mouth. Nope. No sleepovers until they had a bigger bed to share.

Of course, there was no saying he had to leave *now*. He kind of thought if he lay here for a while, snuggling her, that he might regain enough muscle control to do more than snuggle. Say, to start all over again and go nice and slow, now that he'd taken the edge off his hunger, so to speak. Acadia's fingers were idly exploring his chest and she seemed to like having her head tucked so neatly on his shoulder, which made him suspect she might not be averse to round two.

Her hand stroked down over his belly and his body stirred.

Oh, yeah.

WEDNESDAY MORNING, Reeve opened up at the station, a sick feeling in his stomach as he instructed the guy he was leaving in charge, the way he'd heard Walt do a million times.

He did not want to go to Walt's funeral. Had to go. Hoped like hell Mrs. Stenten wasn't one of those crazies who believed in open-casket goodbyes. He'd seen Walt's dead face once, and he'd never forget it. He thought he might puke if the lid of that casket stood open. She wouldn't do that, would she? *Please, no.*

At home again, he shaved, dressed in his Sunday church-going suit and stared at himself in the full-length mirror on the back of the door.

He looked weird. Unnatural. He hadn't gone to church in a while, and the suit didn't fit so great anymore. Even the white dress shirt beneath it didn't. His wrists stuck out and too much of his black socks showed. Man, he was so bony. His cheeks were gaunt. A stubborn cowlick on the crown of his head refused to be subdued by gel and, per usual, stuck up. Oil stayed beneath his nails, no matter what he did. There was nothing dignified about his person.

The misery in his belly intensified. He looked at the toilet. He was this close to puking.

"Reeve?" His mother's voice. She and Dad were going with him to the funeral, of course. In one way he was grateful, and in another way he'd rather have been by himself. It was harder to hide in the crowd when there were three of you.

"Coming," he called, took a last, desperate look at himself and went.

In the family car, he sat in the back, staring at his father's hair and realizing how bare that spot on top was getting. Did that mean he'd get bald, too?

Walt's hair had been real thin on top, too. Reeve had wondered if that's why he'd kept it near-shaved. But after seeing the photo of him in his Marine Corps uniform, Reeve thought probably that's why he'd kept wearing his hair the same way—because that's who he was. A marine.

A hero.

Dad found a parking spot only a block away. In the church, Reeve slid into the first pew he came to. His parents stopped in surprise.

"For God's sake, Reeve." Dad's face was turning red.

"Shouldn't we go up in front?" his mother asked.

"You can if you want."

"Don't be ridiculous," his father snapped, and gestured for Mom to slide in. Then the three of them sat there, all staring straight ahead and not talking. Mom did reach out once and pat Reeve, which told him she sort of understood.

He didn't look at any of the people coming in until, out of the corner of his eye, he saw a face that made his heart slam. Rob…no, not Rob, of course, but his brother. The one who was some kind of high-powered attorney and who had been on television. Three other people were with him— two older women, one of whom had to be his mother, and another guy, tall, skinny and graying.

Reeve kept sneaking peeks. That face made his stomach churn worse. He flickered in and out—here in the church, and back in his garage seeing the black silhouette that had materialized into crazy Rob Owen, armed like some bad-ass commando.

Shit. His pulse was revving, his palms sweating, more

sweat burning his eyes. He wanted in the worst way to climb over his parents' legs and run out of the church.

Why don't you piss your pants? Go hide in the bathroom?

Suddenly David Owen's head turned and his eyes met Reeve's. They stared at each other for a long moment. Finally David nodded, a grave dip that said, *I know I make you uncomfortable. I'm sorry.*

Or, Reeve thought, *I'm going out of my freaking mind.*

But something in him settled. For one thing, David's eyes were gray, not brown like his brother's. They were sane, too.

And he knew something else: David didn't want to be here any more than he did. Had David even known Walt?

He also had a flash of envy. David Owen looked really sharp. *His* suit fit as though it had been made for him. As big as he was, maybe it had been. His tie was narrower than Reeve's or his father's, somehow classier; gold glinted at his wrists and Reeve realized he wore cuff links. Reeve had never seen anyone in cuff links before. Even his dress shoes had the subtle gleam of better quality leather than Reeve had seen. He guessed David really was the fancy attorney people said he was. He had to have lots of money.

Knowing his cheeks were flushed, Reeve turned his head straight ahead again and thought about the brief glimpse into the other man's eyes. He'd keep his cool no matter what happened; Reeve could tell. Word was, David Owen had been the best athlete Tucannon and maybe Eastern Washington had ever seen. Supposedly he'd turned down the chance to go pro. Who would do that?

Walt would've. That's who. He'd known what he wanted to do as soon as he graduated from high school. Reeve bet he'd always wanted to be a marine. Maybe Walt didn't say much, but he was sure of himself, no matter what happened.

Blind to the people filling the church in front of him, Reeve saw again the young Walt, the guy in that crisp parade uniform. He saw the pride in his eyes, the way he held his shoulders square and his head high.

And Reeve wondered—which had come first? Was that confidence always there? Or had earning the right to wear the uniform given it to him?

The pastor had begun to speak. Reeve wasn't listening. Walt hadn't been much of a churchgoer, so the guy in the collar couldn't know him very well. And Reeve was working out the idea in his head.

Maybe a man wasn't born to be a hero. Maybe he could make himself into one.

CHAPTER FIFTEEN

JOYCE REFUSED TO let Jackie help her with dinner.

"This morning was too much for you," she scolded. "I should have realized the heat would get to you."

Her sister sank onto one of the kitchen chairs. She fanned herself with a magazine, her face plum-red. They'd all gone upstairs and changed out of their finery earlier, but Jackie had kept on the wig she'd donned for the funeral. Not that the heavy turban would have been any cooler. "Of course it gets to me! I never could understand how you bear it. Why, at home there's always cool air off the ocean."

"And so much rain you have to fight to keep the moss from growing on your roof and between your toes."

It was an old argument. They grinned at each other, but Joyce was pretending, because she was genuinely worried. Jackie insisted on making light of her health, but Joyce could tell Warren was less confident than he let anyone know, too. Poor Jackie had shrunk, Joyce would swear. And it didn't seem as if she was sweating the way she ought to be, which might be why her color was so awful.

"That wig can't be helping!" Joyce burst out.

"No." Her sister sighed. "I don't know what I think I'm hiding. It's not as if I have anything to be vain about." She tugged off the wig and set it on the table, where it curled like some dead animal.

Jackie still had some hair, but it was thin, almost entirely gray, and wispy, allowing the pink of her scalp to shine through.

"Well," Joyce said, after inspecting her, "we wouldn't want you going outside here like that. You'd burn your head to a crisp."

Jackie almost choked, she laughed so hard.

Pleased, Joyce went about her dinner preparations. She had suggested David invite Acadia tonight and he'd done so, returning to report that she'd be glad to eat with them. Then he'd disappeared down into the basement, where he seemed to be spending his afternoons. She'd worry about him, too, if it weren't for his evening visits to Acadia. Joyce had heard him come in last night at nearly one in the morning. They couldn't have been sitting on the porch talking all that time. Maybe she ought to be more prudish than she was, but far be it from her to disapprove! She and Pete had had some quite enjoyable premarital sex, after all. She hadn't thought about it in a long time, but last night, waking to hear the stair squeak as David tried to make it to his room quietly, she had remembered sneaking in and out of *her* bedroom window, Pete there to catch her. She hoped David and Acadia were having anywhere near as good a time as she and Pete had had. She missed him every day, but it had gotten so the missing was what an ox in the yoke might feel if its teammate had stumbled and gone down. This kind of missing—well, it was different, more poignant.

Oh, she did hope it was possible for Pete to have taken Robbie into his arms, and for both of them to be waiting for her.

"Have you thought about what you're going to do?" Jackie said to her back.

Joyce tried not to visibly stiffen. She kept chopping carrots for the salad. "What do you mean?"

"Surely you don't plan to stay here, in this house."

"I don't know why not." Except, of course, she knew exactly why not. She just wasn't ready to make any decisions. That was always the advice, wasn't it? After a death or a divorce, don't make big changes too quickly.

"I saw the way some people looked at you today," Jackie said.

"Mostly ones I never liked anyway." The knife went still in Joyce's hand and stayed suspended over the cutting board. Why, that was true! More people were being decent to her than she'd expected. Anne Stenten had received Joyce's condolences graciously, as had Betty's sister and Earl's son. It seemed with each funeral more people came up to her to let her know they understood she was hurting, too. It hadn't occurred to her before, but…well, she'd certainly never liked Marvella Hatcher or that nasty Marge Perkins—even long ago, Joyce and Pete had gone out of their way to choose a table at the Bluebird Café so that Marge wouldn't be their waitress. Although once a friend of sorts, Marie Merfeld always had been small-minded, and who cared what someone like that silly young police officer who'd come out to the house the one night thought?

I didn't like his father, either, Joyce decided with a kind of triumph. *Why* did *I ever hide?*

She could hardly remember.

"I suppose David asked you to talk to me," she said, and resumed chopping.

The silence behind her was answer enough. Jackie said, "I was hoping I could persuade you to move to Yachats. I'd love to have you close."

Answer enough, indeed.

"Oh, I couldn't take the climate." She frowned. Could it be that Jackie was asking for her own sake rather than for Joyce's? She turned. "I could come for a nice long visit, though, if you need me."

"If you mean because of this business with the chemotherapy, nonsense! Warren takes good care of me. You know that. It's just that I miss the kids, and you'd be as near to David as you are now. Wouldn't you like a new start?"

Joyce's reaction was instinctive, and powerful. *No.* She tried to imagine selling this house, where she'd come as a new bride, where she'd loved her husband, raised her sons, and knew she couldn't do it despite everything that had gone sour. Rob and Pete both would be in the cemetery, right here in town, and that was where she had every intention of being buried herself.

"I'm not ready to make any decisions," she lied. "Anyway, this would be a terrible time to try to sell the house, with two more on the street already for sale." The sign had been up in front of Charlie's house for a few days, and this afternoon Joyce had seen Betty's sister and a strange man touring the Tindalls' house. He'd given her a business card at the end and shaken her hand. Joyce knew a real estate agent when she saw one.

"That's fair enough," Jackie said grudgingly. "I wonder where Warren took himself off to?"

"Maybe he decided to lie down."

"He never naps. Come to think of it, I heard him talking to David earlier. He might have gone downstairs."

Joyce abruptly became busy peeling cucumber. She didn't want to think about downstairs, or why David had needed a whole Dumpster. He'd mentioned at breakfast this morning that the garbage company would be picking it up tomorrow.

"I'll go see what's up," Jackie announced, and heaved herself to her feet.

"Your wig…"

"Might as well scare my nephew out of half a year's growth," she said cheerfully, and disappeared.

Joyce didn't see any of her family again until she called them for dinner. She'd heard them all head upstairs a while ago. At least two of them took showers. When the doorbell rang, feet thundered on the stairs, and for the first time all day Joyce smiled. Oh, did that sound take her back! Growing boys were seldom quiet, and especially when they wanted most to be. She used to marvel at David's grace on the basketball court compared to the way he thudded through the house.

Acadia looked so pretty tonight, and young, with her hair caught in a ponytail at the crown of her head. She wore capris and a bright yellow T-shirt. She laughed when Joyce told her with that hairstyle she ought to have on a poodle skirt.

At the dinner table, she admitted to being glad she had skipped Walt's funeral.

"He may have pumped gas for us, but that's not the kind of thing you pay attention to when you're a kid."

"I didn't know him or his wife well, either," Joyce said. "But I felt obligated."

No one responded. Of course she had to go to each and every one of the funerals to say, *I'm sorry.*

They'd progressed to coffee and pie when David looked at her, expression serious. "Mom, I showed Aunt Jackie and Uncle Warren the basement today."

Joyce took a sip of coffee.

"Acadia saw it the other day, too."

Well. She didn't know how she felt about that. Joyce frowned. Perhaps it was all right, if Acadia was to be her daughter-in-law.

"I want your permission to have Alan come take some pictures of it."

She finally looked at her son. "What?"

He repeated himself.

Bewildered, she asked, "Why?"

"Because I think what Rob did down there was extraordinary. I think the world needs to see it."

"You want people to see…? I don't understand," she said tremulously.

"Have you never looked down there?"

It shamed her to have to make the admission, but she held her head high and said, "Not in many years. That's how Robbie wanted it."

"Well, then, you need to take a look." He was frowning, but not exactly at her. "You must have known he was buying paint. Or you bought it for him."

"Both," Joyce said in a small voice.

He talked then about how Robbie had painted walls, ceilings, canvases, parts of the floor. He'd asked her to buy drawing paper, too, that thick kind, and she had. Apparently he had left hundreds of drawings, some crumpled, many incomplete, but others that all but crawled from the paper.

"They're not comfortable to look at," David warned, "but he left some remarkable insight into the way he saw the world. It's a chance to offer a window into his kind of mental illness. But I won't do anything without your permission."

Her heart fluttered, but finally she said, "I suppose I should see all this before I decide."

"Weren't you curious?" Jackie asked, looking at her strangely.

Curious? Had she been? She'd regained some sense of pride these past days, but right at that moment what she was most conscious of was the shame that had sunk into the very marrow of her bones.

"No," she said. "It was easier to pretend if…" She couldn't finish. She could not.

Acadia touched her hand. "I understand."

It seemed to Joyce as if Acadia's stare accused David of bullying. Which wasn't fair, of course, she knew wearily; she was a coward and deserved his disappointment.

But then anger flickered inside her, and she stared at him. "Weren't *you* ever curious?"

His mouth twisted. "Touché. No. I didn't want to know. I didn't want him to be my problem. I was a shitty brother and son. You don't have to tell me."

"No. Oh, no." She held out a hand across the table. "Robbie *wasn't* your problem. Your father and I so desperately wanted you to have a normal life. It gave us so much pleasure, knowing you were free to spread your wings. The last thing we'd ever have wanted was for you to be trapped, too."

His big hand closed hard on hers. For a moment, it seemed they were alone. "I didn't know," her Davey said. "I wish I had."

Her smile shook. "But if you had," she said simply, "you'd have felt responsible and that wouldn't have been right."

His jaw muscles spasmed. "God, Mom…" He seemed to shudder.

The next instant, Acadia hugged him. Despite the tears in Joyce's eyes, she also smiled again. Of all the little girls in Tucannon, who would have thought Acadia Henderson would grow up to be a nurturer? No one, Joyce would venture to guess. But then, she had become a nurse, and it was easy to imagine her standing fiercely for her patients. What doctor would dare to give *her* trouble?

"Goodness," Joyce said, surveying the table, "no one is finishing their pie. Please, eat."

Jackie and Warren labored to produce bland conversation thereafter, and of course Acadia joined them even as David and Joyce remained rather quiet. After dinner,

Acadia asked if she could help clear the table. When Joyce said, "Don't be silly, you're a guest," she excused herself.

"You know Mom is coming Friday?"

"Yes, I'm so looking forward to seeing her," Joyce said. "I wish the circumstances were different, of course…"

"She asked about you, too. But, well, I'm trying to make more progress on the house before she gets here. Before…"

Her father's funeral.

"Of course," Joyce said hastily.

Acadia said good-night and David rose with her. "I'll walk you home."

She didn't look surprised. Why would she? They'd been spending every evening together. Joyce wondered if he'd be sneaking in at 1:00 a.m. tonight, too.

THE SKY WAS a lovely shade of lilac streaked with pale yellow and orange as Acadia and David walked home. It wasn't quite twilight, but already a sliver of moon had risen, and above it a startlingly bright star. No, not a star. A planet, surely.

Acadia realized she'd spoken aloud when David said, "Venus, maybe. Wouldn't Jupiter be fainter?"

"I have no idea. Once I realized astronomy was all mathematics, I lost interest."

He laughed. His hand sought hers, and she loved the warmth and security of walking this way.

As a couple.

The thought stirred the queasiness inside that she'd felt ever since she awakened this morning. Probably she was being dumb, but…

"I've been thinking all day about last night," she began hesitantly.

He stopped her at the foot of her porch steps. "Me, too," he murmured, voice deep, rough.

"It was wonderful, but…" Oh, she hated to be so confused. "Do you feel, well, at all guilty?"

David's fingers bit into her. His whole body had gone rigid. "Do I feel guilty because in the middle of all this tragedy and grief we had a damn good time in bed last night?"

Anger flared. A damn good time in bed? That's all it was to him? Wow, that put her in her place.

She lifted her chin. "That's what I'm asking."

He growled an obscenity, and his hands dropped from her. "What do you think? Of course I do, goddamn it!"

Her heart thudded heavily in her breast. This *hurt*. She hadn't wanted him to agree. "I'm not saying…"

"That it wasn't fun?"

His disdain stung more. It pissed her off, too.

"That there's anything wrong with finding happiness in the middle of tragedy. That's…human nature."

"But you don't like knowing you didn't give your father a thought last night. Is that it?"

His tone drove her back a step. "Maybe."

"Then call it a mistake," he suggested, and now his voice was devoid of any expression at all. "Go don your sackcloth and ashes."

"What? You're mad because I'm not ripping your clothes off?"

"I'm mad because…" Apparently taken aback to find himself shouting, he clamped his teeth shut. "Forget it. Just forget it, Acadia." He backed away. "See ya."

He loped away so fast she never had the chance to stop him. She wasn't sure he would have stopped even if she'd begged him and said, *Please, please tell me it wasn't really meaningless sex. I need to know because I'm in love with you.*

Miserably watching until she lost sight of him beyond the Tindalls' house, Acadia thought, *I hurt his feelings, too.* Of course she had. There had to have been a better way to ask for reassurance. To say, *Is it wrong to be so happy when I'm also in mourning?*

Feeling ten years older than she had fifteen minutes ago, Acadia plodded up the steps. So much for feeling happy. She'd taken care of that, hadn't she?

DAVID ALMOST WENT back. He'd been such an asshole. He didn't even know why. No, who was he kidding? Of course he knew. *He* felt guilty. It had been eating at him the whole damn day, though he hadn't let himself acknowledge it. He'd stood at yet another graveside, his gaze fixed on a shining, forest-green casket, and seen Acadia naked, arms held out for him. It had been like a double exposure, no longer possible with digital photography but something his mind apparently accomplished, no problem. Death and sex. Just as he'd turned his head, recognized Reeve Hadfield, looked into the boy's eyes and seen his agony, while still being able to cling to a kernel of happiness that glowed warm and comforting.

He couldn't go in the house yet. He walked around the yard, head tipped back, eyes on the night sky, and made himself breathe deeply. *I can fix this.* Tomorrow morning, first thing. Acadia had been able to make love with him despite what his brother had done. She'd been able to comfort his mother, publicly forgive Rob. She would understand that his emotions felt raw right now, even though he didn't.

On impulse he lay down in the middle of the backyard, arms flung wide. When was the last time he'd felt the grass tickle the back of his neck?

Had he ever been such a goddamned mess before?

He laughed, a harsh, unpleasant sound.

Maybe he'd been a goddamned mess for near twenty years, and never let himself notice. No, he thought, not twenty years; sixteen. Since the summer Acadia had been home. He'd still been…open then. Able to feel. He'd had her to talk to. After that, there'd never been anyone, not the same way. How could there be? A couple of his best friends knew his brother was schizophrenic. But he hadn't been able to say to either, *My parents love him more than me.* He hadn't wanted to tell them how much Rob suffered or how self-centered he, David, had been, putting his anger at how his brother's illness had impacted his life ahead of the compassion he should have felt.

The stars were coming out now. The light in his mother's bedroom window, too, and then the one in the guest room that had once been Rob's.

The love that had shone in Acadia's face back then, the faith in him, would have made him a better man, if he hadn't lost it.

So, what? he asked himself. *You think now she should take up where she left off? Believe in you with all the purity of an innocent girl's first love?* Not allow herself a moment of bitterness or anguish because Saturday morning, it would be her father's coffin being lowered into the dry, volcanic soil of the town he'd never left?

He said a foul word, glad he was utterly alone, and sat up.

His hometown, he was discovering, was serving as a mirror, and he didn't much like the reflection he saw in it.

He made himself stand up and walk around to the front of the house. Without any conscious volition, his feet took him twenty feet down the sidewalk, but Acadia's house was now dark. She probably still had a light on upstairs; he couldn't imagine she'd be ready for bed this early, but a dark facade did not welcome visitors.

Especially one who'd lashed out so viciously at her twenty minutes ago. He heard again the whispery hesitation with which she'd asked, "Do you feel at all guilty?"

Of course, what she'd really been saying was, *I feel guilty. Help me come to terms with it.*

He took a last look at her dark windows. *Yup. I am a worthless piece of scum.*

New knowledge of himself, perfect to soothe him to sleep. Adding to his corrosive self-doubt. *Do I deserve Acadia Henderson, compassionate in a way I'm not sure I've ever been? How could she really* want *me?*

His mood black, he let himself in his house and made his way as silently as he could up to his bedroom, a childish bedroom that was such an ill fit to the man he'd become.

"I CAN bring the drawings up here for you to look at if you don't want to go downstairs."

"No." David's mother closed the dishwasher and faced him, holding herself straight. "I need to see."

He thought she did, too, or he would have tried to deflect her.

"Where's Aunt Jackie?" he asked.

"Lying down." Mom's worry showed. "She's not feeling well today."

He'd thought at breakfast she looked like crap. Warren had set out to do the shopping, for which David was grateful. No one would recognize him. Jackie hadn't suggested accompanying him.

His thoughts took a sharp right turn. Maybe he could try calling Acadia again quickly while Mom nerved herself for the plunge into Rob's personal hell....

David blinked and realized Mom had passed him and started down the hall. With his longer strides, he caught up with her by the time she opened the door to the basement.

"Careful on the steps," he warned.

She gave him a scathing look over her shoulder. "I've lived in this house for thirty-seven years, you know."

He didn't say, *Thirty-seven years ago, you were a young woman.* Truth was, Mom still wasn't an old one. She just looked like she was.

Wishing he'd thought to suggest they enter from the backyard instead of going down the steep, crude, lumber staircase from the house, he stuck close enough to grab her if she faltered. He could tell the minute she really let herself look around. She was a couple of steps from the bottom when she stopped dead.

"Oh, dear Lord," she whispered.

The impact had lessened on him, but he understood her shock. Being down here was like being shrunk inside a kaleidoscope. Garish colors and dizzying images seemingly spun around you. The difference was, kaleidoscopes usually formed random, bright, beautiful images, not scenes depicting the hell only a crazy man would have been able to envision.

David looked around again, as if for the first time. It *was* dizzying; talk about double exposure. Having pictures superimposed over others was a challenge to the eyes. That face…did it peer from behind the smoldering remnants of a burned-out house, or was it part of the picture that lay beneath? Over there, the black creature seemed to be crawling out of the stomach of a towering, God-like figure with blazing red eyes. The whole thing was surreal beyond belief.

Mom seemed to sag. Clutching the railing, she went down the last steps, then sank onto one. "I had no idea."

David passed her, then squatted in front of her. "Who could have?"

"It's like…like the Sistine Chapel, except…"

A devil's disciple had painted it.

No, David thought, not fair; the painter hadn't worshipped the devil, he'd feared him. He'd lived in constant, bowel-loosening terror of the evil that taunted and haunted him.

"Did he never have peace?" David asked huskily.

"I think…when he was on his medication." His mother continued to gaze around, lingering on one detail after another. "I could never understand why he'd start refusing it. But now…now I think I do."

"Yeah." Sickening as it was to understand, David did, too. Rob had been an artist. His vision was horrifying, but he had needed it in all its clarity and shocking colors. Mind-dulling peace must have been as unbearable in another way as was his illness at full throttle.

"I thought," David heard himself saying in an odd voice, "that I'd find something down here to tell us why he went off the deep end like that. Some last writing. I don't know, a confession."

For the first time since she started down the stairs, Mom looked at him. "But you didn't."

"Nothing."

"I think…" She swallowed. "I think it happened gradually. It wasn't until the last few years that I was frightened of him at all. Two weeks before was when I knew I couldn't sleep if he was in the house. His pictures…" Her head turned again. Her voice had dropped, become a shattered whisper. "The ones on top are the ugliest of all."

"Yeah. They are."

She nodded, squared her shoulders. "Yes. Please do call Alan. Let him take his pictures and publish them anywhere he can find. And then…" Her voice broke. "And then do we paint over all of this? Or do we preserve it? Oh, dear God."

David knew a prayer when he heard one.

He rocked forward and drew her too-frail body into his arms. "I'm so sorry, Mom. So sorry."

Her arms closed around him and she cried. Quietly, but her tears wet his shirt. When she was done, she straightened. "I love you, Davey. You may not believe that, but I always did."

Oh, damn. His own cheeks were wet. "I knew that, Mom. Deep inside. I let myself be a fool, that's all."

She actually, sort of, laughed. "We're all capable of that, aren't we?"

He kept his arm around her as they climbed those rough wood stairs to the sanity of the home above. He thought they both breathed a sigh of relief when he shut the door behind them.

"I was thinking I'd deadhead Wayne's roses," he said. "Give 'em a soaking, too. It would be a shame if they died before a new owner takes possession. You want to help?"

He braced himself for, *Do you know how hot it is out there?*

His mother looked at him in astonishment, all right, but also pleasure. "Why...what a lovely idea. Of course I would."

She trotted off to get her gardening gloves while he grabbed his. Waiting for her at the back door, David had the unpleasant notion that his childhood home was an allegory. For heaven and hell? Hell, of course, being the secret depths beneath the outwardly normal. Or was the story really Cain and Abel's? Had Rob hated his brother? Would he have killed him, if David had been here when his rage became uncontainable?

David grunted.

No. Damn it, he didn't believe it. He'd never seen hate festering in his brother's eyes. He had to have been jealous. How could he not be? But corroding hatred? David wouldn't believe it.

And who, he asked himself, was Cain, and who Abel? Sure, he'd been the Good Son—and also the one who abandoned his family, for all intents and purposes.

Maybe not so good.

He couldn't go back. Couldn't undo his part in the tragedy. Could only strive for redemption by being the son his mother now needed.

Acadia, I need you.

But she hadn't answered earlier, when he called. He'd left a message, but his phone, in one of the pockets of his cargo shorts, hadn't rung.

'Cadia, forgive me.

He bumped his forehead against the doorframe.

Mom, forgive me. Rob, forgive me.

Then he dragged the soaker hose out of Mom's garage, found two pairs of pruning shears and set about making things right, as well as he could.

CHAPTER SIXTEEN

AFTER A SLOW start to the morning, Acadia concentrated on the kitchen, unearthing the most ridiculous things from the depths of cupboards. A rice cooker? A *hot dog cooker?* If her father ate hot dogs, she felt reasonably sure he'd dropped them in boiling water in a pan on the stove. Confirming her belief, both small appliances were in their original boxes, unopened. Somebody must have thought these to be reasonable gifts for him. Shaking her head, she put both in the carton intended for a thrift store.

She discovered he had owned a set of now very tarnished sterling silverware. A wedding present? Mom probably hadn't wanted it. Keep—until she figured out how to sell the set.

She left the basics in cupboards and drawers—after all, she'd be here at least another week, and with Mom here over the weekend she would need two of everything. Otherwise, she made swift decisions: trash, keep, thrift store. There wasn't much in the "keep" box, not from the kitchen.

The sound of voices drifted through the open back door and she peered out the window above the sink, able to see over the fence. Was that *Joyce* in Wayne and Betty's yard? And David?

Yes, Acadia confirmed, it was. They seemed to be gardening.

"Well, crap," she said aloud. Damn it, every time David did or said something lousy, he'd turn around and then do something so kind or thoughtful it set her emotions head over tails.

It wasn't as if she'd planned to keep sulking for long. She understood why he'd reacted the way he had. She could probably blame herself for being the trigger. But she hadn't felt able to deal with him yet today, although she'd listened twice now to his phone message.

"I was a shit, 'Cadia. You don't have to tell me. Are you going to give me a chance to apologize?" Long pause. "Please call." Voice rougher.

Mom would be here tomorrow night. This evening would be her last chance until next week—and then their days would be running out—to sit on the porch with David and talk.

Don't you mean, to make love?

Maybe. She didn't know. Yes, she wanted him. She thought she always had. But she knew increasingly how hard it was going to be to say goodbye, and that scared her.

With a sigh, she closed the top of the closest carton, went upstairs to swipe on some suntan lotion and grabbed Dad's way-too-big work gloves kept by the back door. Then she went outside and through the gate into the Tindalls' yard, the sun beating down on her.

"Hey," she called. "Need a hand?"

David turned, as if in slow motion. "Acadia?"

Joyce beamed. "We'd love to have help. Poor Wayne's roses are in sad shape."

They were. Acadia had noticed, without it occurring to her to do anything for them.

"Oh, you're watering," she said. "I should have thought of it. I've soaked Dad's few roses."

"It was David's idea." Joyce shone with pride in her son. "Wayne babied his roses. Did you know he won ribbons every year at the fair?"

"I had no idea," David said hoarsely. His eyes, intense and electric, had stayed on Acadia's face.

"We constantly battered his bushes," she said ruefully. "Threw our bikes down on the ones in front, sliced blooms off with a Wiffle ball, broke off new shoots cutting through his yard… No wonder he finally put up the fence here in back. It wasn't unfriendly, it was self-defense."

"Yeah, that's what I was thinking," David admitted, sounding a little more normal. "I guess, if he's anywhere he can know, I didn't want him to have to watch his roses die. Once there are new owners, well, the yard will be their problem. But we can keep them going through the heat of August."

"I'm happy to help," Acadia said. "Should I go get Dad's soaker hose and lay it out in another bed?"

David set down the hand clippers he'd been using and started toward her. "Yeah, if you have one, that would be great. Mom only has the one. Let me help."

Neither spoke as they circled her house to the garage. He heaved up the rolling door and looked around the shadowy interior. "I was afraid this would be full of junk, but it's not too bad. Are you going to sell his car?"

"Yes." Acadia sighed. "I finally listed it in the *Walla Walla U-B* this week. The ad will be coming out Sunday. I should have done it sooner."

"There was a lot to do." His voice was gentle. His eyes, she realized, still held that intensity. "'Cadia…"

"You don't have to tell me you're sorry. It was a stupid thing for me to say. Of course you feel guilty. Of course I do." She looked around, not really seeing her dad's neatly stowed tools but not wanting to meet those unnerving gray eyes, either. "I should probably apologize, not the other way around."

"I'm the one who went off the deep end." He wrenched

off a glove and scrubbed a hand over his head, making sweat-damp hair stand on end. "Part of me thinks I ought to be wallowing in grief and misery 24/7. What am I doing instead? Rejoicing, because you're back in my life. So, yeah, guilt's part of the picture." His emotions were suddenly there on his face, raw, for her to see.

She caught her breath.

"That doesn't mean," he went on, "that I really believe the only way to mourn someone is to shut out anything that makes us feel good. I remember when my grandmother died. I was, I don't know, thirteen or fourteen. Mom took me when we went to Portland for the funeral and to help clear out her house. She and Jackie did a lot of laughing. It was part of remembering Nanna. The first time I saw them really cracking up, I was shocked, but, knowing her, I'm pretty sure she'd have been laughing with them." He frowned. "Not that what happened here is the same," he added with sudden awkwardness. "She was an old lady…"

"I know what you mean," Acadia said, cutting him off. "And you're right. It *was* a stupid thing for me to say. Of course I feel sad. But I've been remembering stuff I thought I'd long since forgotten, too. In a weird way, it's been… good. You know?"

"Yeah." David looked at her but didn't take a step closer. "Me, too. Mom and I are, uh, saying things that we should have said a long time ago. Like you say, it's been good."

She nodded. The awkwardness had infected his stance, too. She couldn't bear to let it continue.

"Um, here's the hose," she said, turning away. Dad had kept it coiled, hung neatly in its place. She reached for it, but David was there to heft the heavy roll over his shoulder. "I'll grab some clippers," she said hurriedly.

"You're sure you don't have too much to do to take time to help out?"

Oh, boy. Did that mean he'd rather she not work outside with him and his mom?

"Up to you." Acadia tried to sound easy, unruffled. Uncaring.

"Acadia…" His voice came out so gruff he cleared his throat. "I want you with me all the time."

Her feet stopped moving. She probably quit breathing, too. There seemed to be a buzzing in her ears. Her heart—oh, it was beating. Exploding. "That's, um…" Mind blank.

"You probably don't believe me, after I stalked away last night."

Was that *uncertainty* in his eyes?

She was going to faint if she *didn't* take a breath. "I do," she managed to say. "We've been…each other's refuge."

"It's more than that." He swore. "Never mind. This isn't the time or place for this."

"No," Acadia agreed, but the explosion in her chest had settled into an insistent drumbeat. They were supposed to go *garden* after this?

Yep. That's exactly what they were going to do. What they did do.

Neither said anything else until they were back in the Tindalls' yard. David and she laid out the hose, hooked up to the faucet at the back of her house.

"This isn't the best time of day," she murmured, watching the droplets appear on the porous black hose and probably evaporate as quickly.

"No," he said, "but I was thinking we could keep them going into the evening. Move them a couple of times. Do the same this weekend."

After Daddy's funeral? *Why not?* she thought. *He'd approve.*

She followed Joyce's example and began ruthlessly deadheading. David weeded. Dry as the ground was, not much had taken root, but the sharply edged lawn had crept where it wasn't wanted, and after a few minutes he went back to his house and returned with an edger.

His aunt appeared at one point, said she was going to sit in the shade and disappeared again.

"She's losing her hair," Acadia observed. *Well, duh.*

"Yeah. And she's quit hiding the fact."

"Good for her."

Warren came home, refused help unloading groceries and disappeared within. Joyce or Acadia made an occasional observation, but the heat was getting to them all. Acadia had to keep blinking away sweat that stung her eyes. Her T-shirt stuck to her. Her ponytail did the same. Ugh. Maybe she should cut her hair off. Go bald in sympathy for Jackie.

If it hadn't been so hot, she'd have laughed. Yeah, right. The bald part would be okay—the Little Orphan Annie do that would follow, not so much.

David was looking at her. "What's that smile for?"

She told him and he laughed. "Oh, yeah. Even Mom remembers that summer."

"What do I remember?" Joyce asked, pausing to look up.

When Acadia told her, she chuckled, too. "Your mom parked in the driveway after taking you to the hairdresser. I happened to be outside to see you get out of the car and stomp inside. You were furious."

Laughing again, David peeled his T-shirt off over his head and used it to wipe his face. Oh, heavens, he had a beautiful body. Lean, long muscles, a torso that tapered from broad shoulders to a narrow waist. The dark hair on his chest was matted with sweat. Riveted, Acadia could *taste* the saltiness of his skin. She wanted…

Oh, damn. Her eyes lifted to meet his. They glittered in

the long moment before she could tear her gaze away. By that time, her cheeks were painfully heated.

Seemingly oblivious, Joyce announced, "I think I need to go in. It's roasting out here! Maybe tomorrow we could come out in the morning, while it's cooler."

"Yeah. Yeah," he said again, voice scratchy. "We've probably all had enough."

Helpless, Acadia looked at him again.

"Let me move the hose to another bed," he said to his mother, "and then I'll follow you in."

Joyce thanked Acadia again for helping and left to join her sister at the back of her own house.

David said, "I want to take a shower with you."

She shivered with longing, but said, "Fat chance."

He groaned. His arousal was very obvious. "It was wishful thinking."

"Mom'll be here tomorrow."

"Can I come over tonight, 'Cadia?"

"Yes." The word all but burst from her. "Please." Inconsistency seemed to be her watchword these days. *He loves me, he loves me not...*

I am going to get hurt.

Maybe not.

"Count on it," he told her, keeping his distance, then muttered, "Oh, hell. I can't go in like this."

Feeling a little steadier, a little more cheerful, Acadia said, "Nope. See you later."

He took a step, tapped her nose. "I'd complain about you deserting me, but…"

"I'm looking Rudolph-like."

"Yeah, you're not made for sun, are you? I'd forgotten how you used to spend all summer every summer peeling."

"And you have a tan even though you live in Seattle. There's no justice."

He flashed a wicked grin. "None, despite my best efforts."

Laughing, she turned on her heel and left him. One cold shower later, her pulse still fell in the abnormal range.

DAZED, REEVE stumbled out of the recruitment office, a sheaf of papers and brochures in his hand, and turned his head looking for Dad's car. He hadn't signed anything, not yet, but he knew he'd made the decision. If the Marine Corps would have him. There was some kind of test— a vocational aptitude battery, the major who'd talked to him called it. Reeve had thought "battery" was something that went with "assault," but he guessed not. Or maybe the poor wannabes who took the test felt as if they'd undergone a battery when they were done. Maybe that's why it was called that. And the recruiter wanted to sit down with Reeve's parents, too.

His mind spun with everything he'd learned today, but what rose to the top was the stuff about the U.S. Marine Corps' core values. Reeve wasn't stupid; he knew from the news that marines screwed up like anyone else. That some of them didn't live by those values, if they'd ever believed in them. But Walt—Walt *had* believed. And lived, and died, what he believed.

Honor. Courage. Commitment.

Reeve knew that, more than anything, he wanted to live by those values, too.

During the drive home from Kennewick, where the recruiting office was, he worried about what his parents would say and how long he'd have to wait before he could leave for basic training in San Diego. He'd explained why he couldn't go until Mrs. Stenten had somebody to replace him. The major had nodded with respect and said, "I'm glad you're set on doing the right thing, son." That felt

good. Lately Reeve had had trouble believing he deserved
to be respected.

He sort of thought his dad might be okay with Reeve
enlisting. Dad had served in the navy. Mom, though… She
might understand why he wanted to enlist, but she wouldn't
like the idea of him going into danger.

He didn't like it, either, but he also did. He'd never get
back the part of himself he'd lost the day Walt died for him
if he *didn't* face his worst fears and come out the other side
with his head held high. In the back of his mind was the
scary thought that he might fail—that he'd crumble when
guns started firing. But ever since Mrs. Stenten had showed
him that picture of Walt in his uniform, Reeve had started
carrying himself with his shoulders square and his back
straight. He'd found out what it was like to despise himself, and he was willing to do anything, face any terror, to
feel proud instead.

Man, he'd have to start running and weight lifting, like
yesterday, or he wouldn't make it through the first day of
training. Washing out was *not* an option. He glanced side-
long at the heap of papers. There was stuff he was supposed
to memorize, too. He was okay with that. He wanted to be
confident when he got off the plane in San Diego.

He started rehearsing aloud what he was going to say to
his parents tonight at the dinner table.

"Mom, Dad, you know how Walt was a U.S. Marine?
Well, I want to be one, too."

Hearing his voice, sort of timid, like when you spoke
up in class and thought everyone might laugh at you, he
cleared his throat and tried again.

"Mom, Dad, I've decided I want to be a U.S. Marine
like Walt was."

He hoped he wouldn't have to say, *Why? Because I don't
want to ever be so scared again I piss my pants. I want*

*someday to be able to look at a camera the way Walt did. I
want to know that* I *would die without hesitation for someone else.*

He gave a weak grin. Yeah, Mom really wouldn't like
that part.

"OH, HONEY!" Deborah Henderson slammed the car door
and rushed for the house as Acadia bounded down the porch
steps.

They met midlawn and hugged as exuberantly as if they
hadn't seen each other in years instead of a mere month.
Then her mom pulled back, sniffed and said, "I swear you
look like a little girl again."

Acadia laughed. "I might believe you if I didn't wear a
C-cup bra."

"No, but there's something…" Mom shook her head and
looked toward the street and neighbors' houses. "This town
hasn't changed a bit, has it?"

"Not much," Acadia admitted, not wanting to say, *Not
at all.* "Now…well, it'll have to change some. I don't know
what will happen to the hardware store, for example. Betty's
sister was here for the funeral and she put the house up for
sale, but I have no idea whether she inherited the store, too.
Or how hard it will be to find a buyer for it. I'm guessing
Mrs. Stenten will sell the Shell station, too. I can't imagine it would be very profitable if she had to pay a full-time
manager and mechanic."

Her mother's face had sobered while Acadia talked, and
now she nodded. "Everyone who died will leave a hole. And
some of the others might move away. Will Wendi Rowe
want to come back to Tucannon when she's released from
the hospital, for example?"

"I don't know."

Mom lowered her voice. "What about Joyce?"

"I don't think she's decided yet."

Acadia carried her mother's suitcase in and upstairs. There she hesitated on the threshold of her father's bedroom. "If you don't want to sleep here, I can let you have my bed." She didn't say, *I'll sleep downstairs on the sofa,* although that's what she meant.

Mom had a funny look on her face, but she shook her head. "No, this is fine." She entered the room very slowly, though, and stiffly, as though she had to unlock every joint to make it swing forward. "Nothing in the house has changed, either."

"Except that I've emptied most of the closets and drawers and cupboards. It's beginning to feel like a ghost town. The facades are there, but the wind whistles through what was once behind them." Well, that sounded bleak. *Way to go, 'Cadia.*

Her mother lowered her carry-on to the dresser top. "His clothes?"

"The only thing left in here is the furniture. Oh, and I put fresh sheets on the bed, of course."

Mom nodded. "Oh, my," she whispered, and sank onto the edge of the bed. "I knew, but..."

"A part of you thought he was still here?"

Her mother wiped at suddenly damp cheeks. "Yes, damn it."

Acadia joined her on the bed, putting her arm around her mother's waist. "Maybe I shouldn't have asked you to come."

"I'd have been hurt if you didn't. And...regretful if I'd said no."

"Okay, then." Once again they hugged, the emotions different this time.

Finally Acadia left her to put her toiletries in the bathroom and, probably, to pull herself together. Eventually

Mom reappeared downstairs, her eyes puffy but her grief controlled. Not surprisingly, she spent five minutes complaining about the heat.

"How could I have forgotten?" she whined.

Acadia laughed and told her the San Francisco fog had crept into her bones. "Maybe drying out some would be good for you."

They did get serious, over dinner discussing tomorrow's service and how much Acadia still had to do to get the house in shape to sell.

"I've already had one looker," she said, "which surprised me. I mean…Tucannon. It's a long commute even to Walla Walla."

"You may not get a quick sale, that's for sure. On the other hand…" Mom grimaced. "Tucannon may get some newcomers. I doubt a local will buy the hardware store or the gas station. And the high school will need a new English teacher. Some of the people besides Wendi who were wounded may decide they want a fresh start somewhere else."

"That's true." Why any of this was new to her, Acadia wasn't sure, but it was. There was a Before Rob Owen's murderous spree, and an After. Of course Tucannon wouldn't stay the same. She found that made her sad anew.

She told her mother about the people she'd seen, let herself be catty about the ones she despised, and Mom told her a few eye-popping stories about old-timers. Acadia made a mental note to share those with David, who would appreciate them.

Of course Mom asked about him. Images of last night played in her head: his eyes darkening to charcoal just before he kissed her, the sight of his head bent over her breast as he suckled, her own fingers gripping his shoulders and savoring the bunching of his muscles as he surged inside her. David over her, in her.

Inevitably, she blushed, knowing her mother's sharp eyes didn't miss the heat beneath her skin.

"You'll meet him tomorrow." *Don't ask more; don't ask me to give you answers I don't know.*

"Will Joyce be coming to the funeral, too?"

"Yes, and her sister, Jackie—do you remember her? And Warren, her husband."

Mom's face relaxed. "Of course I remember Jackie. Warren, too, although I don't recall him having much to say for himself."

"I haven't heard much out of him."

Her mother's eyebrows rose but she didn't comment on how much time Acadia must be spending at the Owen home to have formed an opinion of David's uncle.

"If we feel up to it tomorrow," Acadia continued, "Joyce has asked us to dinner. She knows we may not want to socialize after the funeral, but she said she'd love to have a chance to visit with you and that might be the only chance."

Mom nodded. "We have to eat. And since you were smart enough to schedule the service for morning, that'll give us time to weep for hours afterward, if we want."

Want? Acadia shuddered. She'd cried more already than she had in all her life. More than she had even after her mother had dragged her away from Tucannon, Dad and David.

Mom helped clear the table and clean the kitchen, then decided to shower so she didn't have to in the morning— "Two women having to share one bathroom boggles the mind"—and get ready for bed. She'd worked the night shift, napped for a couple of hours, then packed and hurried to the airport. Two flights later, she'd rented a car and driven the forty-five minutes to Tucannon. "And I'm beat," she concluded, kissed Acadia's cheek and went upstairs.

Acadia's gaze strayed to the clock and she thought, *It's not that late. I could call David.* She made a face. *Can't go one evening without seeing him? That's pathetic.*

No, she thought—that was desperate. One more week— that's what she was allowing herself to be done with Daddy's house. She *had* to get back to the hospital. The nursing administrator had been nice as it was to give her so much time off. And…she didn't even know for sure that David was staying in town that long. He must be under enormous pressure to get back to work, too. He'd been here two weeks now. Of course he'd stay for Rob's funeral, but then…

Then they'd go their separate ways.

No, she decided, *I am not calling him tonight. It'll be worse if he guesses quite how hungry I am for his time, his touch, his attention.*

For him.

Instead, she walked through the downstairs, noting what she'd accomplished, what she still had to do, and wondering what her father would think if he could know his wife was once again sleeping in his bed.

DAVID WAS SURPRISED at how little Acadia's mother had changed. Intrigued, too, to see more of her daughter in her face than he'd realized. Unless the resemblance was startling, kids didn't think that way: *oh, she looks like her mom.* And they didn't share the coloring or the freckles; those were Acadia's own.

Her mother's hair was curly, though, if not as exuberantly as hers, and he thought it was natural. She had a sharp little chin, too, and something of the same independence and spirit in eyes that were more hazel than brown, but shaped rather like Acadia's.

There was an irony, he thought, in the fact that it was the personality mother and daughter shared—yes, the independence, and also the curiosity, the impatience with rules and the mundane—that had likely led Deborah Henderson to leave her husband and take her daughter off to a new life in the big city.

He wondered if Acadia had understood that.

Six was too many people for his Lexus, so to his displeasure Acadia and her mother had driven separately to the church. He intended to offer to drive them home after the service and burial. He didn't like the idea of 'Cadia behind the wheel when she was distraught. Uncle Warren could drive his car.

Because her father had been, at most, an irregular churchgoer, Acadia had chosen to hold the entire service at graveside, like Earl Kennedy's son had. The pastor of the Congregational church had known Charlie well enough to be happy to conduct the service, she'd told David.

They'd arrived ahead of him and his family, of course, and were already greeting neighbors and friends when the Owen clan walked across the grass toward the bright-colored canopies and the rows of folding chairs. That was when he got his first look at Acadia's mother since those long-ago days when he'd been of an age to be oblivious to most adults.

When he kissed Acadia's cheek, she murmured, "Will you sit up front with us?"

"If you're sure you want us."

She gave him one swift look, an odd one. "Of course I do" was all she said.

His mother and hers hugged, and then Aunt Jackie and Deborah hugged. Uncle Warren kissed both women's cheeks.

He told his mother where Acadia wanted them to sit, and she and the rest went ahead, leaving him standing patiently to one side. It was while he was waiting, keeping his distance enough so he didn't have to participate in every meet and greet, that it occurred to him it hadn't once crossed his mind today to worry about the reception he or his mother would receive at this, yet another, funeral. He hadn't automatically glanced around to see who was glaring or avoiding their eyes.

Bemused, he turned his head and saw several people had paused up front to talk to his mother with every appearance of sympathy or kindness. *I didn't worry,* he realized with faint shock, *because people mostly haven't acted the way I thought they would.* Early on, maybe—there'd been the rock thrower, the kids who'd egged the house. The few townspeople who were unpleasant at the grocery store. But the groundswell of opinion had swung, to remembering that Joyce Owen was one of them and David Owen had been a good kid, a great athlete in whom they'd taken pride. A hometown boy.

He gave his head a slight shake. *Huh.* Then he looked around, from face to face, and grappled with the understanding that the world had once more shifted beneath his feet in the disconcerting way that defied logic.

Eventually he walked Acadia to the front. She sat next to her mother, and he took the chair on her other side.

The first time her body lurched with an incipient sob, he also took her hand.

The pastor talked simply about a good, quiet, generous man, a friend to all, incapable of resentment or hatred. "We all heard Acadia Henderson talk about how certain she felt that her father would hold no grudges, that he would feel pity for the tortured soul who ended his life, never anger. Even though, like everyone in this community, my first reaction was horror, shock and, yes, anger, I immediately thought, *Of course.* Charlie often spoke up for Rob Owen, as he did for other members of this community. Rob's final act wouldn't have changed Charlie's mind a bit." He paused. "Acadia has asked me to read some of the notes she's received from her father's former students."

He did that, and tears ran down her face although she seemed unaware. He glanced past her to see that her mother cried, too, as quietly. His mother held her hand.

The weirdness struck him, and for a minute he couldn't get past it. Here they sat in a row, together in every way that mattered: the dead man's ex-wife and daughter, and the murderer's mother, brother and aunt. How was it that Acadia and her mother could turn to Rob's family for strength? It made no sense, and yet he'd never been more grateful for anything than he was for her forgiveness.

The pastor asked God to comfort Charlie Henderson's family, his friends, this entire, sorrowing community. "Let our faith be our consolation," he said, "and eternal life our hope." He smiled gently at the congregation. "And now, Acadia wants to tell you a little bit about the man her father was."

Acadia wiped her face, blew her nose with a defiant honk and cast a wild look at David. He managed a sort of smile and squeezed her shoulder encouragingly. This had to be one of the hardest things anyone ever did.

Panic moved in him. Oh, damn—would he have to say something about Rob when they buried him? God. Maybe not, given how few people would be there. Then he grimaced, knowing his mother would want him to.

Acadia showed no self-consciousness about her blotchy face or tear-clogged voice. She faced the people who had come to mourn her father and the TV cameras at the back and said, "Many of you know that my parents divorced when I was thirteen, and I never lived full-time again with my father. In a very real way, this has been a homecoming for me. I've gotten to know him all over again. Remembered who he was." She shared memories: how willing he always was to run up and down the street holding up the bike until she learned to ride herself, to pitch a softball to her even after she broke a window in a neighbor's house—twice. "I'm here to tell you he was a lousy pitcher," she said, earning chuckles. "Daddy wasn't much of an athlete." When the laughter died down, she went on. "What he loved was reading. Books." She smiled softly, and David guessed she wasn't seeing these faces anymore, that her inner eye saw only her father. "Of course Mom read to me." Momentarily her gaze did touch her mother, who was openly sobbing now. "But Dad kept on reading to me, even when I was in third or fourth grade. Glorious books, long before I could have managed them. *The Once and Future King, 20,000 Leagues Under the Sea, The Prince and the Pauper*. Greek myths—oh, he did love those stories. We talked about going one day to Greece, but he never did. He was many things, but he wasn't an adventurous man. He found adventure enough between the pages of his books, and in the imaginations and dreams and achievements of his students. My father was a generous, thoughtful man. I believe, if he could ask one thing of you today, it would be forgiveness." She nodded, made her way back to her seat, her eyes looking curiously blind, and David, not caring what anyone thought, had an arm waiting to go around her.

Other people went up and talked—a couple of Charlie's students from the community college, and a couple of townspeople. The service ended and David didn't think of leaving Acadia's side as she endured the endless stream of condolences.

And finally, it was over. He took the keys from her unresisting hand, handed his off to Warren and escorted the two women to Acadia's rental car.

This funeral was the last, he thought during the drive. The last—except for Rob's. Decency suggested he tell Acadia she needn't come. For all her generosity, she had still to be harboring some of that rage he'd seen on her face while she washed away her father's blood. But he also knew he wouldn't ask, because he'd never spoken truer words than when he told Acadia he needed her.

CHAPTER SEVENTEEN

ALAN FINLEY CAME with his camera on Sunday, stared in predictable shock for a long time, then got to work photographing Rob's murals. David let him take with him some of the best—or most horrifying—drawings, too. Alan intended to scan them into his computer. David's mother signed her permission for him to send the photos out.

Alan agreed, though, that they ought to give reporters from the Walla Walla paper the opportunity to come and see for themselves, take their own photos if they preferred.

"I can damn near guarantee some of these pictures will be in *People, Time, Newsweek*," he said. "What do you want me to do if any of them offer payment?"

That jolted David. "I'll talk to Mom. There must be a reputable nonprofit raising money for research into schizophrenia. You're entitled to keep some, too, Alan."

"Don't be ridiculous," his friend said brusquely.

They exchanged back slaps and promises to keep in better touch, and he left.

David saw several visitors arrive at Acadia's on Sunday, too. She'd backed her father's car out, and a couple of the strangers took it for a spin. Midafternoon, the father of a teenage boy shook her hand and soon the boy drove the car away, his father following in the family sedan. Seeing how alone she looked watching it go, David walked over.

"Hard to see it go?" he asked.

When he put his arm around her as naturally as if it

belonged there, she rubbed her cheek against him. "It's a dumb thing to be sentimental about. But I feel as if I just gave Daddy's poor, bewildered, old dog away."

David smiled and kissed the top of her head. "To a loving new owner. Imagine if it had been a wreck and you'd had to send it to the great junkyard in the sky."

She made a rude sound and separated herself from him. "I suppose you're telling me you don't mourn at all when you sell a car?"

"I give a few passing thoughts to good times I had in it." He grinned. "When I was a teenager, especially to the good times in the backseat." He pasted a reminiscent look on his face. "Not much privacy in Tucannon unless you find a dark gravel road...."

Acadia punched him.

He laughed. "I missed you last night," he said more seriously.

"I missed you, too."

They *had* had dinner together, of course, along with her mother and his family. It had been a happier occasion than he'd have expected; maybe the evening had been a sort of wake for Charlie, the real goodbye. They'd talked about him, smiling at the memories. There'd been hugs all around when Acadia and Deborah left to walk back to the house that hadn't been home for either in a long time.

The house that wouldn't belong to a Henderson much longer.

David had seen a hearty man in a suit usher a couple through it in the late morning, when Acadia was outside chatting with one of the strangers come to look at the car. The three went through the Tindalls' house, too, pausing to admire the roses. A part of him hoped Acadia would sell her dad's house soon; he didn't like the idea of it sitting empty for a year, her maybe having to hire firms to do outside and inside maintenance. There was a lot of competition, though; he'd driven around town one day, out of curiosity, and noticed several other places already for sale. Old man Tackett had died in June, David's mother had told him. That was one. The Bunkers had moved to Boise to be close to their son. That was another. Not surprisingly, Mr. Baron's house had a for-sale sign in front of it now, too. Maybe the Stentens' soon. He found himself wishing some young families would move here. Tucannon had been a good place to grow up. For all his later desire to escape, David wouldn't trade his childhood here.

Acadia's mother called to her and she went back inside. He would have liked to kiss her, at least on the cheek, but hadn't since he had no idea what she'd said about him to her mother. He didn't want to embarrass her.

The idea that he might be an embarrassment had him frowning as he walked home.

He went straight to the kitchen where he found his mother taking a roast from the refrigerator.

"I thought we'd have a nice dinner tonight." She checked to be sure they were alone. "Warren says Jackie doesn't feel very good after her treatments," she said, keeping her voice low. "She's going for one tomorrow, you know."

He nodded. They'd set Rob's burial for Wednesday to give Jackie a day to recover in between.

He grabbed a soda from the refrigerator, opened it and sat. "Mom, you don't want to move, do you?"

The bluntness of his question made her jerk, but after a moment she faced him. "This is my home."

"You won't be lonely?"

"No lonelier than I've been," she said, equally blunt.

He couldn't help flinching.

But his mother was already shaking her head, not seeming to notice his reaction. "No, that's not true. I've been realizing how much of my isolation was my own fault. I pushed people away. I have friends again. If there are other people who think I should disappear out of shame, well…" She shrugged. "I can ignore them. It beats starting all over somewhere else."

He nodded, understanding how she felt if not convinced her decision was right. What was she doing, staying in Tucannon to be near the graves of her husband and son? That seemed downright morbid to him.

"You know I'd be happy if you'd come to Seattle."

They looked at each other, her expression slowly softening. The knowledge was between them that a year ago he'd have just as soon she—and Rob—*had* kept their distance. He was ashamed to accept that about himself, but also glad something important had changed between him and his mother.

"Thank you, but you're busy," she said. "You work long hours, you have friends, I assume you date."

"Assume" was all she could do, since he had never told her about any of the women he'd spent time with. Why would he, when the relationships weren't serious?

"That's true," he agreed, "but one of these days I'll get married. Start a family."

"Tucannon isn't that long a drive. Or maybe then I'll decide it's time to move to a nice condo close to my grandchildren."

"Okay, Mom." He guessed he'd known all along what her decision would be. This *was* home. "You know I love you." More shame followed when he thought about how long it had been since he'd bothered telling her that. Or Dad. He regretted not having time with his father before he died.

She came to him, kissed his cheek and said, "My little boy." Then laughed, a hitch in it giving away her emotions. "Not so little anymore."

He caught her around the waist, gave a squeeze and laughed, too. "I passed you by when I was, what, ten years old?"

"Oh, earlier than that, I think. You were as tall as your dad by the time you were thirteen or so."

A fuzzy memory came to him. "That's funny. I remember suddenly realizing I was looking *down* at him. Freaked me out. He was supposed to stay bigger than me, stronger. He was my *dad*."

She chuckled, then got sad again. "He shouldn't have died so soon, either, should he? I wish he'd lived long enough to see grandkids."

That would have set David to squirming a few weeks ago. But here he was, imagining a redheaded toddler who already knew how to stomp her feet and poke her pointy chin out when she was indignant. Big, melting brown eyes, too. Yeah, he hoped when he had a little girl, she'd be a redhead.

"Me, too," he said gruffly, then nodded at the roast looking kind of bloody on the pan. "Don't you have to do something with that?"

Flustered, she returned to her dinner preparations, pausing only to ask when Acadia's mother was leaving. "If it isn't before dinner, maybe she'd like to join us."

He didn't comment on the fact that it seemed half the time Acadia sat down to dinner with them, mainly because, to hell with half the time, he'd have been happier if she'd been here *every* evening. "I'll check with her," he said, tossing his empty can in the garbage.

He called, only to discover that her mother had already gone.

"Are you sure?" she asked. "I don't want everybody feeling sorry for poor Acadia, all by herself in that house."

"Mom likes you," he said simply. *I love you.* Man, did

that cause a cramp of shock in his chest, and he didn't even know why. Not that it was a surprise. He just hadn't been that straight-out with himself, David guessed. He groped for the right words. "You feel like part of the family."

There was a funny silence. "Thank you," she said, sounding choked. "Tell your mother I'd love to come for dinner."

"Good." He was smiling. Leaning against the wall in the hall, keeping his voice low so no one overheard. "I'm looking forward to walking you home."

"I kept thinking about you the past two nights," she admitted. "Friday, Mom went to bed early and I almost called you."

He sighed with regret but also the knowledge that he couldn't have gone up to her bedroom with her, or brought her home to his. "We could have christened the backseat of my Lexus," he said thoughtfully, making her laugh.

They did a fair amount of laughing at dinnertime, too, until Acadia asked when they were holding the service for Rob.

"Wednesday morning, ten o'clock," his mother said, voice constricted.

In the silence, he knew this was the moment when he should say, *Don't feel you have to come.* He opened his mouth and closed it, then did it again. Seeing Acadia's astonished stare, David realized he probably looked like a guppy.

"We'd be glad if you want to attend," his mother said. "But don't feel you have to, Acadia. You've been gracious enough already."

He braced himself.

"Don't be silly," Acadia said firmly. "Of course I'll come. You were right there beside me yesterday morning, weren't you? And Rob—" she broke off. "Rob was a big part of my childhood, too, you know."

David found her hand beneath the tablecloth and squeezed. Acadia squeezed back and he could breathe again.

"Thank you." Mom had tears in her eyes. "You and Davey both…well, you've turned into such fine people." She nodded, as if confirming her assessment.

Shame pricked again, because he hadn't always been someone he could be so proud of, but maybe everyone carried the knowledge of times they should have said or done something different. Times they'd been silent, times they'd been mean. Not many people were saints. He knew one thing—he'd be weighing his own behavior and choices on a new scale from here on out.

He and Acadia were both maybe a little quiet when he walked her home. He was still dealing with his realization that he was in love with her. In one way it wasn't a surprise, but in another… He'd never been in love, unless it was with her that long-ago summer. How could it happen so fast? How could he be so sure of what he felt?

They'd almost reached her front porch when she stopped so suddenly he lurched off stride.

"I keep thinking about how awful I was to you that day," she burst out. "I am perfectly capable of being…oh, selfish and pigheaded and not very nice at all." She made that sound like the worst sin of all: *not very nice.*

When he laughed, she didn't like it at all. "Why is that funny?" she exclaimed.

Telling her his own reflections sobered him up, and had her wrapping her arms around his waist as if holding him when he bared his soul made perfect sense to her.

When he was done, they stood in silence for quite a while. This was his favorite time of night. It was getting hard to see, but kids were still out playing down the street. He heard a whoop and then a mother's voice. Porch lights were on. Overhead, a bat flashed by. The moon had gotten a little fatter as the week went on.

He was glad his mother was staying in Tucannon. The thought was disconcerting, but also settled something in him. She was right. This was home. It could keep being home for him, too. Rubbing his cheek on Acadia's head, he thought, *For 'Cadia, too. If she marries me.*

Though seeing someone else living in her dad's house might always make her sad.

Maybe not so much, David reflected, if it was a family. It would be okay if the lawn got shaggier than her father had kept it, if a kid's bike lay toppled on the lawn, if maybe, some night, the parents sat out on the front porch and called to their children.

His arms tightened around her. Yeah, he thought, that would be all right.

Would she think he was as crazy as Rob if he told her tonight he wanted forever with her?

He imagined himself introducing the subject. *Two weeks ago, I was no more than a pleasantly nostalgic memory to you. So...wanna get married?*

Cheek against her hair, he winced. Yeah, this maybe was too soon.

When, then?

He had no idea. He'd undergone a seismic shift since he came home to Tucannon, and was still finding his feet. Trying to get a handle on emotions he hadn't known he was capable of feeling. None of what he felt for Acadia was comfortable. The worst and most crippling part was his uncertainty. He'd spent most of his life believing he was the unloved son.

If Acadia couldn't love him...that might kill him.

Closing his eyes, he thought, *Let me get through Rob's funeral first.* Then, if he was still standing, he'd do it. Right now, even if his silence made him a coward, he was desperate to hold on to the dream: he and Acadia coming home regularly in the years to come, bringing their own kids, who would love Tucannon, too.

Just for a few more days.

"I THOUGHT you ought to be made aware that his mother intends to bury Rob Owen in our cemetery here in Tucannon," Marge told Earl Kennedy's son.

This was her third call. She planned to spend the entire evening letting as many people as possible know. She'd been shocked to her soul today after church to overhear Pastor Young telling Naomi Kastner that Rob was to be laid to rest beside his father this very week. She had frozen right there on the church steps, listening in outrage. He had been speaking quietly, but sounding as if he thought Naomi might want to attend. Was he planning to pray over the body of a mass murderer?

"It's all right by me," George Kennedy said after a minute. "Joyce Owen is a nice lady. If this is what she wants to do, I won't say anything against it."

"How can you bear to think of your father and that… that *monster* resting side by side?" she asked.

"Don't suppose where the earthly remains are much matters, Ms. Perkins. Good night."

The quality of the silence told her he was gone. Hanging up her phone—*she* still had one that was attached to the wall, why anyone would want a telephone in their pocket was beyond her—Marge said, "Well!"

Dismay and incomprehension sat like undigested oatmeal in her stomach. She didn't understand people at all. Someone like Alice Simmons, that was one thing—*she* hadn't lost a loved one. But how Earl's son could be fine with his father sharing the hereafter with his killer—no, that was simply unacceptable!

Anne Stenten had said only, "Thank you for informing me, Miss Perkins."

Miles Degamo had professed to be as outraged as Marge was, but wouldn't commit to calling Pastor Young or standing outside the cemetery Wednesday to be sure the Owens knew the community opposed having Rob remain part of it. Of course, all *he* could think about was what his customers would think. If she could marshal enough of those customers, perhaps he'd appear with them.

Marie Merfeld gasped when Marge gave her the news, and at first agreed that of course all right-thinking people should express their belief that Rob Owen didn't belong in holy ground at all, far less in *their* town. "But I'll have to talk to Kirk," she added less strongly, leaving Marge guessing she wouldn't appear Wednesday morning. Kirk was one of those people who seemed to believe Joyce's feelings took precedence over the grief of those hurt by her crazy son.

Marge didn't even think of calling Charlie Henderson's daughter. *She* was firmly in the Owen camp. Marge thought it was disgraceful the way she'd been leaning on David Owen yesterday, at her own father's funeral.

Midway through the evening, her phone rang.

"Ms. Perkins, this is Chief Bolton." He sounded stern. "I understand you're attempting to rally people to hold some kind of demonstration Wednesday while Rob's mother is burying him."

Demonstration? That wasn't a word she cared for. It was hippies and militants who *demonstrated*. But there was a time and place for everything, she thought, shoulders firming.

"That's right," she said. "And don't you try to tell me we aren't entitled to express our opinion."

"I won't tell you any such thing," he said, "but I'll arrest anyone who accosts any member of the Owen family, and I'll ask you to stay outside the cemetery grounds."

"I had intended that," she said stiffly.

"Fine." There was a pause. "You're making a mistake, Ms. Perkins. No matter what happened, Robbie was one of ours."

"Robbie should have been put away somewhere else fifteen years ago. If he had been, some good people would still be alive."

"I know Pete and Joyce, and I know they tried their best. And I also know that you keep loving your children no matter what. Maybe you should keep loving your neighbors' children, too. Good night, Ms. Perkins."

She did *not* appreciate people hanging up on her. Or trying to intimidate her.

Determined, she moved her finger down the list of names in the thin Tucannon directory, put out by the chamber of commerce. Unlike some people, she knew what was right.

As she dialed, she wondered if she ought to inform the television stations what was happening. Not that she was doing this for attention.

ACADIA WAS PAINFULLY aware that David hadn't asked when she intended to go home; nor had he told her his end date, if he had one. Surely he wouldn't be staying much past his brother's funeral. Why would he, now that his mother had made the decision to stay in her house? In cleaning out the basement and standing by her side in front of the press and at the funerals, David had done what he needed to for her. Perhaps he'd stay the rest of the week, but no more than that.

I *won't be staying beyond the rest of the week, either.*

Why would I? The thought balled a fist beneath her breast-bone. On her few visits home, leaving Tucannon had always been a bittersweet experience. Driving across the bridge, pausing at the stop sign, although there was rarely traffic coming either way on the two-lane highway. Turning left, accelerating, looking ahead and into the rearview mirror, both.

This time, she knew, the goodbye would be all bitter and no sweet. It would be goodbye to Daddy, goodbye to her childhood, goodbye to David, finally and forever.

Lying in her bed with him, her head on his shoulder, she begged silently. *Say something. This doesn't* have *to be goodbye, Acadia. I want to keep seeing you.*

She could say it. She'd never stayed timidly silent in her life.

Yeah, so what if he said, *Sure, I'd like to keep seeing you?*

That would work out so well, she mocked herself, him in Seattle and her two states away in Sacramento. She could imagine it, them getting together a couple of times, him flying down for a long weekend, her coming up there. The length of time between phone calls or emails stretching. It was the old dilemma—peel the bandage off slowly, or yank it off quickly.

She'd always been an advocate of the quick, get-it-over-with approach to life.

He lifted his head and peered at her face. "I suppose I'd better get home."

Acadia murmured something he could take as either agreement or protest, whatever suited him.

He planted a kiss on her forehead, groaned and heaved himself to a sitting position. But after reaching for his pants, he made no move to put them on. "This really sucks," he said suddenly, explosively.

Alarmed, Acadia rose to her elbow. "What sucks?"

"Having to trot home like a good little boy when all I want is to stay."

"You're respecting your mother, that's all."

He made a harsh sound that might have been intended to be a laugh. "I think it's safe to say she knows damn well we're sleeping together."

"Then…" Oh, God. "Stay," she whispered.

He yanked at his hair. "Damn it, I don't want any of them looking differently at you. I'm not going home out of respect for my mother, 'Cadia. I'm going out of respect for you."

Feeling a delirious and painful cramping inside, she stroked a hand down his powerful back. "That's…old-fashioned."

His muscles shivered beneath her touch. "We agreed a long time ago that Tucannon is old-fashioned," he said, voice husky.

"That's true." Acadia closed her eyes. "We won't be here forever."

She thought he stiffened beneath her hand.

"No." Long pause, his gray eyes searching her face for the secrets he must know she harbored. "Not much longer."

This doesn't have to be goodbye, Acadia. I want to keep seeing you.

And, finally, she knew why she wouldn't be the one to say it. A too-big part of her was still thirteen years old and loving him from afar while knowing it was hopeless. She'd never been able to tell him how she felt. She still couldn't.

Stupid, pathetic, but true.

"Damn, I'm dreading Wednesday," he said abruptly.

A lump in her throat, she took back her hand, feeling as if she'd singed her fingers. "I don't blame you."

"Thank you for saying you'd come. For staying until we've buried Rob. It means a lot to Mom and me both."

She supposed she should be touched instead of hurt. He was being sincere and kind. He'd no doubt always think fondly of her. After all, they shared a wealth of memories and had needed each other for these few weeks. *He* hadn't been in love with her since he was thirteen years old.

It wasn't really *love.*

Oh, who are you kidding? she scoffed at herself. *No other guy has ever measured up and, gee, why is that?*

She couldn't make herself do any more than nod.

"Maybe I'll stay a little longer," he said suddenly.

Oh, lucky her. Acadia didn't think she could bear it.

"I'm sure you're past your curfew." She managed a teasing smile. "You're just grumpy because you're the one who has to get dressed and drag yourself half a block home. While I—" she stretched luxuriantly "—get to stay snug in bed."

As she'd hoped, he relaxed, laughed and began to get dressed. "Maybe you're right. Although…" He reached out and squeezed her thigh, poking out from beneath the cover. "You are tempting."

She gave an indelicate snort. "Right, that's me. The temptress. At the hospital I'm better known as the holy terror."

David laughed again. "You've always been that, too, haven't you?" He tugged his T-shirt over his head and pulled it down. "Damn. Well, I'll see you tomorrow."

A quick kiss and he was gone, leaving her achingly aware of what he *hadn't* said.

This doesn't have to be goodbye, Acadia.

MRS. STENTEN surprised Reeve at the station on Tuesday. He'd been planning to call her tonight anyway. Last night the recruiter had come, sitting down with Reeve and his parents at their dining room table and talking for a long time. It had gone better than he expected. Reeve now had a date and time to take the aptitude test, and an assurance from the major that, if he passed, he was in. He wasn't that worried; he'd been an okay student.

When she arrived, he'd been checking the brake and transmission fluid on a car in for an oil change. He straightened, leaving the hood up, and wiped his greasy hands on a rag.

She looked around the garage, then at him in that grave way she had. He wondered if she'd ever again become the soft, smiling woman he remembered.

"Do you have a minute?" she asked. "I thought we ought to talk."

"Sure," he said. "Why don't we go in the office."

He sat behind the desk, a battered old thing, and she perched on one of the straight chairs kept for customers who chose to wait while a tire was replaced or other work done. For a minute, they only looked at each other. Reeve couldn't imagine what she saw. A week ago he might have squirmed, but new pride kept him still.

"I haven't asked you what your plans are," she said, straight out. "I'm giving thought to selling the station, which I'm assuming you expected."

He nodded. "It doesn't make much sense for you to keep it. Uh…do you think you *can* sell it?"

"I've actually had an inquiry." For a moment she gazed down at her clasped hands, then back at him. "I did want to give you first refusal, in case there's any chance you'd hoped…"

Reeve shook his head. "I'm joining the marines." It was the first time he'd said it to anyone but his parents.

She went completely still. "Because of Walt."

"Partly," he admitted. "I never intended to stay in Tucannon. Or to work at a gas station all my life."

He could tell that made her feel better.

"He was good to me. He…well, he inspired me." Telling her felt awkward, but necessary.

She nodded. Her face worked, and he thought, *Oh, crap, she's going to cry,* but she didn't. She took a deep breath. "Will you send me a picture of you in your uniform?"

Oh, man, now *he* felt like crying. But he didn't, either. "I'll be proud to do that," he said, then cleared his throat. "There's something I need to tell you."

Mrs. Stenten looked inquiring.

"I'm going to Rob Owen's funeral tomorrow." When she said nothing, he felt compelled to go on. "Maybe I shouldn't. I mean, considering Walt and all… But I've been thinking I could have treated Rob better. That maybe… Not that what he did was my fault, but I didn't help any. I figured it might mean something to his mom. You know, if I go."

Mrs. Stenten dipped her head. "I intend to be there as well, Reeve."

"Oh." He flushed. "I could pick you up. If, uh, you'd rather not go alone."

She smiled. It didn't reach her eyes, but she tried. "Thank you, Reeve. That would be kind of you. I'd appreciate that."

They agreed on a time, and she told him she'd let him know if the station really was selling.

Then she left. Reeve had risen out of respect, but sank back down feeling shaky. It took him a minute to reason out why.

Everything was changing. Him, maybe, most of all.

And this was only the beginning.

CHAPTER EIGHTEEN

"Why, that bitch," David growled.

Acadia, sitting directly behind him in the Lexus, straightened and craned her neck to see what he was talking about. She felt Warren and Jackie, squished here in back with her, doing the same.

And then, as he turned the car to drive into the cemetery, she saw the woman standing alone just outside the gate, holding a sign.

He's Not Welcome Here.

Marge Perkins, of course, planted there in the middle of the road as if to block their passage. Dressed to the nines, for her, in a flower-printed dress, her gray curls carefully styled, and her expression self-righteous. Against the wrought-iron fence that enclosed the cemetery rested half a dozen other hand-printed placards. The one that Acadia fixated on said "No Rest Here for the Wicked."

A rumble coming from his throat, David didn't even slow. She stepped back at the last second, calling something at them as they swept by.

Joyce said not a word, only sat rigid in front, staring straight ahead as if she hadn't seen that nasty woman.

"How dare she," Acadia muttered, furious, and Warren reached over and gave her hand a brief squeeze. She saw that he was already holding his wife's hand. "Where is Chief Bolton when we need him?" she said more loudly.

"She's not breaking the law." David now sounded steady and unemotional, in contrast to his first flare of anger.

Acadia seethed. "Damn her."

An unexpected chuckle from Warren brought everyone's heads around. Even David stared at him in the rearview mirror.

"You notice she's all by herself," Warren pointed out comfortably.

"We're early," David snapped.

"Well…that's true. Still, you'd think if there was going to be any kind of serious demonstration, the others would be with her."

Nobody said anything. Yes, you would expect the crowd to have gathered if there was going to be one. After all, family usually arrived early for a funeral. But the half-dozen placards suggested Marge *was* expecting others.

Acadia sighed and leaned back against the seat. Marge wasn't doing or saying anything they hadn't expected. Honestly, Acadia wouldn't have been surprised if half the town had been blocking the way, shouting ugly threats.

Joyce quietly directed her son to the plot. As if he didn't know; he'd surely been to his father's grave.

They arrived to find the hearse already parked on the verge of the paved lane that wound through the cemetery grounds. Pastor Young was already here, too. He'd either hitched a ride in the hearse or walked. He hurried to open Joyce's door and help her out.

"I can't believe Ms. Perkins could be so uncharitable," he fussed.

Getting out on her side after David opened the door for her, Acadia didn't hear his mother's response. What she did hear was another car coming. They all turned to look.

It parked behind the Lexus, and two women got out. David's hand on Acadia's arm relaxed when he saw that

Alice Simmons had been the driver. Acadia didn't know the other women, but both went immediately to Joyce, enveloping her in hugs as they exclaimed anxiously that they hoped she didn't mind them attending.

"Of course not," she said, sounding choked.

"David," Acadia whispered.

He looked down at her, then followed the direction of her gaze.

Other cars had turned into the cemetery and were proceeding sedately in their direction. Three. Four. No, they kept coming.

"What the hell?" he breathed.

They parked in turn, more and more of them, until the line of vehicles snaked through the cemetery.

MOST HEADS DIDN'T even turn as the cars passed Marge, defiantly holding her sign. The few people that looked at her shook their heads.

Television crews had come, briefly filmed her, then lost interest. Half a dozen people had promised to stand beside her this morning, and not a one had showed up. Pride hadn't allowed her to gather her signs and go home. She'd said she would be here protesting, and here she was. None of them had the courage of their convictions, but she did. That was something to hold on to. Or so she told herself. But as car after car entered the cemetery and she understood that most of the townspeople had come out of respect and sympathy for Joyce, who had let that monster run wild, Marge felt so odd.

Hollow, and brittle. As if there was no substance to her body. Her blood still rushed through her veins; she knew that, because it painted her cheeks hot with humiliation.

The last car that arrived had a rack of lights atop it and the insignia for the Tucannon Police Department on the door. It stopped abreast of her. The driver's-side window rolled down and Chief Bolton looked at her. She expected pity, and saw something implacable instead.

"I tried to tell you, Marge. You've made a mistake."

"He was a monster. He doesn't belong here." So why did her voice shake? Why did it lack the conviction that had gripped her so hard?

"He was driven by demons we couldn't see. But somewhere inside, Robbie Owen was still the boy we all knew. He was one of us." The chief shook his head. "I'm not so sure you are."

His window glided up. He was no longer bothering to look at her. The squad car glided forward and disappeared into the cemetery.

Marge stood stricken. Shocked. *I'm going to have to move away,* she realized, and was scared near to death. Tucannon was all she knew.

"But I'm right," she whispered, and knew it didn't matter.

DAVID AND ACADIA joined his mother. Staring at the unexpected arrivals, she had her fingers pressed to her mouth, tears glittering in her eyes.

"Oh, my," she whispered. "The Daleys. And Dr. Cole! Who could have told him that it was today? And Alan Finley and his mother—he drove all the way from Portland—and…and George Kennedy."

There were so many others. Kirk Merfeld—Acadia recognized him. Mrs. Skott and Mrs. Kastner, plus several teachers from the high school including Mr. Montalvo. David's hand spasmed at the sight of them. Acadia was shocked to see the Sonnenbergs, the sweet old couple who lived on the corner next door to the Owens. They moved slowly, Mrs. Sonnenberg looking especially frail.

She clutched the arm of a middle-aged woman who must be their daughter. Mrs. Stenten escorted by, of all people, Reeve Hadfield, who nodded gravely at Robbie's family.

They kept coming, each pausing in turn to hug Joyce, shake David's hand and murmur, "We're so sorry." Acadia didn't know most, but Joyce obviously did, and Pastor Young stood to one side beaming.

This was his doing.

One of the last people Acadia saw arrive was Lieutenant Sykes. He was out of uniform today, wearing instead an ill-fitting suit, and had a plump woman with a nice face at his side.

David said something under his breath Acadia couldn't make out. She knew only that he sounded shaken.

"He left that first bouquet, didn't he?"

Her eyes stinging, she looked up at him. "I think so."

"Damn."

There were only a handful of chairs set up graveside, and those were there only because of Jackie's weakness. David had requested them, he'd told Acadia. As it was, almost everyone stood, the chairs reserved for Jackie and Joyce and the Sonnenbergs and another elderly couple Acadia didn't remember.

After this endless week, the brief service should have felt familiar, but didn't. The pastor spoke of forgiveness, of pity for the troubled young man who had been, despite his horrific last act, a member of this community. Acadia turned her head and saw only acceptance on the faces around them. She was barely holding herself together, and suspected David, for all his formidable self-control, was doing the same. He gripped her hand so hard it hurt, and she saw the muscles in his jaw bunching repeatedly. The two of them stood right behind his mother. His free hand was on her shoulder. He held himself rigidly, his gaze leaving the casket only long enough to rest now and again on her head. Probably he couldn't see her face, but Acadia could. Her tears ran freely.

At the end, Pastor Young smiled kindly at David. "Rob Owen's brother, David, would now like to say a few words."

Acadia hadn't known he intended to, given that this funeral was supposed to be private. Oh, poor David. Was he going up there entirely unprepared?

He let go of Acadia's hand, squeezed his mother's shoulder and walked to the front. His eyes burned as he surveyed the crowd.

"First, I thank you all for coming. The fact that you chose to do so means more than I can tell you. To me, and to my mother. Your generosity and forgiveness..." His voice splintered. He cleared his throat, his eyes finding Acadia's. She read sheer desperation in them.

"All of us," he said finally, "I think even Mom and Dad, certainly myself, forgot who Rob was. These past two weeks, I've been trying to remember. I loved my big brother. He was...the best brother in the world. I learned everything from him—how to dribble a basketball, how to throw a baseball, how to ride a bike with no hands." From somewhere, he summoned a smile, this one for his mother. "See, Ma?"

Laughter shimmered through the crowd of friends and neighbors.

"How to sneak out of the house at night, how to catch a frog and how to scare little girls." Again he smiled, although his eyes were too bright. "Except Acadia Henderson, of course. She didn't scare."

There was more laughter.

"The one thing he never could do was teach me to draw. We shared some talents, but not that one. He was the artist." He paused, and Acadia saw him gathering his fraying control. "Illness stole so much from Rob. His sense of humor, his athletic ability, the chance to have a girlfriend. His independence. But one thing it couldn't take was his ability to share his vision with pencil or paint. Until the day he died, my brother was an artist." He nodded at someone.

Acadia looked, and saw Warren politely make his way through the crowd, going toward the cars. David talked some more about what Rob had become. When Warren returned, he had a canvas in his hands. He stepped up beside his nephew and lifted it so everyone could see.

"This is how Rob saw himself," David said, still mostly steady. "I don't know when he painted this self-portrait, but I believe it was years ago. It was at the back of a closet."

They all stared. Acadia was probably less shocked than most people, because she'd seen the basement. But still a lump filled her throat. The brushstrokes were choppy, emphatic, reminding her in that sense of a Van Gogh even though the style was very different. She could see the Robbie she remembered in the mouth, the nose, the shape of his face, but the despair in his eyes hurt to see. Tears tracked rivulets down his cheeks, seeming to have carved the flesh. He held a handgun, and the barrel touched his temple. The colors around him were odd, wrong. It was a stunning painting, and painful to look at.

"We saw a handsome young man. Mentally ill, yes, but for a long time retaining many of the qualities that made him our brother, our son, our neighbor. This is who Robbie saw when he looked in the mirror. I suspect he thought every day of his adult life about taking that life. I am so sorry…" Again his voice broke. Again he recovered. "So sorry he took others with him. Despite everything, I can only say again—I loved my brother."

His mother made a sound. Jackie's arms closed around her.

David nodded brusquely and turned. Not coming toward

his mother and Acadia, but walking away between grave markers until he reached one of the old trees that studded the velvet green of the cemetery. There, he flattened his hands on the bark and bent his head.

Acadia hesitated for no more than thirty seconds. Then she hurried after him. Behind her, she heard Pastor Young speaking again, but didn't even try to make out the words. She saw only David. The boy she'd loved, the man she loved, sobbing.

She closed her arms around him fiercely from behind, and he all but lunged around to grab her, too. And then he pressed his wet face in the crook of her neck and cried. She tasted the salt of her own tears as she held him, sheltered him from other eyes, murmured a probably meaningless litany of comfort and love.

It was a long time before the violence of his grief passed and she felt his muscles growing lax. Acadia smoothed his hair and rubbed her other hand over his back.

"God," he mumbled finally. "I made a spectacle of myself, didn't I?"

"No," she whispered. "No. People expect to see grief."

"I didn't even listen to Mom talking about him."

"She didn't." Acadia knew that much. "I think you said enough for both of you. It was...incredibly moving."

The breath he let out made his body shudder. He straightened and tried to smile wryly at her. Acadia's own smile shook.

"Fortunately, I had some foresight." She bent to pick up the small purse she'd brought for this exact reason but had let fall when she reached him. She thrust the first wad of tissues into his hand, then used the next handful to mop her own face and blow her nose.

When they were both done, David still didn't look quite

like himself. "That's my 'Cadia," he murmured, and his voice did sound more normal. "Ready for anything."

"Nurses are good at being prepared."

He dared, finally, to turn enough to look back toward the crowd. Acadia did the same. People were taking turns to hug Joyce and Jackie, to shake Warren's hand, then walking slowly across the grass to their cars.

"It's over." David's hand found hers.

She had to swallow. "Yes. It's all over."

He squared his shoulders. "Stay with me, 'Cadia?"

She nodded, squeezed her hand and did what she wanted most in the world. She stayed with him.

HER HOUSE WAS mostly dark. A faint light through the front window made him think a lamp might be on, somewhere. The rush of relief he felt when he made out her shape sitting in the dark at the top of her porch steps almost brought David to his knees.

"You're here," he said.

"I thought...you ought to have some time with your family." Her voice was very soft. "Without an outsider."

"An outsider?" He stopped at the foot of the steps. "Do you really think that's what you are?"

"You know what I mean."

"I know." Hadn't she realized when they had assumed she'd sit down to dinner with them tonight that she was part of the family in all their eyes? His mother had looked at Acadia with such gratitude that morning when the two of them rejoined the mourners at graveside. She had comforted and held him, and that made her part of the family. "Can I join you?" he asked, nodding toward his spot.

"I was waiting for you," she said simply. "Do you, um, want to go in?"

To her bed? "Yes," David said. "I definitely want to go in. But not yet. Let's sit out here awhile."

"It does feel good," she murmured.

He'd rehearsed what he wanted to say, but now that he was here he had a bad feeling it would sound stilted. For once he wished it wasn't quite so dark. Or maybe he should be glad—darkness could be kind. If her face showed nothing but surprise, or pity, he didn't want to see it.

For a long time he looked out at the night and not at her at all, although he felt her presence with every cell in his body. What kind of idiot was he, to go to Nicaragua that summer and not be here when Acadia came home? Looking back now, he thought he'd known he was in love with her, but then…he hadn't even considered it. Hadn't let himself. It was impossible. They were too young. He'd had dreams.

And yes, they probably *were* too young. Kids. Maybe they'd needed to go their own ways.

Because he had, he'd fulfilled some of his dreams. But he'd been so damn lonely, so emotionally closed. David didn't even want to think what he would have become if this hadn't happened.

He took a deep breath. "Do you have a plan for when you're going back to California?" Not home—he wasn't going to say that.

"Sunday, I think." She sounded unbothered, which bothered *him*. "You?"

"Uh…probably this weekend, too." God, this was hard. "Acadia…"

She scooted a little so she was facing him, one leg tucked under her. "Yes?"

"I'm in love with you," he said hoarsely.

She gaped at him; he might not be able to read the expression in her eyes, but he could see the oval of her mouth hanging open.

David half stood, then made himself sit back down. "Say something."

"You're in love with me?" she whispered.

"God knows, there's every reason in the world for you not to feel the same about me. Rob. And me. You know how petty I've been. Abandoning my family because of hurt feelings. I can understand if you don't think much of me. I've had trouble working up the courage to tell you." He sucked in a deep breath. When she said nothing, he forged on. "To ask if, ah, there's room in your life for me. If you're willing to move, or…I could." He was petering out here, the uncertainty killing him. Was she totally blown away? Never saw this coming?

"You're asking me to…to live with you?" If she'd moved a muscle, he couldn't tell.

"I'm asking you to marry me. Eventually, anyway," he amended quickly. "This has been really fast, I know. I kept thinking that it might be too soon. That there was no way you'd expect this. I guess you might have seen the time we spent together as part of your goodbye."

She laughed. Goddamn it, she laughed. Except…it was choked, nearer tears than humor. She kept laughing so long, he suffered.

It ended with startling abruptness. "I've been praying you'd say, 'This doesn't have to be goodbye, Acadia.' That maybe you might feel something for me." She made another sound, indecipherable. "I said goodbye to my father, but I don't know how I could have said goodbye to you."

She flung herself toward him, ending up halfway across the space between them, on her knees when he met her. He kissed her because he had to. Because it might be the only way to silence all the fear that could so easily crush him.

The kiss was hard and hungry, but not about desire. This embrace was about love and tenderness and hope and happiness. All those things were jammed so tight in his chest, it hurt.

"I love you, 'Cadia. I never got over you."

She pulled back at that. "That's ridiculous. How can you say that? I was stupid in love with you, and you were nice to me. We were friends."

"If anyone was stupid, it was me. Not staying in touch. Just…letting you go."

Her fingers flexed on his shoulders. "I don't think you wanted much to do with Tucannon by then. That's what I was to you. That neighbor girl who amused you. Part of your memories of home."

He shouldn't have been staggered to realize she was right, but somehow he was. In his youthful resentment and hurt, he'd been rejecting everything to do with home. And, yeah, maybe Acadia had been part of that, even though she'd been so sympathetic. His balm, the one summer.

"Stupid," he pronounced again, and loved the fact that when she laughed this time, he could tell she meant it.

"I am so in love with you," Acadia told him. "And I wouldn't mind moving at all. If you really mean it."

More emotion thickened his throat. "I mean it," he managed to get out. "I swear, almost from the minute I saw you again… Say the word, and I'll apply for jobs in Sacramento."

"No." She kissed his jaw. "Mom and I mostly talk on the phone and email anyway. You should stay up here, near enough to come home easily when your mother needs you. I think…she needs you more than my mom needs me."

"Will it bother you? Coming home to Tucannon and seeing other people in your house?"

"Maybe the first time." She was silent for a moment. "In middle school, I secretly practiced writing 'Acadia Elise Owen' over and over." There was a smile in her voice, but something else, too, the yearning of her young self. "I dreamed about sharing your bedroom and your bed upstairs in your house when we came home to Tucannon to see our parents. So, you see, that's what I wanted."

He ducked his head to see her face. "Does that mean you will marry me?"

"Are you kidding?" Her arms snaked around his neck. "Try to get out of it."

He was grinning. All those emotions, all that happiness, didn't weigh him down. Instead, he felt light, as if his knees weren't planted on the porch boards but rather he was floating a few inches above. "And, uh, you're going to take my name?"

"Bet you didn't expect that."

"You can't tell me you're not a raving feminist."

Her chuckle was as airy as bubbles of champagne. "I won't. But this is different. I want to be an Owen. And I want the rest of the world to know it."

He realized what she was saying, and felt a further squeeze of pleasure/pain. She had allied herself with him and his mother from the minute she returned to Tucannon. Now, by taking his name, she was making sure no one would mistake her.

"I love you," he whispered. "*Now* can we go in?"

She giggled. "Yes, we can."

"And you know what?" he said, a minute later as they climbed the stairs to the second story. "I'm not sneaking out in the middle of the night."

"Twin bed," she reminded him.

"We'll manage."

"My reputation," Acadia said primly.

"Tomorrow morning, we are announcing our engagement. And I can confidently predict that my mother will be thrilled."

"Will she?" Uncertainty threaded her question. She tipped her freckled face up, those glorious brown eyes full of hope and some of the stunned disbelief he still felt.

"Why do you think she kept inviting you to dinner?"

"Guilt. Pity."

David made a rude noise. "My mother loves you, too, Acadia soon-to-be Owen. Never doubt it. Besides, you'll give her visions of grandkids to dance in her head."

They stood by her bed, facing each other. He cupped her face in his hands.

"You do want children?" she asked, sounding breathless.

"Yeah," he said. "Yours. You?"

"Oh, yes. Yours."

All that love swelled until he could hardly speak. "I don't want you going back to Sacramento."

"I need to work out a notice."

"I know." He tugged her to him, even though it would make it harder to strip off her clothes. "That doesn't mean I have to like it."

"Anticipation," his Acadia informed him, "is half the pleasure, you know."

"To hell with anticipation." All patience deserted him. He eased her down onto the bed, and made love to his 'Cadia.

* * * * *

Look for the next book by Janice Kay Johnson,
ANYTHING FOR HER!
Coming in March 2013
from Harlequin Superromance.

COMING NEXT MONTH FROM
HARLEQUIN® SUPERROMANCE®

Available February 5, 2013

#1830 WILD FOR THE SHERIFF
The Sisters of Bell River Ranch • by Kathleen O'Brien

Rowena Wright has finally come home to the Bell River Ranch. Most townspeople thought this wild child would never be back, but Sheriff Dallas Garwood always knew it. She *belongs* to this land. He's doing his best to steer clear of her. The last time they tangled, he almost didn't walk away. And now there's too much at stake for him to risk a second round with her.

#1831 IN FROM THE COLD
by Mary Sullivan

Callie MacKintosh is good at her job. That's why she's been sent to this Colorado town—to persuade her boss's brother Gabe Jordan to relinquish his share of the family land. But she soon learns there's more to this situation than she knows. And her skills are no match for a family feud that runs deep...or for her growing attraction to Gabe!

#1832 BENDING THE RULES
by Margaret Watson

Nathan Devereux has big dreams—and they don't include family. After years of raising his siblings, he's ready for some time to himself. But what is he supposed to do when faced with an orphaned thirteen-year-old daughter he didn't know about? He can't turn his back on her—or ignore her very appealing guardian, Emma Sloane. But when Emma announces that she wants to adopt the girl herself, all Nathan's personal rules about family suddenly seem to change.

#1833 THE CLOSER YOU GET
by Kristi Gold

As a country music superstar, Brett Taylor seems to have it all. But appearances are deceiving. He's learned the hard way that relationships and family don't mix with a life on the road. Then Cammie Carson joins his tour group, and the pull between them is intense. Suddenly he sees an entirely new perspective...with her by his side.

#1834 RESERVATIONS FOR TWO
by Jennifer Lohmann

Opening her own restaurant has been Tilly Milek's lifelong dream—and she's finally done it. And all it takes is one bad review to derail everything. Of course The Eater, the anonymous blogger all of Chicago reads, was there on the worst possible night! But when Tilly meets Dan Meier and discovers that he's the reviewer, she's determined to make him change his mind—no matter what it takes.

#1835 FINDING JUSTICE
by Rachel Brimble

For Sergeant Cat Forrester, there is only right and wrong. But when former lover Jay Garrett calls to say their friend has been murdered, those boundaries blur. Especially when he admits he's a suspect in the case. She needs to think like a detective and find the truth. But can she balance these instincts with her feelings for Jay?

YOU CAN FIND MORE INFORMATION ON UPCOMING HARLEQUIN® TITLES, FREE EXCERPTS AND MORE AT WWW.HARLEQUIN.COM.

HSRCNM0113ENHB

Wild for the Sheriff

by Kathleen O'Brien

On sale February 5

Dallas Garwood has always been the good guy, the one who does the right thing...except whenever he crosses paths with Rowena Wright. Now that she's back, things could get interesting for this small-town sheriff! Read on for an exciting excerpt from *Wild for the Sheriff* by Kathleen O'Brien.

Dallas Garwood had always known that sooner or later he'd open a door, turn a corner or look up from his desk and see Rowena Wright standing there.

It wasn't logical. It was simply an unshakable certainty that she wasn't gone for good, that one day she would return.

Not to see him, of course. He didn't kid himself that their brief interlude had been important to her. But she'd be back for Bell River—the ranch that was part of her.

Still, he hadn't thought today would be the day he'd face her across the threshold of her former home.

Or that she would look so gaunt. Her beauty was still there, but buried beneath some kind of haggard exhaustion. Her wild green eyes were circled with shadows, and her white shirt and jeans hung on her.

Something twisted in his chest, stealing his words. He'd never expected to feel pity for Rowena Wright.

She still knew how to look sardonic. She took him in, and he saw himself as she did, from the white-lightning scar dividing his right eyebrow to the shiny gold star pinned at his breast.

Three-tenths of a second. That was all it took to make him feel boring and overdressed, as if his uniform were as much a costume as his son Alec's cowboy hat.

"*Sheriff* Dallas Garwood." The crooked smile on her red lips was cryptic. "I should have known. Truly, I should have known."

"I didn't realize you'd come home," he said, wishing he didn't sound so stiff.

"Come *back*," she corrected him. "After all these years, it might be a bit of a stretch to call Bell River *home*."

"I see." He didn't really, but so what? He'd been her lover once, but never her friend.

The funny thing was, right now he'd give almost anything to change that and resurrect that long-ago connection.

Will Dallas and Rowena reconnect? Or will she skip town again with everything left unsaid? Find out in *Wild for the Sheriff* by Kathleen O'Brien, available February 2013 from Harlequin® Superromance®.